SHUDDERS

SHUDDERS

DESIGNED BY

CYNTHIA ASQUIST

COACHWHIP PUBLICATIONS
GREENVILLE, OHIO

Shudders, designed by Cynthia Asquith
© 2025 Coachwhip Publications edition

First published 1929
CoachwhipBooks.com

ISBN 1-61646-608-1
ISBN-13 978-1-61646-608-4

Contents

The Playfellow

Cynthia Asquith

Laura Halyard wondered whether she would ever grow more accustomed to the loveliness of her new home. Each time she looked at the beautiful Tudor house she still wanted to rub her eyes.

After the din and glare of New York the mellow beauty and green silence of Lichen Hall and its perfect surroundings lay like a spell on its new mistress. It was just six months since her husband Claud Halyard had succeeded to the property at the death of his elder brother who had died childless. Since his marriage to Laura, business had kept Claud in America, so she had never met her poor, paralyzed brother-in-law. Yet she often thought of him, so strongly had his sad story impressed her imagination: The early loss of his adored wife, the accident which left him a hopeless cripple and the ghastly tragedy of his only child, a girl of ten, who had perished in the fire which twelve years ago had destroyed a small wing of Lichen Hall.

The building had been so skilfully restored that it was difficult to believe in that fatal fire. Laura felt herself lapped in an atmosphere of peace and found it impossible to associate anything so hideous as the death of that poor child with this place. Could such a thing have happened here and only twelve years ago? In these serene surroundings it seemed so unimaginable.

Laura Halyard had the extraordinary adaptability of her race, and as she sat in the great hall one December evening, her slim, delicate beauty glowing in the flicker of the firelight, she looked wonderfully in tone with her setting. She was giving tea to the old parson whose faded eyes blinked appreciatively at the grace and beauty of his hostess. He wished he didn't feel it was time to end his visit.

"If I may be permitted to say so," he said, reluctantly dragging his stiff limbs from the depths of the easy chair. "If I may say so, Lady Halyard, it is very pleasant to have a chatelaine here again. Lichen Hall has been a sad place these last twelve years."

"Yes," responded Laura sympathetically, "I don't suppose my poor brother-in-law ever recovered from the terrible tragedy of that poor, poor child."

"A broken man is a phrase one often hears," said the parson, "but I am thankful to say that in the course of a long life it has only been my lot to know one man to whom I felt the phrase could be justly applied. That man was your brother-in-law. He did his duty by this place. No one could have done it better. But after Daphne's death, duty was all the world ever held for him. Nothing else remained. To see such gray ashes and have no power to kindle one spark has been a great pain to me. Such loneliness! Scarcely any one ever came here during these last years. Just a few old friends, but I always felt he only suffered them out of consideration for *their* feelings.

"I often wondered why your husband never came. In spite of the twenty years between them, they had always appeared to be such devoted brothers. It seems strange he should never once have returned to his own home until he succeeded to it."

"I know," said Laura. "Of course he was very tied by business, but still he could have managed it in his summer holiday. I often urged it, but he always said he thought next year would be better. I don't know why it was. Of course, Mr. Cloud, he's very sensitive. He shrinks from things. Perhaps—I sometimes think—he felt he simply couldn't face his brother's misery."

"Possibly," said the parson. "But I wish he had come. It might have made a big difference."

Laura detected a hint of reproach in the kind old voice.

"It isn't that he doesn't love this place," she eagerly assured him. "I can't tell you how much it means to him."

"I know, Lady Halyard, I know. You see, I remember him as a boy. Why, his love for his home was quite a household joke. Once he gave a visiting schoolfellow a black eye because he dared to say his home was more beautiful than this! Bright days those were when he and all his sisters were young." The parson's pale eyes widened as he stared wistfully back into the past. "I always think this garden clamors for children. It's wasted when there's none about. I assure you, it's a real joy to see your little girl tearing up and down the grass slopes."

"I can't tell you how happy Hyacinth is here," exclaimed Laura. "Her day is one long rapture."

"Bless her!" said the parson. "How lovely she is and how extraordinarily like—"

"Like? Like whom?"

"Like her poor cousin—like poor little Daphne. Why, surely the resemblance must have struck your husband?"

"No. At least he hasn't said anything, but then perhaps he wouldn't. Even after all these years he can't bear to speak of his niece. He never mentions Daphne's name."

"I know it was a great shock to him," agreed the parson. "He was so fond of her. I remember he was always playing with her. But then we all loved her. Yes, there was a real fascination about little Daphne."

"And was she really like our Hyacinth?"

"Like?" exclaimed the parson. "Why, it's the most astounding resemblance! I assure you it gave me quite a start the first time I saw your girl peering at me through the bushes. Yes, it took me back twelve years. She's ten, isn't she—your Hyacinth?"

Laura nodded.

"Well, you see poor Daphne was just the same age the last time I saw her—the day before— Yes, yes, I can see her now. Just the same mop of red-gold hair framing the pale, pointed face—the wide eyes and the same eager look— something so extraordinary *vivid.*"

"Really," said Laura. Her voice trembled and the hall swam in a blur of tears.

"Yes, a most extraordinary resemblance," continued the old man. "Voices a good deal alike, too. And your Hyacinth seems to have a similar passion for play. I never saw any being like Daphne for filling the day. She always seemed to want to cram as much fun into each hour as it could possibly hold. It was almost as though she knew she had no time to lose. Do you remember that passage in Maeterlinck about those he calls 'Les Avertis'?"

"Yes, I do," Laura's voice was heavy.

"Well, well, I must be going now," said the old man. "Thanks, dear lady, for a very pleasant afternoon. Give my love to Daph—Hyacinth. She must come to tea with me."

"Good night, Mr. Cloud. Come again soon," said Laura rather mechanically. Turning to the fire she kicked one of the large logs with her foot, and then stirred amongst the embers with a poker, until they blazed into flames. She felt cold and tired. She started when the clergyman re-entered the room. He apologized for having forgotten his gloves.

"Oh, what color are they?" asked Laura absently, as though a variegated assortment of gloves were likely to be lying about the hall.

"Gray. Here they are. I'm so sorry to have troubled you."

"Stop one moment, Mr. Cloud. There was something I meant to ask you. How do you think my husband is looking?"

"Well, Lady Halyard, quite well. He always was a magnificent fellow. Yes, I think he looks quite well. But, since you ask me, the only thing I notice about him is a sort of strained expression on his face—in his eyes, and on his forehead. It's as though he were making some kind of mental effort—as if he were trying to remember something."

"Trying to remember something?"

"Yes, he looks as I feel I must look, when I'm struggling with my daily Crossword. No doubt it's the result of all his work in that office. I'm so glad to see him out of it. Somehow I can't picture any Halyard in an office. Oh, yes, Claud was always made for country life. Good night, Lady Halyard, good night."

Left to herself, Laura crouched over the blazing fire. 'Claud made for country life'? Yes, so she had always thought. In America he had seemed an exile pining for his native land. And yet, now that they were at his beloved home, and it had proved more beautiful than even his rhapsodies had led her to expect, what was the matter? To her growing disappointment she could not help admitting that her husband's spirits—never steady—were on the whole much lower than they used to be. A sultry gloom seemed settling on him. Then that look of strain the parson had noticed. Others had commented on this. What could cause it, now that the present and the future seemed so fair? Business worries? Laura wondered almost hopefully. No! what business worries could he have? He told her everything. Told her everything, did he? Laura almost laughed aloud. That very afternoon she had re-encountered that threadbare phrase. The heroine of the bad novel she was reading, a woman in total darkness concerning her husband, had confidently asserted, 'He tells me everything!' How could any human being ever tell any one everything?

No doubt Claud had got something on his mind. Since their home-coming, she had been conscious of a barrier thickening between them. In old days, if challenged, he would often admit to a fit of depression. Now he seemed rather to resent any inquiry as to his health or spirits. If she said, "Is anything the matter?" he would answer almost irritably, "The matter? No, nothing's the matter. Don't suggest things."

Laura was not left to her reflections for long. Her husband, a tall, handsome man, came into the room with their daughter Hyacinth riding on his shoulders, her mop of red-gold hair shining above his dark head.

The three of them settled round the fire. Hyacinth, with her knees drawn up to her pointed chin, and her wide eyes staring into the flames, made but a poor pretense of listening to her father reading "Ivanhoe" for her benefit. The moment the chapter was finished she sprang on to the tips of her toes and stood quivering, like a flame released.

"May I go now?" her whole eager being seemed to express.

Struck afresh by the gleaming quality of her beauty, her father gazed at her lovingly. So breathlessly full of life! Ought she perhaps to have playfellows of her own age?

"Are you lonely, sprite?" he asked her tenderly.

"Lonely! Oh, no! I'm never, never lonely here!" There was a note of exultation in the child's happy laugh.

"I must go now!" she said, excitedly, and, slipping out of her father's arms, she darted up the dark oak stairs and, with a wave of her hand, disappeared from her parents' gaze. Long after she had turned the corner which took her out of sight, they heard her running footsteps and her voice trilling out: "Come Lasses and Lads, Take Leave of Your Dads."

"Hyacinth's voice matches her face so marvellously, doesn't it, Claud?" said Laura. "Not many people's do. Hers has that piercing quality of crystal youth. It's like cold, cold water or biting into an apple."

Claud rose to throw another log onto the blazing fire.

"Laura, what does Hyacinth mean by saying she's never lonely *here?*"

"I don't know, Claud. But, now you ask, haven't you noticed how different she is since we came here? Do you remember how listless she sometimes used to seem? I often got quite worried and thought that perhaps I ought to borrow some bright child to keep her company, but now she's always as happy as the day is long. In fact to tell the honest truth—I can't help rather missing her moods—or at least her dependence on me. You see, she used so to want me. Don't you remember how she was always imploring me to read to her or tell her stories?"

"Doesn't she now?" asked Claud.

"No, nowadays I can scarcely ever persuade her to stay with me. She's always rushing away as though she had 'something better to do.' It's little I see of her beyond her heels and the back of her head! She's so strangely self-sufficient. Between you and me, Claud, I think she's almost disquietingly happy."

"Disquietingly happy? What do you mean, Laura?"

"Well—I mean—it's almost uncanny. Really, I don't know how to put it into words, but it's—it's as though she had some resource we don't know about. She seems so *occupied*. Yes, that's it—occupied. It sounds too silly, but it's as though being by herself were not being alone. She's grown a queer new sort of smile lately too, a stealthy, sidelong smile, and the comings and goings of that smile don't have any connection with what any of us say or do. Haven't you noticed it? Claud, do you remember what that spooky friend of mine said about Hyacinth?"

"No, I don't," Claud answered shortly. "Some absurdity, I'm sure, from what I remember of her."

"She said, 'Now there's a child that should *see* things. *Her* "muddy vesture of decay" is too transparent to "close her in."' She said she had what she called, 'listening eyes,' and the thinnest lids she had ever seen. Nonsense I thought it at the time, but now, Claud, I sometimes wonder . . . This old place—"

"Oh, Lord! For Heaven's sake don't start any of that psychical rot here."

Surprised at the annoyance in her husband's voice, Laura laughed.

"I know, dear, you think no American can come near a stately home of England without peopling it with ghosts, but I assure you I haven't—to replace into my native tongue—'sensed' anything unpleasant here. I've had neither sight nor sound of Abbots carrying their heads, nor of ladies in blood-speckled shrouds. No, indeed! On the contrary, I am conscious of a something that's happy—gay—blithe—I don't know what to call it, but there seems a sort of *liveliness* about the atmosphere of this house—especially upstairs and most especially in that room Hyacinth insisted on having as her playroom, the old day nursery."

"I didn't want her to use that room," said Claud gruffly.

"I know, dear, I know," his wife responded sympathetically. "But she *insisted.*"

Poor fellow, she thought, how sensitive he is! Of course it had been his little niece, Daphne's playroom. Probably she had romped in it just before her life ended so tragically. Laura reproached herself. She should never have allowed Hyacinth to appropriate that particular room. For Claud, its associations with Daphne were too strong. She should have remembered how he winced at any reminder of that poor dead child. Laura shuddered at the thought of the horror of her death. Ten years old! Just the same age as Hyacinth!

"I promise you there's nothing unpleasant in that room," Laura went on. "But—please don't think me silly—I do feel an atmosphere in it—a happy, youthful one. When I sit in that room, as I often do, memories of my own childhood break out of the past and come thronging round me. I feel the years simply slipping off me." She laughed. "Why, I get funny impulses to play, to dance, to jump about. My toes begin to twiddle. It's as though there were some *invitation* in the room. You'll think me too absurd, but once I actually found myself hiding in the cupboard, just as though I expected some one to come and search for me. And yet all the time I knew Hyacinth must be in bed and asleep. Sometimes I long to mount the old rocking-horse and have a gallop. I would too, only I'm so afraid of being caught by one of those terribly grown-up housemaids.

"Once I thought I heard light, scuffling steps and a sort of soft tittering. Imagination, of course! . . . And yet, I suppose generations and generations of children have played in that room?"

"Yes," said Claud. His voice was very gruff, and as he spoke he raised *The Times,* and held it, like a wall, between him and any further confidences. Conscious of having annoyed him, Laura went away to tell Hyacinth it was bedtime. It was half an hour before she found her in the hayloft and then she had great difficulty in coaxing her indoors. At last she handed her over to her maid, Bessy. The moment she returned to the hall her husband rose, saying he would go and say good night to Hyacinth.

"You won't find that little flibberty-gibbet in bed. I had such a tussle to get her in. It's the same thing every night. However late I leave her, she always says, 'I haven't had nearly time enough to play!'"

"Not nearly time enough to play?" echoed Claud. *"She* doesn't say that; not Hyacinth?"

"Yes, why shouldn't she?" exclaimed Laura, puzzled by the violence of his manner.

But, giving no answer, Claud hastened from the room. That night at dinner when Laura asked him why he had been so struck by those very ordinary words of Hyacinth's that she had repeated, he said he had no idea to what she was alluding, couldn't remember her quoting Hyacinth, and that it must be one of her "silly fancies."

Puzzled and hurt, Laura dropped the subject. Claud did not look well and to-night that expression of strain was very noticeable. How had the old parson described it? "As though he were trying to remember something." No, she didn't think that was what the expression in Claud's cavernous gray eyes suggested. But when she tried to define it to herself, she felt completely baffled.

A few days later, the Halyards were walking in the garden. A strong wind blew, the trees were bare, and crisp leaves, the color of Hyacinth's hair, rustled around their feet. As usual their thoughts turned on their adored child.

"I thought Hyacinth looked very pale at luncheon," said Claud.

"Yes," answered his wife. "Naughty child, she went out of doors last night!"

"Out of doors?"

"Yes. Bessy found her shoes and stockings drenched this morning, and when I asked, the little wretch owned she had gone out long after we were in bed. Just think how cold it must have been! She wouldn't tell me why she had done it, and when I said she must promise not to do it again, she burst into tears."

"Little sprite!" laughed Claud. "She still thinks of sleep as waste of time! I hope it may be— Heavens! Just look at her now! What is she doing? I never saw a child run so fast, all alone."

Hyacinth, her face wildly tense, flashed past them on long, spindly legs. Her speed, surprising for her age, never slackened until, with arms outstretched to touch it, she reached an acacia tree at the foot of which, panting and laughing, she flung herself to the ground.

Her parents approached.

"Well done, Hyacinth! You *were* going fast!"

"I nearly won that time!" exclaimed the excited child, her green eyes blazing. "Oh so, so nearly!"

"You nearly *won!* What do you mean by you 'nearly won'? Were you racing one leg against the other?"

Hyacinth flushed, smiled nervously, sprang to her feet and in an instant had run out of sight behind the great yew hedge.

"Funny child!" said her mother with an uneasy laugh. "She's always running off, just as though she had an appointment elsewhere. She never seems to need me, now. Do you remember how she used to think it such a treat to sleep with me? Now she never wants to. You know, Claud, it sounds ridiculous, but nowadays when I go into that child's room, I feel as if I were—interrupting." As she spoke, Laura gave a slight shiver. Her own words seemed to crystallize vague misgivings of which she had scarcely been aware.

"Interrupting?" echoed Claud. "Interrupting what?"

"I don't know," she answered hopelessly, and turned toward the house.

Claud whistled for his dogs and set off for a long walk.

That evening Laura went to see Hyacinth in bed.

"Darling," she said, wheedlingly, "wouldn't you like to come and sleep with Mummie to-night? We'll have early morning tea together and play Ludo on my big pillow."

An anxious look flitted across the child's sweet but rather set face.

"Thank you, Mummie darling," she answered, shyly, but decidedly, "only I'm so happy in my own lovely room. I love it and I don't think it would like to be left."

Intense relief shone in her bright eyes when, in silent acquiescence, her mother kissed her good night.

"Good Mummie," she cooed, and with a little ecstatic wriggle, she turned her radiant face toward the window.

That night, it was very late before Laura rejoined her husband after dinner. The great bow window in the hall was uncurtained and the moonlight streamed in, its slanting green shafts mingling with the flickering red from the blazing fire by which Claud sat, an unopened book on his knee.

"Where have you been all this time, Laura?" he asked, glancing up at her face. "What have you been doing? I hope Hyacinth hasn't been up to any more of her pranks?"

"No," Laura answered quickly. "But I have."

"What do you mean?"

"I mean, I've been what you'd call silly. You remember what I told you about those funny feelings I get in the playroom? Well, directly after I left you over your coffee, I felt I wanted to go to the playroom. Don't frown, Claud, I couldn't help it. I simply had to go. My feet just took me there. Well, as I went along the passage, I heard a faint noise—a queer sort of a noise. I opened the door. What do you think I saw? Claud, the rocking-horse was plunging to and fro going furiously—*without a rider!*"

"Well," said Claud, "no doubt Hyacinth heard you coming, and, knowing she should be in bed, jumped off and ran out of the door."

"So I thought—so I hoped! But I rushed straight to her room, and found her fast asleep."

"Well, then it must have been one of the maids."

"No, there was no one about. They were all down at their supper. When I got back to the playroom, the rocking-horse was gradually subsiding. I watched it and soon it was quite motionless."

"No! You *do* surprise me!" jeered Claud.

"The queer thing," said Laura solemnly, "was that even while the rocking-horse was galloping so fast, the stirrups were not swaying as they naturally would. No, they were quite taut—stretched out forward—just as if—"

"Look here!" exclaimed Claud, angrily. "What are you driving at? What have you been reading? What have you been eating? Rocking-horse, indeed! It sounds more like a nightmare! I never knew Hyacinth had a rocking-horse. Who gave it to her?"

"No one. We found it here. It was Daphne's. You must have seen it. Vermilion nostrils and minus a tail. But, do you mean to say—haven't you ever been in the playroom since you came home?"

"No."

"How extraordinary!"

"Why should I?" Claud's voice was fierce and he glared at his wife.

"Quite, quite!" said Laura nervously. She was surprised and shocked at the tone of his voice, and the expression on his face. Why, for a second he had looked at her as though he hated her. Was it possible? Claud! her gentle, courteous husband, whose devotion to her was almost a joke to their friends. "Oh, I've forgotten my spectacles," she said confusedly, "I'll run up and fetch them. I shan't be two minutes."

With this excuse she ran upstairs, leaving her husband moodily staring at her spectacles which lay conspicuous on the table where she had just placed them.

Five minutes later she returned. Glancing at her, Claud knew that if she had not been flushed, she would have been very pale.

"What is it now?"

With her back to him, Laura stood facing the fire. She spoke quickly, in a very low voice as though she feared to hear her own words.

"As I got near the playroom, I heard the gramophone playing. I thought I heard dancing feet, but when I opened the door there was no one in the room. You won't believe me, Claud, but there was no one in the room. No one! And yet a *record had just been set going.* It was 'Come Lasses and Lads, Take Leave of Your Dads.' Before I found the electric switch, I thought I felt something very light brush past me. Almost before I was aware of it, it had gone. Oh, so quickly!—just like a puff of wind. Just to make sure, I went to all the maids' bedrooms. One of them might have started the gramophone, but they were all in bed. Then I went to Hyacinth's room. I crept in, so as not to wake her, if she was asleep, and she was—yes, sound asleep. But as I looked at her, I heard a tap-tap at the window. It *might* have been a branch. Anyhow it woke her. She sprang up in a second, wide, wide awake, with such a joyful welcoming expression on her excited little face. . . . Then she saw me, and she looked sort of scared and sorry—yes, *very* sorry to see me. Oh, Claud! I couldn't bear the look on her face when she saw me!"

Laura's last words came from her like a cry, and she turned to Claud with outstretched arms, as though appealing against she knew not what.

"Damnation!" he cried, springing to his feet. "I can't stand any more of this! Look here, Laura darling, we'll all three go away to-morrow. It's obvious you need a change. We've been here too long. After all, you aren't used to staying like a tree in one place. Besides, it will be great fun to take Hyacinth to London, won't it? Laura, my sweet, darling Laura, say you like this plan?"

"Of course I should love it," murmured Laura, clasped in his arms.

It was such joy to feel herself carried on this wave of tenderness back into the haven of love, in which, until recently, she had felt so secure, that any proposal would have seemed welcome.

If only he would go on looking at her as now with love in his eyes, what matter where they went? And yet, even in the intensity of her relief, Laura was conscious of the irony of his wishing to leave the home he had always described as the Earthly Paradise. It was decided that they should leave the very next day, but alas! when to-morrow came, their plan could not be carried out. Hyacinth had sprained her ankle very badly and was unable to put her foot to the ground. When told the news, Laura hurried to her daughter's room. She found her sitting up in bed. Her face was flushed and she looked shy.

"Poor darling! This is too sad. However did it happen?"

"I'm so sorry, Mummie." Hyacinth spoke hurriedly and nervously. "But I'm afraid I've been naughty again. Don't be very angry with me, but I went out again last night and—"

"You went out? Oh, Hyacinth darling, you promised you wouldn't!"

"I'm so sorry, Mummie, but it was such a lovely night— such bright, bright moonlight. It made me forget I mustn't and I simply *couldn't* say no."

"The sooner you learn to say 'no' to yourself, the better. I shan't be able to trust you any more. You've hurt yourself, so I won't scold you, but you must never, never do such a thing again. Anyhow, what happened? How did you hurt your silly self?"

"I had a fall."

"What, running?"

"No," answered Hyacinth reluctantly. "I was climbing a tree."

"Climbing a tree? Good heavens! You might have broken your leg and lain out all night. Which tree?"

"The big elm. The one Daddy made a house in when he was little. A branch broke—"

"Well, you've had what Nannie used to call a 'natural punishment.' So I won't say any more. Lie still now, until the doctor comes."

After the doctor had bound up Hyacinth's ankle, her mother went to look at the elm tree. She was appalled at the height of the broken branch. It seemed almost a miracle that the child was not more seriously hurt.

She returned to question her.

"You don't mean to tell me you fell from where a branch is broken off right up near the top of the tree?"

"Yes, but you see there were so many branches that I paused on all the way down. I only really fell just the last bit."

"But I had no idea you could climb so high. Surely you can't have got all that way up without any help?"

"Oh yes, I did!" cried Hyacinth triumphantly. "And she climbed even higher, but then of course her legs are a little longer."

"She? Who is She?"

Hyacinth flushed scarlet and in confusion flung her arms round her mother's neck. Glancing quickly all round the room, she put her finger in front of her mouth.

"Don't tell Daddy. Oh, Mummie, *please, please* don't tell!" she said in a scared, panting voice. Not one word more would she say. After that one unguarded moment, her whole being was clenched in silence. At first her mother tried to coax her into an explanation, but alarmed by her flushed, excited face, she took her temperature. Finding her a little feverish, she did not like to press her any further. She seemed so troubled.

Laura did not tell her husband of Hyacinth's strange slip.

"*She* climbed even higher"? How could she tell him of that? She dreaded to hear him speak in that new, sharp way so utterly unlike his old self.

After all, Hyacinth's fall must have been a considerable shock. Perhaps she had not known what she was saying. The next day the child seemed better and Laura made another attempt to cross-question her about her accident, but at the first word of inquiry, the child's flower-like mouth set in a thin hard line, and an expression came into her eyes that was like a shutter between her and her mother.

During the following days she was affectionate but somehow guarded, and Laura felt strangely out of touch with her. On every one's account she longed for a change and chafed at the enforced postponement of their plans. Claud, though now uniformly gentle in his manner, seemed increasingly depressed. Laura was determined to leave the first possible day, but unfortunately Hyacinth's injury proved more serious than had been supposed, and her ankle took a long time to recover.

No bed-ridden child has ever been so little trouble. In fact, she seemed almost unnaturally contented. Whenever her mother read aloud to her, she was politely acquiescent, but her manner was that of one who makes a necessary concession, and waits with as good a grace as can be commanded.

Her gladness when the book was closed was evident, and when her mother turned to leave the room she would wave her hand over-gratefully, and raise herself a little on her pillows, with a look of relief and a hovering smile of happy expectancy. Though Laura tried to shut her mind to the impression made by Hyacinth's manner, she could not succeed. Stung out of her usual self-control, she once cried out, "What is it, Hyacinth; why are you always waiting now—waiting for me to go?"

A look of fear quivered across the child's sensitive face.

"Waiting? What do you mean, Mummie? Why do you think I want you to go?" and with unskilled evasiveness she began to talk of irrelevancies—the cat's kittens—the new gardener, the pony that had kicked the groom—anything that came into her head.

With a heavy heart and a sense of absurdity, Laura acquiesced in making conversation with the child whose confidence she had once so completely possessed.

Though Hyacinth was full of strange whims, the one her mother thought the queerest was her insistence on having the rocking-horse brought into her bedroom.

"But darling, it will take up so much room. And whatever is the use of having a rocking-horse you can't ride?"

But Hyacinth's pale, peaked face set in obstinacy.

"I want it. I need it," was all she would say.

So the shabby old rocking-horse was dragged along the passage and stood in arrested prance at the foot of the child's bed.

That evening as Laura came into the room, Hyacinth gave an obvious start, and, turning to her mother in flushed uneasiness, said querulously:

"Aren't I old enough yet, Mother, for people to knock at my door before they come into my room? You always tell me I must knock at your door."

Amazed and hurt, Laura looked at the usually so gentle child, whose worried gaze she noticed was now fixed on the rocking-horse. Glancing at it herself, her glance became a stare. Was it her fancy, or was it slightly, almost imperceptibly moving?

"Have you been out of bed, Hyacinth?" she asked suspiciously.

"Oh, no, Mummie. Why?"

"Only I thought perhaps you had been very naughty and got on the rocking-horse. When I came in I thought it was just moving, as if it had been in motion and wasn't yet quite still. But of course, it must have been my fancy."

With unwonted eagerness, Hyacinth said:

"Will you read to me now, Mummie?"

Laura readily consented.

"Before I begin though," she said, "I must tell you some good news. The doctor says you may get up in a week, and the very day after you get up we are going to take you to London."

"You're going to take me to London?" Hyacinth's voice was sharp with dismay.

"Yes, darling. Won't it be fun?"

To her distress Hyacinth burst into tears.

"Oh no, Mummie! No, no, no! Please don't take me away from here. I can't go! I won't go! It wouldn't be fair!"

"What do you mean, you absurd child? You'll have a lovely time in London. We'll take you to the Zoo and Madame Tussaud's and have pink ices at Gunther's. We'll do all the treats I used to tell you about in New York."

Hyacinth's eyes welled with tears.

"Oh, please, Mummie," she implored, "don't take me away from lovely here."

"But my darling, I love you to love this place, but you can't always be here. It will be all the more fun to come back to it." She tried to laugh the child out of her distress. "After all, you goose, it won't run away because we leave it. Everything will be exactly the same when we return."

"I don't know, Mother," sobbed Hyacinth. "You can't tell. I'm afraid to go—besides it wouldn't be fair."

"Not fair, what do you mean?" questioned Laura, now completely bewildered.

"Oh! I don't know, Mummie! But I'm so happy here. Mayn't I stay? *Please,* please, *please!*"

Seeing Hyacinth so hysterically excited, Laura said firmly: "We won't talk about it any more now," and began to read aloud to unlistening ears.

The next day, Hyacinth seemed much more sensible. Laura told her their departure was quite settled, and she made an obvious effort to accept the inevitable with as good a grace as possible, but she looked pale and strained and her manner was even more than usually preoccupied.

"She looks as though she were trying to propitiate herself," Laura explained to her husband.

"Trying to propitiate herself? What an absurd phrase!" he laughed. "The ideas you have about that child!"

"I haven't any ideas about her." Laura was astonished at the vehemence of her own voice.

Laura spent most of Christmas Eve decorating a small tree for Hyacinth. When she brought it upstairs, gay with glittering tinsel, gilded walnuts and shiny ornaments, the child clapped her hands with delight. Saying she would return in about an hour to light the candles, Laura placed the tree on a table in front of the fire.

When she came back she was surprised to find the room illuminated by the glimmer of little wax candles. Hyacinth seemed asleep, but sat up as the door opened. Assuming the child had prevailed on Bessy the maid to light the candles, Laura merely said:

"Well, I must say, after all my trouble, I do think you might have waited for me. Never mind. Now let's pull the crackers together."

Shamefacedly Hyacinth pointed to the colored tatters of two dozen exploded crackers. Her bed was strewn with paper caps, mottoes, and little tin musical instruments.

"Sorry, Mummie, I just couldn't wait," she mumbled. "I *love* candles. Flames are such fun, aren't they? May I have some toy fireworks? Please, Mummie!"

"I don't know. I think they're rather dangerous."

"Oh no, Mummie. They aren't! Please say I may have some. I know! I'll ask Daddy to give me some. He told me to tell him what I wanted."

Laura went to find Bessy.

"You should have asked me before lighting the candles on the Christmas tree," she said severely. "It wasn't at all safe to leave Miss Hyacinth alone in the room with all those candles alight. They often set fire to a bit of the tree. There should always be some one at hand with a wet sponge. I'm surprised at you, Bessy."

"I didn't never light no tree, my lady," said the astonished maid. "I haven't been into Miss Hyacinth's room, not for two hours."

Laura hurried back to Hyacinth.

"I don't want to scold you on Christmas Eve, but it was very naughty of you to get out of bed to light the candles, when you know perfectly well you're still forbidden to put your foot to the ground. And isn't it rather selfish to pull crackers by yourself?"

Hyacinth blushed, but the expression on her face was unmistakably one of relief.

"Sorry, Mummie," she said. "So sorry," and impetuously she flung her arms around her mother's neck and kissed her quickly—lovingly—just as she used to in the days when she was lonely.

At last Hyacinth's ankle was sufficiently recovered to allow the Halyards to make all their plans for leaving the next day.

That evening, Claud was to dine out with an old school fellow who lived about four miles away. Before starting he went up to say good night to Hyacinth. Her half-packed trunk was open and she was practising getting about the room.

"Don't ruin my tie!" he cried, as hopping toward him she flung her thin arms around his neck.

"Bother your tie!" she laughed. "Oh, Daddy, darling Daddy. Thank you for the lovely, lovely box of fireworks. They came by the afternoon post. Aren't they gorgeous?

Look at the lovely pictures on the lid. Whizz-bangs, Catherine wheels and all!"

"Oh, they've come, have they? Well, mind, you aren't on any account to touch them. I'll let them off for you the first evening we come home. I'll carry them away now and lock them up somewhere safe."

"Oh, mayn't they stay here, Daddy? I like looking at the pictures."

"Certainly not. I can't trust you not to touch them."

Hyacinth stood flushed and pouting. Suddenly she turned toward the window.

"Oh look, Daddy," she cried pointing. "Look at that great white owl. Oh! what a lovely Mrs. Fly-by-Night."

"Where, Hyacinth? I can't see it."

"No, Daddy. You aren't looking where I'm pointing; can't you see? She's just flown over the Church Tower."

But look where he might Claud could see no owl. He was still trying to be guided by Hyacinth's erratically pointed finger, when the butler came in and announced his car.

"Well, then, I must give the owl up," he said. "My friend's a great stickler for punctuality," and kissing Hyacinth, who made no effort to detain him, he left the room, quite forgetting the box of fireworks he had left lying on the table.

As he was about to step into his car, he overheard a mocking, "To whit a Whoo." Remembering an accomplishment of Hyacinth's—she could imitate an owl by whistling through her hands—he looked up toward her window. There she was, leaning far out, her red head gleaming, her pale face strangely elfin in the moonlight. Claud was startled by her beauty.

"Go to bed, sprite," he called.

Hyacinth waved her thin white arms.

"Good night, Daddy. See you in the morning!"

Though bitterly cold, the still, starlight night was so beautiful that Claud decided to walk home and dismissed his car. He and his friend found much to say to one another, and it was past midnight before he started home. As he strode across the frozen fields, he began to regret his dismissal of the car. The cold, clear silence was only broken by his own footsteps; the occasional hoot of an owl, and the far, far away bark of a lonely dog. He felt too much alone in a white, unshared world.

The Present—in which Claud always strove to enwrap himself—receded and faded. Quite powerless to protect him from the Past, it became a mere dissolving mist.

A man maimed by one memory, he depended on contact with immediate external things to preoccupy him, to claim his attention so urgently that his senses might not be re-assailed by certain ineffaceable impressions.

Just now he felt abandoned to the Past, unprotected by the passage of time. What were time and space but modes of thought? There could be no putting distance between yourself and any experience. What had all the intervening years availed to release him? Nothing.

Claud Halyard had paid dearly for his inheritance. That strained expression friends noticed on his face was due not to the effort to remember, but to the effort to forget—to expunge from his consciousness a haunting memory from which there was no release.

> "And if I seek oblivion of an hour,
>   So shorten I the stature of my soul."

In Claud's life there is one hour of which he ceaselessly and desperately seeks oblivion. Struggle as he may, he is now caught back in that hour, forced to relive each agonizing instant. It is superimposed on his present and all the impressions of twelve intervening years are powerless to soften any of its intensity.

Twelve years ago; it is a moonlight night and as now he is walking toward Lichen Hall, the beautiful home of his childhood, the home which so obsesses his imagination that to him it seems the core of the entire world. Such love, he feels, should surely establish ownership, but Lichen Hall is not entailed on the male line and, at the death of its present owner, his widowed and crippled brother, it will pass to that brother's only child, Daphne, who in time will marry and transfer all that wonderful beauty to strangers. He reaches the edge of the park. What is it that so startles him? What strange terrifying sounds? God! the alarm bell in the great tower is clanging furiously. "Fire! Fire!" he hears the word shouted.

Sick with dread he rushes toward the house from which his horror-struck eyes see wreaths of smoke curling. Terrible crackling sounds are coming from one wing and from the little turret tower in that wing long ribands of flame flutter toward the white moon.

Breathless, he reaches the lawn. The distracted servants have just carried some one out of the house. It is his brother. Claud rushes to him. Struggling to raise his paralyzed body, the agonized man clutches at Claud, and, pointing toward the house, shrieks, "Daphne! Daphne!"

Claud realizes the situation. The fire brigade has not yet arrived and Daphne, who sleeps in the turret tower of the burning wing, has not been got out. The alarm has only just been given as it is merely a few minutes since the servants were aroused, the fire having gained a strong hold before any of them awoke. So far they have only just had time to carry down their helpless master. The child they hoped would have woken and escaped. They expected to find her outside but, to their dismay, she is nowhere to be seen.

With a reassuring shout, Claud dashes into the house. The staircase leading up to the burning wing is already dense with smoke. Claud smashes a window, and, choking, fights his way up and into the suffocating room where he sees Daphne on the floor—lying close to the window. The smoke has been too much for her. She is unconscious—quite unconscious, but breathing. He is in time! Quite easy to fling that light burden over his shoulder, to dash down the stairs and carry her safely out into the blessed air. Vividly Claud sees himself doing this—sees the joy blaze in his brother's eyes.

Simultaneously, an alternative picture presents itself. The child left lying as she is—unconscious—quite unconscious, not suffering, not dreading, not knowing, just *not reawakening*. Unaware. His own future? Lichen Hall?

His body seems to act without any conscious volition. Something takes command of his limbs. "I never told myself to do it! I never told myself to do it!" How often thereafter was he to mutter these words.

Stooping, he lifts the light body. The burnished red hair brushes against his cheek. In a moment he has shoved her safely out of sight. Now for the stairs, they have become almost impassable. He emerges choking. "I can't find her!" he gasps to the horrified crowd. "She's not in her room. She must have got out." A frantic scream from his brother. Two minutes later the fire brigade dashes up. Claud takes control, directs the firemen to search for Daphne in every room except her own.

Now he sees the glowing, writhing roof of the little turret tower fall in. Soon the flames are extinguished. All the pictures are saved. The body of a child is found.

"Unfortunately the poor girl had taken refuge beneath her bed and therefore her gallant uncle was unable to find her." The coroner's verdict.

Daphne's father. Oh God, his eyes!

Claud has lived through each moment just as intensely as twelve years ago. Shaking, dripping with perspiration, he drops back into the present.

He still sees his brother's eyes.

Had he loved his Daphne as I love my Hyacinth? At the thought Claud's heart contracts agonizingly. Suppose he had. Why not? Was she not as lovely, as piercingly sweet and young? Her eagerness! Had he not loved her himself— his dear little niece? The "perfect playfellow" he used to call her. That last evening he had gone to say good night to her in her little Carpaccio bed.

"Time to go to sleep," he had said.

"Oh, bother sleep!" she had exclaimed, imploring him to remain. "I haven't had nearly time enough to play!"

Once more he feels the light burden in his arms, the unconscious little body that would so easily have revived to entertain its eager spirit—to welcome it back to the life it loved.

"Not nearly time enough to play?" Claud's mind struggled from the past to the present, to the past again and back to the present. Not nearly time enough to play.

The galloping, riderless rocking horse? Hyacinth running races alone? His wife's strange impulses? Hide and seek? These and other things flit through his strained mind.

He is nearly home now—home to Laura and Hyacinth— and to-morrow night they will all three be far from here. Yes, but in the meantime he is still so much in the grip of that fatal hour twelve years ago, that he seems actually to hear that awful clanging and the cries of "Fire! Fire!"

Heavens! how *real*, how outside himself these hideous sounds now seem! But this is past bearing. Are his senses hopelessly haunted? This way lies madness. He must go away—let the house—return to America.

The sounds are insistent—grow louder. The illusion is complete.

God! can it really be *now?*

Turning the corner which brings the distant house into view, Claud stares. Yes, it is true! The present and the past have fused. The bell—the shouts are actual—immediate!

It is twelve years later, but Lichen Hall is again on fire, and burning—burning furiously. How can a fire have taken so strong a hold? Every modern device for extinguishing an outbreak had been installed.

Claud tears up the hill and reaches the lawn. This time it is the other wing that has caught fire, that in which he, Laura and Hyacinth sleep. Its top storey is already blazing. A crowd is gazing upward—pale faces red in the reflected glow. That shrieking woman, struggling to escape from arms that hold her back, can that be Laura? Disjointedly, from various voices, Claud learns the situation. The water-supply is frozen—all the pipes useless. The telephone wires are broken down, but the car has gone for the fire brigade. Any moment now they should be here. In the meantime the child—his child—is upstairs, and the wooden staircase is impassable; was already so before any one was aware of the outbreak. His wife had not yet gone up to bed, and, as only the family sleep in that wing, no one was there. The child is alone, up there, trapped in that red horror, and the longest ladder cannot reach to the window of her room. A second ladder? Yes, they are tying two together with ropes and several men have offered to climb up.

Claud says he will go himself. Thank God the ladders are now securely fastened together. There is still time, but none to lose. The roof must soon fall in.

The ladder has been placed against the wall under Hyacinth's room. Claud's foot is already on its second rung when something catches his eye. At a window three to the right of the one to which he is climbing he sees a child appear. The window is open. Her long, thin arms are outstretched, her red head gleams in the flaring light.

"Move the ladder, quick, quick!" Claud yells distractedly. "She isn't in her bedroom. She's gone into the other room—the playroom. There! There! Can't you see her? There, hanging out of that window!"

No one sees anything, but blindly they obey. There is a rush and eager arms carry out his orders. The ladder is dragged away to the other window, at which Claud is pointing. It's ready now. Cheers ring out. Claud climbs up, up, up.

Near the top he raises his head and finds himself staring into the smiling face of the girl who had perished in the flames twelve years ago. As Claud stares transfixed, the lovely, smiling face blurs and fades away. No one is there.

With a cry no one below could ever forget Claud hurls himself down the ladder.

"The other window!" he gasps. "Back to the other window!"

Wonderfully quickly the ladder is moved and replaced, but not quickly enough. The delay has been fatal. Just as the fire engines roar up the drive, the roof falls in.

Again every picture is saved, and a little body is recovered.

The Travelling Grave

L. P. Hartley

Hugh Curtis was in two minds about accepting Dick Munt's invitation to spend Sunday at Lowlands. He knew little of Munt, who was supposed to be rich and eccentric and, like most people of that kind, a collector. Hugh dimly remembered having asked his friend Valentine Ostrop what it was that Munt collected, but he could not recall Valentine's answer. Hugh Curtis was a vague man with an unretentive mind, and the mere thought of a collection, with its many separate challenges to the memory, fatigued him. What he required of a week-end party was to be left alone as much as possible, and to spend the remainder of his time in the society of agreeable women. Searching his mind, though with distaste, for he hated to disturb it, he remembered Ostrop telling him that parties at Lowlands were generally composed entirely of men, and rarely exceeded four in number. Valentine didn't know who the fourths was to be but he begged Hugh to come—

"You will enjoy Munt," he said. "He really doesn't pose at all. It's his nature to be like that."

"Like what?" his friend had inquired.

"Oh, original and—and queer, if you like," answered Valentine. "He's one of the exceptions—he's much odder than he seems, whereas most people are more ordinary than they seem."

Hugh Curtis agreed. "But I like ordinary people," he added. "So how shall I get on with Munt?"

"Oh," said his friend, "but you're just the type he likes. He prefers ordinary—it's a stupid word—I mean normal, people, because their reactions are more valuable."

"Shall I be expected to react?" asked Hugh with nervous facetiousness.

"Ha! Ha!" laughed Valentine, poking him gently—"we never quite know what he'll be up to. But you will come, won't you?"

Hugh Curtis had said he would.

All the same, when Saturday morning came he began to regret his decision and to wonder whether it might not be honorably reversed. He was a man in early middle life, rather set in his ideas, and though not specially a snob he could not help testing a new acquaintance by the standards of the circle to which he belonged. This circle had never warmly welcomed Valentine Ostrop; he was the most unconventional of Hugh's friends. Hugh liked him when they were alone together, but directly Valentine fell in with kindred spirits he developed a kind of foppishness of manner that Hugh instinctively disliked. He had no curiosity about his friends, and thought it out of place in personal relationships, so he had never troubled to ask himself what this altered demeanor of Valentine's, when surrounded by his cronies, might denote. But he had a shrewd idea that Munt would bring out Valentine's less sympathetic side. Could he send a telegram saying he had been unexpectedly detained? Hugh turned the idea over; but partly from principle, partly from laziness (he hated the mental effort of inventing false circumstances to justify change plans) he decided he couldn't. His letter of acceptance had been so unconditional. He also had the fleeting notion (a totally unreasonable one) that Munt would somehow find out and be nasty about it.

So he did the best he could for himself; looked out the latest train that would get him to Lowlands in decent time for dinner, and telegraphed that he would come by that. He would arrive at the house, he calculated, soon after seven. "Even if dinner is as late as half-past eight," he thought to himself, "they won't be able to do much to me in an hour and a quarter." This habit of mentally assuring to himself periods of comparative immunity from unknown perils had begun at school. "Whatever I've done," he used to say to himself, "they can't kill me." With the war, this saving reservation had to be dropped: they could kill him, that was what they were there for. But now that Peace was here the little mental amulet once more diffused its healing properties; Hugh had recourse to it more often than he would have admitted. Absurdly enough he invoked it now. But it annoyed him that he would arrive in the dusk of the September evening. He liked to get his first impression of a new place by daylight.

Hugh Curtis's anxiety to come late had not been shared by the other two guests. They arrived at Lowlands in time for tea. Though they had not travelled together, Ostrop motoring down, they met practically on the doorstep, and each privately suspected the other of wanting to have his host for a few moments to himself.

But it seemed unlikely that their wish would have been gratified even if they had not both been struck by the same idea. Tea came in, the water bubbled in the urn, but still Munt did not present himself, and at last Ostrop asked his fellow-guest to make the tea.

"You must be deputy-host," he said; "you know Dick so well, better than I do."

This was true. Ostrop had long wanted to meet Tony Bettisher who, after the death of some one vaguely known to Valentine as Squarchy, ranked as Munt's oldest and closest friend. He was a short, dark, thickset man, whose appearance gave no clew to his character or pursuits. He had, Valentine knew, a job at the British Museum, but, to look at, he might easily have been a stock-broker.

"I suppose you know the place at every season of the year," Valentine said. "This is the first time I've been here in the autumn. How lovely everything looks!"

He gazed out at the wooded valley and the horizon fringed with trees. The scent of burning mould drifted in through the windows.

"Yes, I'm a pretty frequent visitor," answered Bettisher, busy with the teapot.

"I gather from his letter that Dick has just returned from abroad," said Valentine. "Why does he leave England on the rare occasions when it's tolerable? Does he do it for fun, or does he have to?" He put his head on one side and contemplated Bettisher with a look of mock despair.

Bettisher handed him a cup of tea.

"I think he goes when the spirit moves him."

"Yes, but *what* spirit?" cried Valentine, with an affected petulance of manner. "Of course our Richard is a law unto himself: we all know that. But he must have some motive. I don't suppose he's *fond* of travelling. It's *so* uncomfortable. Now Dick cares for his comforts. That's why he travels with so much luggage."

"Oh, does he?" inquired Bettisher. "Have you been with him?"

"No, but the Sherlock Holmes in me discovered that," declared Valentine triumphantly. "The trusty Franklin hadn't time to put it away. Two large crates. Now would you call that *personal* luggage?" His voice was forever underlining; it pounced upon "personal" like a hawk on a dove.

"Perambulators, perhaps," suggested Bettisher laconically.

"Oh, do you think so? Do you think he collects perambulators? That would explain everything!"

"What would it explain?" asked Bettisher, stirring in his chair.

"Why, his collection, of course!" exclaimed Valentine jumping up and bending on Bettisher an intensely serious gaze. "It would explain why he doesn't invite us to see it, and why he's so shy of talking about it. Don't you see? An unmarried man, a bachelor, *sine prole* as far as we know, with whole *attics-full* of perambulators! It would be *too* fantastic. The world would laugh, and Richard, much as we love him, is terribly serious. Do you imagine it's a kind of vice?"

"All collecting is a form of vice."

"Oh, no, Bettisher, don't be hard, don't be cynical—a *substitute* for vice. But tell me before he comes—he *must* come soon, the laws of hospitality demand it—am I right in my surmise?"

"Which? You have made so many."

"I mean that what he goes abroad for, what he fills his house with, what he thinks about when we're not with him—in a word, what he collects, is perambulators?"

Valentine paused dramatically.

Bettisher did not speak. His eyelids flickered and the skin about his eyes made a sharp movement inward. He was beginning to open his mouth when Valentine broke in:

"Oh no, of course, you're in his confidence, your lips are sealed. Don't tell me, you mustn't, I forbid you to!"

"What's that he's not to tell you?" said a voice from the other end of the room.

"Oh Dick!" cried Valentine, "what a start you gave me! You must learn to move a little less like a dome of silence, mustn't he, Bettisher?"

Their host came forward to meet them on silent feet and wearing a kind of soundless smile. He was a small, thin, slightly-built man, very well turned out and with a conscious elegance of carriage.

"But I thought you didn't know Bettisher?" he said, when their greetings had been accomplished. "Yet when I come in I find you with difficulty stemming the flood of confidences pouring from his lips."

His voice was slightly ironical, it seemed at the same moment to ask a question and to make a statement.

"Oh, we've been together for hours," said Valentine airily, "and had the most enchanting conversation. Guess what we talked about."

"Not about me, I hope?"

"Well, about something very dear to you."

"About you, then?"

"Don't make fun of me. The objects I speak of are solid and useful."

"That does rather rule you out," said Munt meditatively. "What are they useful for?"

"Carrying bodies."

Munt glanced across at Bettisher, who was staring into the grate.

"And what are they made of?"

Valentine tittered, pulled a face, and answered, "I've little experience of them, but I should think chiefly of wood."

Munt got up and looked hard at Bettisher, who raised his eyebrows and said nothing.

"They perform at one time or another," said Valentine, enjoying himself enormously, "an essential service for us all."

There was a pause. Then Munt asked:

"Where do you generally come across them?"

"Personally I always try to avoid them," said Valentine. "But one meets them every day in the street and—and here, of course."

"Why do you try to avoid them?" asked Munt rather grimly.

"Since you think about them, and dote upon them, and collect them from all the corners of the earth, it pains me to have to say it," said Valentine with relish, "but I do not care to contemplate lumps of human flesh lacking the spirit that makes flesh tolerable."

He struck an oratorical attitude and breathed audibly through his nose. There was a prolonged silence. The dusk began to make itself felt in the room.

"Well," said Munt at last, in a hard voice. "You are the first person to guess my little secret, if I can give it so grandiose a name. I congratulate you."

Valentine bowed.

"May I ask how you discovered it? While I was detained upstairs, I suppose you—you—poked about?" His voice had a disagreeable ring; but Valentine, unaware of this, said loftily:

"It was unnecessary. They were in the hall, plain to be seen by any one. My Sherlock Holmes sense (I have eight or nine) recognized them immediately."

Munt shrugged his shoulders, then said in a less constrained tone:

"At this stage of our acquaintance I did not really intend to enlighten you. But since you know already, tell me, as a matter of curiosity, were you horrified?"

"Horrified!" cried Valentine. "I think it a charming taste, *so* original, so—so human. It ravishes my aesthetic sense; it slightly offends my moral principles."

"I was afraid it might," said Munt.

"I am a believer in birth control," Valentine prattled on. "Every night I burn a candle to Stopes."

Munt looked puzzled. "But then, how can you object?" he began.

Valentine went on without heeding him.

"But of course, by making a corner in the things you *do* discourage the whole business. Being exhibits they have to stand idle, don't they? You keep them empty?"

Bettisher started upon his chair, but Munt held out a pallid hand and murmured in a stifled voice:

"Yes, that is, most of them are."

Valentine clapped his hands in ecstasy.

"But some are not? Oh, but that's too ingenious of you. To think of the darlings lying there quite still, not able to lift a finger, much less scream! A sort of mannequin parade!"

"They certainly seem more complete with an occupant," Munt observed.

"But who's to push them? They can't go of themselves."

"Listen," said Munt slowly. "I've just come back from abroad, and I've brought with me a specimen that does go by itself, or nearly. It's outside there where you saw, waiting to be unpacked."

Valentine Ostrop had been the life and soul of many a party. No one knew better than he how to breathe new life into a flagging joke. Privately he felt that this one was played out; but he had a social conscience, he realized his responsibility toward conversation, and summoning all the galvanic enthusiasm at his command he cried out:

"Do you mean to say that it looks after itself, it doesn't need a helping hand, and that a fond mother can intrust her precious charge to it without nurse-maid and without a tremor?"

"She can," said Munt, "and without an undertaker and without a sexton."

"Undertaker? Sexton?" echoed Valentine. "What have they to do with perambulators?"

There was a pause during which the three figures, struck in their respective attitudes, seemed to have lost relationship with each other.

"So you didn't know," said Munt at length, "that it was coffins I collected."

An hour later the three men were standing in an upper room, looking down at a large oblong object that lay in the middle of a heap of shavings and seemed, to Valentine's sick fancy, to be burying its head among them. Munt had been giving a demonstration.

"Doesn't it look funny now it's still?" he remarked. "Almost as though it had been killed." He touched it pensively with his foot and it slid toward Valentine, who edged away. You couldn't quite tell where it was coming; it seemed to have no settled direction, and to move all ways at once, like a crab. "Of course the chances are really against it," sighed Munt. "It's very quick and it has that funny gift of anticipation. If it got a fellow up against a wall, I don't think he'd stand much chance. I didn't show you here, because I value my floors, but it can bury itself in wood in three minutes and in newly turned earth, say a flower-bed, in one. It has to be this squarish shape, or it couldn't dig. It just doubles the man up, you see, directly it catches him—backward, so as to break the spine. The top of the head fits in just below the heels. The soles of the feet come uppermost. The spring sticks a bit." He bent down to adjust something. "Isn't it a charming toy?"

"Looking at it from the criminal's standpoint, not the engineer's," said Bettisher, "I can't see that it would be much use in a house. Have you tried it on a stone floor?"

"Yes, it screams in agony and blunts the blades."

"Exactly. Like a mole on paving-stones. And even on an ordinary carpeted floor, it could cut its way in, but there would be a nice hole left in the carpet to show where it had gone."

Munt conceded this point, also. "But it's an odd thing," he added, "that in several of the rooms in this house it would really work, and baffle any one but an expert detective. Below, of course, are the knives, but the top is inlaid with real parquet. The grave is so sensitive—you saw just now how it seemed to grope—that it can feel the ridges, and adjust itself perfectly to the pattern of the parquet. But of course I agree with you. It's not an indoor game, really: it's a field sport. You go on, will you, and leave me to clear up this mess. I'll join you in a moment."

Valentine followed Bettisher down into the library. He was very much subdued.

"Well, that was the funniest scene," remarked Bettisher, chuckling.

"Do you mean just now? I confess it gave me the creeps."

"Oh no, not that: when you and Dick were talking cross-purposes."

"I'm afraid I made a fool of myself," said Valentine dejectedly. "I can't quite remember what we said. I know there was something I wanted to ask you."

"Ask away, but I can't promise to answer."

Valentine pondered a moment.

"Now I remember what it was."

"Spit it out."

"To tell you the truth I hardly like to. It was something Dick said. I hardly noticed at the time. I expect he was just playing up to me."

"Well?"

"About those coffins. Are they real?"

"How do you mean 'real'?"

"I mean could they be used as—?"

"My dear chap, they have been."

Valentine smiled, rather mirthlessly.

"Are they full-size—life-size, as it were?"

"The two things aren't quite the same," said Bettisher with a grin. "But there's no harm in telling you this: Dick's like all collectors. He prefers rarities, odd shapes, dwarfs and that sort of thing. Of course any anatomical peculiarity has to have allowance made for it in the coffin. On the whole his specimens tend to be smaller than the general run—shorter, anyhow. Is that what you wanted to know?"

"You've told me a lot," said Valentine. "But there was another thing."

"Out with it."

"When I imagined we were talking about perambulators—"

"Yes, yes."

"I said something about their being empty. Do you remember?"

"I think so."

"Then I said something about them having mannequins inside, and he seemed to agree."

"Oh yes."

"Well, he couldn't have meant that, it would be too—too realistic.

"Mannequins aren't very realistic."

"Well then, any sort of dummy."

"There are dummies and dummies. A skeleton isn't very talkative."

Valentine stared.

"He's been abroad," said Bettisher hastily. "I don't know what his latest idea is. But here's the man himself."

Munt came into the room.

"Children," he called out, "have you observed the time? It's nearly seven o'clock. And do you remember that we have another guest coming? He must be almost due."

"Who is he?" asked Bettisher.

"A friend of Valentine's. Valentine, you must be responsible for him. I asked him partly to please you: I don't know him. What shall we do to entertain him?"

"What sort of man is he?" Bettisher inquired.

"Describe him, Valentine. Is he tall or short?"

"Medium."

"Dark or fair?"

"Mouse-colored."

"Old or young?"

"About thirty-five."

"Married or single?"

"Single."

"What, has he no ties? No one to take an interest in him, or bother what becomes of him?"

"He has no near relations."

"Do you mean to say that very likely nobody knows he is coming to spend Sunday here?"

"Probably not. He has rooms in London, and he wouldn't trouble to leave his address."

"Extraordinary the casual way some people live. Is he brave or timid?"

"Oh, come, what a question! About as brave as I am."

"Is he clever or stupid?"

"All my friends are clever," said Valentine, with a flicker of his old spirit. "He's not intellectual: he'd be afraid of difficult parlor games or brilliant conversation."

"He ought not to have come here. Does he play bridge?"

"I don't think he has much head for cards."

"Could Tony induce him to play chess?"

"Oh no, chess needs too much concentration."

"Is he given to wool-gathering then?" Munt asked. "Does he forget to look where he's going?"

"He's the sort of man," said Valentine, "who expects to find everything just so. He likes to be led by the hand. He is perfectly tame and confiding, like a nicely-brought up child."

"In that case," said Munt, "we must find some childish pastime that won't tax him too much. Would he like Ring-a-ring-a-Roses?"

"I think that would embarrass him," said Valentine. He began to feel a tenderness for his absent friend, and a wish to stick up for him. "I should leave him to look after himself. He's rather shy. If you try to make him come out of his shell, you'll scare him. He'd rather take the initiative himself. He doesn't like being pursued, but in a mild way he likes to pursue."

"A child with hunting instincts," said Munt pensively. "How can we accommodate him? I have it! Let's play Hide and Seek. We will hide and he shall seek. Then he can't feel that we are forcing ourselves upon him. It will be the height of tact. He will be here in a few minutes. Let's go and hide now."

"But he doesn't know his way about the house."

"That will be all the more fun for him, since he likes to make discoveries on his own account."

"He might fall and hurt himself."

"Children never do. Now you run away and hide while I talk to Franklin," Munt continued quietly, "and mind you play fair, Valentine—don't let your natural affections lead you astray. Don't give yourself up because you're hungry for your dinner."

The motor that met Hugh Curtis was shiny and smart and glittered in the rays of the setting sun. The chauffeur was like an extension of it, and so quick in his movements that in the matter of stowing Hugh's luggage, putting him in and tucking the rug round him, he seemed to steal a march on time. Hugh regretted this precipitancy, this interference with the rhythm of his thoughts. It was a foretaste of the effort of adaptability he would soon have to make; the violent mental readjustment that every visit, and specially every visit among strangers entails: a surrender of the personality, the fanciful might call it a little death.

The car slowed down, left the main road, passed through white gate-posts and followed for two or three minutes a gravel drive shadowed by trees. In the dusk, Hugh could not see how far to right and left these extended. But the house, when it appeared, was plain enough. A large, regular, early-nineteenth-century building, encased in cream-colored stucco and pierced at generous intervals by large windows, some round-headed, some rectangular.

It looked dignified and quiet, and in the twilight seemed to shine with a soft radiance of its own. Hugh's spirits began to rise. In his mind's ear he already heard the welcoming buzz of voices coming from a distant part of the house. He smiled at the man who opened the door. But the butler didn't return his smile and no sound came through the gloom that spread out behind him.

"Mr. Munt and his friends are playing 'Hide and seek' in the house, sir," the man said, with a gravity that checked Hugh's impulse to laugh. "I was to tell you that the library is home, and you were to be 'He,' or I think he said, 'It,' sir. This is the way to the library. Be careful, sir, Mr. Munt did not want the lights turned on till the game was over."

"Am I to start now?" asked Hugh, stumbling a little as he followed his guide, "or can I go to my room first?"

The butler stopped and opened a door. "This is the library," he said. "I think it was Mr. Munt's wish that the game should begin immediately upon your arrival, sir."

A faint coo-ee sounded through the house.

"Mr. Munt said you could go anywhere you liked," the man added as he went away.

Valentine's emotions were complex. The harmless frivolity of his mind had been thrown out of gear by its encounter with the harsher frivolity of his friend. Munt, he felt sure, had a heart of gold which he chose to hide beneath a slightly sinister exterior. With his travelling graves and charnel talk he had hoped to get a rise out of his guest, and he had succeeded. Valentine still felt slightly unwell. But his nature was remarkably resilient, and the charming innocence of the pastime on which they were now engaged, soothed and restored his spirits, gradually reaffirming his first impression of Munt as a man of fine mind and keen perceptions, a dilettante with the personal force of a man of action, a character with a vein of implacability, to be respected but not to be feared. He was conscious also of a growing desire to see Curtis; he wanted to see Curtis and Munt together, confident that two people he liked could not fail to like each other. He pictured the pleasant encounter after the mimic warfare of Hide and Seek—the captor and the caught laughing a little breathlessly over the diverting circumstances of their introduction. With every passing moment his mood grew more sanguine.

Only one misgiving remained to trouble it. He felt he wanted to confide in Curtis, tell him something of what had happened after tea, and this he could not do without being disloyal to his host. Try as he would to make light of Munt's behavior about his collection, it was clear he wouldn't have given away the secret if it had not been surprised out of him. And Hugh would find his friend's bald statement of the facts difficult to swallow.

But what was he up to, letting his thoughts run on like this? He must hide, and quickly too. His acquaintance with the lie of the house, the fruit of two visits, was scanty and the darkness did not help him. The house was long and symmetrical; and its principal rooms lay on the first floor. Above were servants' rooms, attics, box rooms, probably—plenty of natural hiding places. The second storey was the obvious refuge.

He had been there only once, with Munt that afternoon, and he did not especially want to re-visit it; but he must enter into the spirit of the game. He found the staircase and went up, then paused; there was really no light at all.

"This is absurd," thought Valentine, "I must cheat." He entered the first room to the left, and turned down the switch. Nothing happened; the current had been cut off at the main. But by the light of a match he made out that he was in a combined bed and bathroom. In one corner was a bed, and in the other a large rectangular object with a lid over it, obviously a bath. The bath was close to the door.

As he stood debating he heard footsteps coming along the corridor. It would never do to be caught like this, without a run for his money. Quick as thought he raised the lid of the bath, which was not heavy, and slipped inside, cautiously lowering the lid.

It was narrower than the outside suggested, and it did not feel like a bath, but Valentine's inquiries into the nature of his hiding-place were suddenly cut short. He heard voices in the room, so muffled that he did not know at first whose they were. But they were evidently in disagreement.

Valentine lifted the lid. There was no light, so he lifted it farther. Now he could hear clearly enough.

"But I don't know what you really want, Dick," Bettisher was saying. "With the safety catch it would be pointless, and without it would be damned dangerous. Why not wait a bit?"

"I shall never have a better opportunity than this," said Munt, but in a voice so unfamiliar that Valentine scarcely recognized it.

"Opportunity for what?" said Bettisher.

"To prove whether the Travelling Grave can do what Madrali claimed for it."

"You mean whether it can disappear? We know it can."

"I mean whether it can effect somebody else's disappearance."

Then was a pause. Then Bettisher said—"Give it up. That's my advice."

"But he wouldn't leave a trace," said Munt half petulant, half pleading, like a thwarted child. "He has no relations. Nobody knows he's here. Perhaps he isn't here. We can tell Valentine he never turned up."

"We discussed all that," said Bettisher decisively, "and it won't wash."

There was another silence, disturbed by the distant hum of a motor car.

"We must go," said Bettisher.

But Munt appeared to detain him. Half imploring, half whining, he said:

"Anyhow, you don't mind my having put it there with the safety catch down?"

"Where?"

"By the china-cabinet. He's certain to run into it."

Bettisher's voice sounded impatiently from the passage.

"Well, if it pleases you. But it's quite pointless."

Munt lingered a moment, chanting to himself in a high greedy voice—greedy with anticipation: "I wonder which is up and which is down."

When he had repeated this three times he scampered sway, calling out peevishly: "You might have helped me, Tony. It's so heavy for me to manage."

It was heavy indeed. Valentine, when he had fought down the hysteria that came upon him, had only one thought: to take the deadly object and put it somewhere out of Hugh Curtis's way. If he could drop it from a window, so much the better. In the darkness the vague outline of its bulk, placed just where one had to turn to avoid the china-cabinet, was dreadfully familiar. He tried to recollect the way it worked. Only one thing stuck in his mind: "The ends are dangerous, the sides are safe." Or should it be, "The sides are dangerous, the ends are safe?" While the two sentences were getting mixed up in his mind, he heard the sound of "coo-ee," coming first from one part of the house, then from another. He could also hear footsteps in the hall below him.

Then he made up his mind, and with a confidence that surprised him, put his arms round the wooden cube and lifted it into the air. He hardly noticed its weight as he ran with it down the corridor. Suddenly he realized that he must have passed through an open door. A ray of moonlight showed him that he was in a bedroom, standing directly in front of an old-fashioned wardrobe, a towering majestic piece of furniture with three doors, the middle one holding a mirror. Dimly he saw himself reflected there, his burden in his arms. He deposited it on the parquet without making a sound; but on the way out he tripped over a footstool and nearly fell. He was relieved at making so much clatter, and the grating of the key, as he turned it in the lock, was music to his ears.

Automatically he put the key in his pocket. But he paid the penalty for his clumsiness. He had not gone a step when a hand caught him by the elbow.

Left by himself in the library, Hugh Curtis took stock of his position. In all the many visits he had paid, he had never met a reception quite like this. But it might have been worse. Adults, when they play children's games, are never so formidable and relentless as when they play their own. He wondered how much effort was expected of him; how far he ought to sacrifice his worn, but still respectable train-clothes. He had never caught any one in his life, and did not expect to do so now. He would just patrol the main thoroughfares like a good-natured policeman, not looking out for trouble, but ready to take in charge any one who ran into him. He had mounted the stairs and was marching majestically along the landing, when he heard a noise so loud that even his curiosity was aroused. For once completely forgetting himself he plunged clumsily forward and caught his quarry.

"Why it's Valentine!" he cried. "Now come quietly, and take me to my host. I must have a drink."

"I should like one too," said Valentine, who was trembling all over. "Why can't we have some light?"

"Turn it on, idiot," commanded his friend.

"I can't—it's cut off at the main. We must wait till Richard gives the word."

"Where is he?"

"I expect he's tucked away somewhere. Richard!" Valentine called out. "Dick!" He was too self-conscious to be able to give a good shout. "Bettisher, I'm caught! The game's over!"

There was silence a moment, then steps could be heard descending the stairs.

"Is that you, Dick?" asked Valentine of the darkness.

"No, Bettisher." The gaiety of the voice did not ring quite true.

"I've been caught," said Valentine again, almost as Atalanta might have done, and as though it was a wonderful achievement reflecting great credit upon everybody. "Allow me to present you to my captor. No, this is me. We've been introduced already."

It was a moment or two before the mistake was corrected, the two hands groping vainly for each other in the darkness.

"I expect it will be a disappointment when you see me," said Hugh Curtis in the pleasant voice that made many people like him.

"I want to see you," declared Bettisher. "I will, too. Let's have some light."

"I suppose it's no good asking you if you've seen Dick?" inquired Valentine facetiously. "He said we weren't to have any light till the game was finished. He's so strict with his servants; they have to obey him to the letter. I daren't even ask for a candle. But you know the faithful Franklin well enough."

"Dick will be here in a moment, surely," Bettisher said, for the first time that day appearing undecided.

They all stood listening.

"Perhaps he's gone to dress," Curtis suggested. "It's past eight o'clock."

"How can he dress in the dark?" asked Bettisher.

"He kept us waiting to-day because he knows us so well," remarked Valentine. "I don't think he will keep you."

Another pause.

"Oh, I'm tired of this," said Bettisher. "Franklin! Franklin!" His voice boomed through the house and a reply came almost at once from the hall, directly below them. "We think Mr. Munt must have gone to dress," said Bettisher. "Will you please turn on the light?"

"Certainly, sir, but I don't think Mr. Munt is in his room."

"Well, anyhow—"

"Very good, sir."

At once the corridor was flooded with light, and to all of them, in greater or less degree according to their familiarity with their surroundings, it seemed amazing that they should have had so much difficulty, half an hour before, in finding their way about. Even Valentine's harassed emotions experienced a moment's relaxation. They chaffed Hugh Curtis a little about the false impression his darkling voice had given them. Valentine, as always the more loquacious, swore it seemed to proceed from a large gaunt man with a hair-lip. They were beginning to move toward their rooms, Valentine had almost reached his, when Hugh Curtis called after them:

"I say, may I be taken to my room?"

"Of course," said Bettisher turning back. "Franklin! Franklin! Franklin, show Mr. Curtis where his room is. I don't know myself." He disappeared and the butler came slowly up the stairs.

"It's quite near, sir, at the end of the corridor," he said. "I'm sorry, with having no light we haven't got your things put out. But it'll only take a moment."

The door did not open when he turned the handle.

"Odd! It's stuck," he remarked, but it did not yield to the pressure of his knee and shoulder. "I've never known it to be locked before," he muttered, thinking aloud, obviously put out by this flaw in the harmony of the domestic arrangements. "If you'll excuse me, sir, I'll go and fetch my key."

In a minute or two he was back with it. So gingerly did he turn the key in the lock, he evidently expected another rebuff; but it gave a satisfactory click and the door swung open with the best will in the world.

"Now I'll go and fetch your suitcase," he said as Hugh Curtis entered.

"No, it's absurd to stay," soliloquized Valentine, fumbling feverishly with his front stud, "after all these warnings, it would be insane. It's what they do in a 'shocker,' linger on and on, disregarding revolvers and other palpable hints, while one by one the villain picks them off, all except the hero, who is generally the stupidest of all, but the luckiest. No doubt by staying I should qualify to be the hero; I should survive; but what about Hugh, and Bettisher, that close-mouth rat-trap?" He studied his face in the glass; it looked flushed. "I've had an alarming increase in blood pressure; I am seriously unwell, I must go away at once to a nursing-home, and Hugh must accompany me." He gazed round wretchedly at the warm, bright room, with its chintz and polished furniture, so comfortable, safe and unsensational. And for the hundredth time his thoughts veered round and flew from the opposite quarter. It would equally be madness to run away at a moment's notice, scared by what was no doubt only an elaborate practical joke. Munt, though not exactly a jovial man, would have his joke, as witness the game of Hide and Seek. No doubt the Travelling Grave itself was just a take in, a test of his and Bettisher's credulity. Munt was not popular, he had few friends, but that did not make him a potential murderer. Valentine had always liked him and no one, to his knowledge, had ever spoken a word against him. What sort of figure would he, Valentine, cut after this nocturnal flitting? He would lose at least two friends, Munt and Bettisher, and cover Hugh Curtis and himself with ridicule.

Poor Valentine! So perplexed was he that he changed his mind five times on the way down to the library. He kept repeating to himself the sentence, "I'm so sorry, Dick, I find my blood pressure rather high and I think I ought to go into a nursing-home to-night—Hugh will see me safely there," until it became meaningless; even its absurdity disappeared.

Hugh was in the library alone. It was now or never; but Valentine's opening words were swept aside by his friend who came running across the room to him.

"Oh, Valentine, the funniest thing has happened."

"Funny? Where? What?" Valentine asked.

"No, no, don't look as if you'd seen a ghost. It's not the least serious. Only it's so *odd*. This is a house of surprises. I'm glad I came."

"Tell me quickly."

"Don't look so alarmed. It's only very amusing. But I must show it you, or you'll miss the funny side of it. Come on up to my room, we've got five minutes."

But before they crossed the threshold Valentine pulled up with a start.

"Is *this* your room?"

"Oh, yes. Don't look so upset. It's a perfectly ordinary room, I tell you, except for one thing. No, stop a moment, wait here while I arrange the scene."

He darted in, and after a moment summoned Valentine to follow.

"Now, do you notice anything strange?"

"I see the usual evidences of untidiness."

A coat was lying on the floor and various articles of clothing were scattered about.

"You do? Well then—no deceit, gentlemen." With a gesture he snatched the coat up from the floor. "Now what do you see?"

"I see a further proof of slovenly habits—a pair of shoes where the coat was."

"Look well at those shoes. There's nothing about them that strikes you as peculiar?"

Valentine studied them. They were ordinary brown shoes, lying side by side, the soles uppermost, a short pace from the wardrobe. They looked as though some one had taken them off and forgotten to put them away, or taken them out, and forgotten to put them on.

"Well," pronounced Valentine at last. "I don't usually leave my shoes upside-down like that, but you might."

"Ah," said Hugh triumphantly, "your surmise is incorrect. They're *not* my shoes."

"Not yours? Then they were left here by mistake. Franklin should have taken them away."

"Yes, but that's where the coat comes in. I'm reconstructing the scene you see, hoping to impress you. While he was downstairs fetching my bag, to save time I began to undress; I took my coat off and hurled it down there. After he had gone I picked it up. So he never saw the shoes."

"Well, why make such a fuss? They won't be wanted till morning. Or would you rather ring for Franklin and tell him to take them away?"

"Ah!" cried Hugh, delighted by this. "At last you've come to the heart of the matter. He couldn't take them away."

"Why couldn't he?"

"Because they're fixed to the floor!"

"Oh rubbish!" said Valentine. "You must be dreaming."

He bent down, took hold of the shoes by the welts, and gave a little tug. They did not move.

"There you are!" cried Hugh. "Apologize. Own that it is unusual to find in one's room a strange pair of shoes adhering to the floor."

Valentine's reply was to give another heave. Still the shoes did not budge.

"No good," commented his friend. "They're nailed down, or gummed down, or something."

"The dinner-bell hasn't rung; we'll get Franklin to clear up the mystery."

The butler, when he came, looked uneasy, and surprised them by speaking first.

"Was it Mr. Munt you were wanting, sir?" he said to Valentine. "I don't know where he is. I've looked every-where and can't find him."

"Are these his shoes by any chance?" asked Valentine.

They couldn't deny themselves the mild entertainment of watching Franklin stoop down to pick up the shoes, and recoil in perplexity when he found them fast in the floor.

"These should be Mr. Munt's, sir," he said doubtfully, "these should. But what's happened to them that they won't leave the floor?"

The two friends laughed gaily.

"That's what *we* want to know," Hugh Curtis chuckled. "That's why we called you: we thought you could help us."

"They're Mr. Munt's shoes right enough," muttered the butler. "They must have got something heavy inside."

"Damned heavy," said Valentine, playfully grim.

Fascinated, the three men stared at the upturned soles. They lay so close together that there was no room between for two thumbs set side by side.

Rather gingerly the butler stooped again, and tried to feel the uppers. This was not as easy as it seemed, for the shoes were flattened against the floor, as if a weight had pressed them down.

His face was white as he stood up.

"There *is* something in them," he said in a frightened voice.

"And his shoes were full of feet," carolled Valentine flippantly. "Trees, perhaps."

"It's not as hard as wood," said the butler. "You can squeeze it a bit if you try."

They looked at each other, and a tension made itself felt in the room.

"There's only one way to find out," declared Hugh Curtis suddenly, in a determined tone one could never have expected from him.

"How?"

"Take them off!"

"Take what off?"

"His shoes off, you idiot."

"Off what?"

"That's what I don't know yet, you bloody fool," Curtis almost screamed; and kneeling down, he tore apart the laces and began tugging and wrenching at one of the shoes.

"It's coming, it's coming," he cried. "Valentine, put your arms round me and pull, that's a good fellow. It's the heel that's giving the trouble."

Suddenly the shoe slipped off, disclosing a slender brown object, the shape of a dog's tongue.

"Why it's only a sock," whispered Valentine; "it's so thin."

"Yes, but the foot's inside it all right," cried Curtis in a loud strange voice, speaking very rapidly. "And here's the ankle, see, and here's where it begins to go down into the floor, see. He must have been a very small man, you see I never saw him, but it's all so crushed—"

The sound of a heavy fall made them turn.

Franklin had fainted.

Those Whom the Gods Love . . .
Hilda Hughes

David Williams walked slowly and wearily up the path to the farmhouse. The sun cast shadows over the meadows, but the hills in the background were dark and ominous. It had been a very red sky that morning.

He was a tall man with a rather handsome and refined face, but time had already imprinted itself upon it. He walked with long steps like one whose business it is to walk across open spaces, across land in the midst of cultivation. But to the observant there was something more in his gait than the characteristic tread of the farmer. He was a little weary of life—not merely tired through work that was well done.

He looked across at the forbidding hills as his hand touched the garden gate latch, and then he entered the farmhouse which was typical of so many Welsh homesteads.

There was a row of copper kettles upon the kitchen mantelpiece which made it a thing of splendor, and an enormous fire roared up the chimney, although it was summer. The teapot was, as almost always, to be seen upon the hob. And there, stretched before the fire was Nan, the black and tan collie with her sensitive face and faithful eyes—an excellently trained sheep dog, while Bob, the other dog, an equally good worker though a less beautiful creature, peered through the door, as if master and mistress would not care for him to enter.

The rosy-faced girl who did the housework and made herself generally useful, put the finishing touches to the table, and Blodwyn, David's wife, seated herself opposite her husband.

She was a healthy, good-looking woman, some six years older than her husband. But her face expressed discontent.

She carved the joint, handed David his portion, speaking but little.

He made a brave attempt at conversation, telling her of Mrs. Jones of Penmaenmawr, who had a new baby, and Mrs. Williams whose son had gone to South Wales, and the Vicar, who was going to organize a concert in aid of the Church School.

When he mentioned music her face clouded still further.

Deirdre, the girl he loved, had won the prize at the Eisteddfod at Pwhlleli that year. Deirdre was a beautiful girl who worked at a neighboring farm, a lovely, delicate creature; she helped Mrs. Thomas with her baby, and milked the cows though she looked too fragile to carry a milking pail.

David had lived with Blodwyn long enough to read her mind, to know what kind of thought was about to seek expression, even if he could not actually foresee the words.

Before the phrase rose to her lips, the color tinged his face and neck.

"Have you seen her to-day?"

"Who?" he asked, pretending not to understand her reference.

"You should know better than I, David—Deirdre, of course."

His cheeks grew a deeper red.

"No," he said rather vexedly. "You didn't want me to, I suppose—though how I could help seeing her if she chanced to come along the hill, Heaven alone knows."

Blodwyn was not soothed. She loved this husband of hers whose eye had wandered to some one years younger and fairer than herself. And her jealousy burned into her very flesh. She would have given much to know if Deirdre ever thought of him so—Deirdre who, she had heard it said, had had the cheek to refuse him before he married her. Deirdre was now being courted by both the sons at the farm where she worked. Why did she not accept one of them? This girl with her beautiful body, sensitive face and fanciful name might have changed her mind, maybe, since David's marriage five years ago.

At any rate, Blodwyn knew that in spite of the money she had brought him—enough to buy their farm—David repented of his bargain very often. And, if Deirdre cared it must make it all the more bitter to him. Blodwyn could not bear to face facts as they were. He was very good to her—he did all that she expected of him.

But the fever in her blood would not be quieted.

"It's not so strange that I should be babbling of her," she said, "after all I know."

"I've never been untrue to you," David said sharply. "You know that. You've talked of that girl to me until I can't stand it any longer. You'll go crazy if you keep on. Besides, I thought we decided not to speak of it any more."

She was silenced then; silenced, but not soothed. She handed him the potatoes and her mind all the time rushed on in the same channels.

He finished his dinner. He sat by the fire and put on his gaiters. He was going to the market town. Usually he went to market early in the morning. To-day, he merely wished to see one or two of the farmers before they left for home. He would be able to discuss business with them before they took out their horses and motors. It was unfortunate that he had been hindered from going into town as usual that morning, but in any case he should not be too late.

"Give me a kiss, Blodwyn, before I go," he said, his huff turning suddenly to tenderness.

And, even as his kiss was fresh upon her cheek, she cursed Fate because she could not control his mind, his heart, his innermost spirit. She could nag him and extract promises and see his obedience to her every whim, but his heart, his mind with all its dreams—were out of her reach.

Blodwyn could not rest at home that day. Her troubled spirit urged her to be off. And since her thoughts were dwelling on Deirdre, she found herself walking to Mrs. Thomas's farm, where the girl worked, as if to see that she were still there.

There was a keenness in the air, and storm clouds were gathering. Yet the sun still shone, and the clouds, passing quickly, cast shadows over the exquisite expanse of green hills. Nature's temper changes in an instant in a mountainous country. Blodwyn, gazing at the dark outline of the mountains before her, knew that rain would fall before night time.

She walked on past babbling mountain streams. Welsh sheep with graceful bodies, small pointed faces and long tails skipped out of her way, or peered at her as she passed from behind some boulder or furze bush. The way was violet and pink before her with heather and ling. Little ferns grew all around and one or two seagulls wheeled overhead.

The solitude would have been terrible to any city dweller.

Rain suddenly began to fall.

Mrs. Williams looked down at the lake between the mountains. It was black like some evil thing—black and threatening. Where, before, the sun had danced upon a shimmering blue surface, all was now chill and black and foreboding. There was a scream of wild birds in the air. Blodwyn turned up her coat collar and began to run.

She reached the farm at last, opened a peculiar iron gate almost like the door of an oven—North Wales is full of these—and took a short cut across the fields.

Outside the house there were white pebbles. It is the fashion for some farmers and many peasants to accumulate pebbles for the sake of decoration, but they must be white.

A dog barked as she advanced toward the door. And a woman, who was working in the scullery, peered out to see who was coming. But Mrs. Thomas herself opened the front door. It creaked a little, as though it were not used very often. Indeed the side door was in greater demand. The room into which Blodwyn was ushered had sporting pictures upon the walls, a case of stuffed birds and a text over the piano—"God is love."

"I wondered if you'd have gone to market," Blodwyn said to Mrs. Thomas, "but I thought in any case I'd just look in to see how you were. Has the gout left you yet?"

"My foot's a bit troublesome," returned Mrs. Thomas, "and Deirdre went in my place. She's a very good girl. I can depend upon her."

Mrs. Williams sat down. This surely was what she had wanted to know.

"Your son's walking out with her, isn't he?" she asked, knowing that this was not the case, but finding it impossible to get the girl out of her mind.

"I wish he was. Both of the boys would give their eyes for her—but she's keeping her own counsel. She's driven into market with William to-day. She's more like one of the family. I hope she will be before she's done. Did you see her prizes? She's been very lucky at Eisteddfods this season."

And Mrs. Thomas proudly displayed the trophies.

"A very fortunate girl all round. A darling of the gods, you might say," replied Blodwyn putting the trophies down before she had so much as looked at them. This talk was going to her head.

They chatted about market prices and the new organ, and had a good deal to say about the vicar's lady. Time after time Blodwyn looked at the clock and always she delayed her departure.

The hour was getting late and Deirdre had not come home. Mrs. Thomas could not think what had kept them.

At last Blodwyn stirred. She decided to go home over the cliffs, since the path there would be drier. But she had left it rather late, and to any one who had not been so sure of the way, the route must have been fatal.

The tide was in and water dashed and swirled against the cliffs. A light flashed and faded, flashed and faded, out at sea. The gorse bushes looked almost like human forms in the uncanny dusk. The moaning of the sea was in her ears, the salt upon her lips and in her nostrils. A seagull wheeled overhead and pierced the darkness with its screams. A sheep crept out from behind a boulder and made Blodwyn start. Thunder rumbled in the distance.

And all the time Blodwyn's thoughts tortured her. She could see a pale and lovely face in her imagination, a pair of laughing eyes, a beautiful young figure. If only she could possess her husband's mind—if she could lay the ghost for once and all.

The wind whistled shrilly about her. Heavy drops of rain fell. She stumbled, picked herself up, went on her way. It was an evil night. Her thoughts were evil too. She hated this girl to whom the gods had been so kind. As long as she lived she could not be sure that her husband would lose his dream. How could she rid herself of this girl for ever—this thorn in the flesh?

Her hatred grew, fed by a tortured imagination.

To live and see this girl till old age came! She could not face the prospect. Rather would she herself drain the life-blood from her veins—crush the flower beneath her heel, strangle the laughter on her lips. If only she might smother her in bed.

"God!" she cried and it was a prayer from the heart, "hear me I beseech you! Let her die! Let her die!"

The significance of the act did not strike her. She wanted death for Deirdre. It was natural to her to call to her God, for her race was religious by instinct and religious from tradition.

"God!" she screamed, "God! Kill her! Kill her! Let her die!" She shrieked the words aloud in the wind. She felt herself stiffen with passion and anger.

"If she were here now," she told herself, "I'd push her over the cliff, let her beautiful body fall into the sea, hear her scream, see her white face when the coastguard found her body later. It would be an accident. I would be able to escape the law. I'd stumble against her when the path was narrow, hurl her below to sudden death."

Was murder committed by people like herself, she asked—ordinary people. "Whoso hateth his brother, the same is a murderer." But she did not care.

And then it seemed as though there was a wailing in the wind, a heart-piercing cry.

Something—she was sure she was not dreaming—brushed against her as she walked, seemed to clutch her skirt, made her heart stand still. Her knees trembled. She could scarcely walk. Her breath came in gasps. The tears were streaming down her face. She heard a distant clock strike nine, but the fact that the church was so near, that humanity itself would soon be within reach, brought no comfort to her. She was possessed with evil spirits. And phantoms seemed to pass her in the darkness. She felt something touch her face—heard ominous noises. Could it only have been the wind? She saw her husband's face distinctly in the darkness—ashen white—with repulsion upon it for her.

She was moaning as she walked. Prayers and curses came
in a strange jumble from her lips. She must be going mad.
Even the white faces of sheep brought the perspiration out
upon her brow. She felt that any moment she might fall,
wished that death might come to her and bring relief.

She turned and left the sea behind her, crossed the
range and found herself wading in a mountain stream.
She turned again, and picked her way carefully between
some cows, caught her ankle against a gorse bush and then
pressed on as before. As she neared home her passion gradually died down. She found herself strangely calm after
such a fury. She was tired physically and mentally. Strong
emotion had worn her out.

She dragged her aching limbs along. Her shoes were
sodden. She believed there was a blister on her heel. Her
hair too was wet through and as her damp clothes clung to
her, she shivered with cold—with cold and fatigue.

She opened her own garden gate, passed up the path,
opened the front door.

Some one stirred in the sitting-room.

She saw William Thomas's face, very white in the lamplight.

Her servant girl hovered about her and was gone. "Mrs.
Williams, Mr. Thomas has been waiting for you. He has
something to tell you, dear."

Blodwyn caught the note of endearment and turned a
beseeching face to William Thomas.

His lips were blue.

"I've bad news, Mrs. Williams. It's a rotten world. Poor
Deirdre . . ."

"Go on!" said Blodwyn, her voice quiet, her body icy cold.

"She's dead. Crumpled up like a flower as she crossed
the road. It was just before nine."

And then his words verged into a sob.

"Just before nine!" The phrase re-echoed in her brain.
She remembered hearing the clock strike. She had been

planning murder, praying to God, just before then. She was a murderess—a murderess. She ought to hang. What was it, they said, "hang by the neck until you are dead"? She wanted to scream and yet she was fighting for breath. Her tongue clove to her mouth and her knees were trembling.

At last she forced herself to speak. "Poor lad!" she said. "It's cruel! But don't take on so!"

No blood had been shed, she thought, some higher power had stepped in.

"Just like a flower," said William Thomas brokenly.

Deirdre dead. She had killed her. . . . It must have been her spirit that had swept past her on the cliff.

"I've killed David's dream. I shall have him for myself now—nothing to come between."

"You mustn't grieve too much," she said aloud, "it's hard, poor boy, I know."

She thought with a rush of relief, "God has answered my prayer." She must really calm herself. Later she would be able to rejoice. Never would she and her man be separated in thought again. She would be very good to him.

"There's something else I must say," continued William Thomas, trying to drain the anguish from his voice.

"David . . . He went to market as you know. He was leaving the 'Swan' when he saw her fall. A car was dashing round the corner. He thought she had fainted and the car would get her. He decided to throw himself between her and the car. So he rushed out into the road—pushed her back—not knowing she was dead already—had died suddenly in the street—something wrong with her heart I suppose—and . . . the car got him . . . poor David!"

"Killed?" said Mrs. Williams dully, knowing how he must reply.

And then she screamed aloud—screamed until there seemed no quieting her.

The Hanging of Alfred Wadham

E. F. Benson

I had been telling Father Denys Hanbury about a very extraordinary séance which I had attended a few days before. The medium in trance had said a whole series of things which were unknown to anybody but myself and a friend of mine who had lately died, and who, so she said, was present and was speaking to me through her. Naturally, from the strictly scientific point of view in which alone we ought to approach such phenomena, such information was not really evidence that the spirit of my friend was in touch with her, for all this was already known to me, and might by some process of telepathy have been communicated to the medium from my brain and not through the agency of the dead. She spoke, too, not in her own ordinary voice, but in a voice which certainly was very like his. Then again, however, his voice was known to me; it was in my memory even as were the things she had been saying. All this, therefore, as I was remarking to Father Denys, must be ruled out as positive evidence that communications had been coming from the other side of death.

"A telepathic explanation was possible," I said, "and we have to accept any known explanation which covers the facts before we conclude that the dead have come back into touch with the material world."

The room was quite warm, but I saw that he shivered slightly, and hitching his chair a little nearer the fire, he spread out his hands to the blaze. Such hands they were; beautiful and expressive of him, and so like the praying hands of Albert Dürer; the blaze shone through them as through rose-red alabaster. He shook his head.

"It's a terribly dangerous thing to attempt to get into communication with the dead," he said. "If you seem to get into touch with them, you run the risk of establishing connection not with them but with awful and perilous intelligences. Study telepathy by all means, for that is one of the marvels of the mind which we are meant to investigate like any other of the wonderful secrets of Nature. But I interrupt you; you said something else occurred. Tell me about it."

Now I knew Father Denys's creed about such things and deplored it. He holds, as his Church commands him, that intercourse with the spirits of the dead is impossible, and that when it appears to occur; as it undoubtedly does, the inquirer is really in touch with some species of dramatic demon, who is impersonating the spirit of the dead. Such a thing has always seemed to me as monstrous as it is without foundation, and there is nothing I can discover in the recognized sources of Christian doctrine which justifies such a view.

"Yes! now comes the queer part," I said. "For, still speaking in the voice of my friend, the medium told me something which instantly I believed to be untrue. It could not therefore have been drawn telepathically from me. After that the séance came to an end, and in order to convince myself that this could not have come from him, I looked up the diary of my friend which had been left me at his death, and which had just been sent me by his executors, and was still unpacked. There I found an entry which proved that what the medium had said was absolutely correct. A certain thing—I needn't go into it—had occurred precisely as she had stated, though I should have been willing to swear to the contrary. That cannot have come into her mind from mine, and there is no source that I can see from which she could have obtained it except from my friend. What do you say to that?"

He shook his head. "I don't alter my position at all," he said. "That information, given it did not come from your mind, which certainly seems to be impossible, came from some discarnate agency. But it didn't come from the spirit of your friend: it came from some evil and awful intelligence."

"But isn't that pure assumption?" I asked. "It is surely much simpler to say that the dead can, under certain conditions, communicate with us. Why drag in the devil?"

He glanced at the clock.

"It's not very late," he said. "Unless you want to go to bed, give me your attention for half an hour, and I will try to show you."

The rest of my story is what Father Denys told me, and what happened immediately afterward.

"Though you are not a Catholic," he said, "I think you would agree with me about an institution which plays a very large part in our ministry, namely Confession, as regards the sacredness and the inviolability of it. A soul laden with sin comes to his Confessor knowing that he is speaking to one who has the power to pronounce or withhold forgiveness, but who will never, for any conceivable reason, repeat or hint at what has been told him. If there was the slightest chance of the penitent's confession being made known to any one, unless he himself, for purposes of expiation or of righting some wrong, chooses to repeat it, no one would ever come to Confession at all. The Church would lose the greatest hold it possesses over the souls of men, and the souls of men would lose that inestimable comfort of knowing (not hoping merely, but knowing) that their sins are forgiven them. Of course the priest may withhold Absolution, if he is not convinced that he is dealing with a true penitent, and before he gives it, he will insist that the penitent make such reparation as is in his power, for the wrong he has done. If he had profited by his dishonesty he must make good; whatever crime he has committed he must give warrant that his penitence is sincere. But I think you would agree that in any case the priest cannot, whatever the result of his silence may be, repeat what has been told him. By doing so he might right or avert some hideous wrong, but it is impossible for him to do so. What he has heard, he has heard under the seal of Confession, concerning the sacredness of which no argument is conceivable."

"It is possible to imagine awful consequences resulting from it," I said. "But I agree."

"Before now awful consequences have come of it," he said, "but they don't touch the principle. And now I am going to tell you of a certain confession that was once made to me."

"How can you?" I said. "That's impossible surely."

"For a certain reason, which we shall come to later," he said, "you will see that secrecy is no longer incumbent on me. But the point of my story is not that: it is to warn you about attempting to establish communication with the dead. Signs and tokens, voices and apparitions appear to come through to us from them, but who sends them? You will see what I mean."

I settled myself down to listen.

"You will probably not remember with any distinctness, if at all, a murder committed a year ago, when a man called

Gerald Selfe met his death. There was no enticing mystery about it, no romantic accessories, and it aroused no public interest. Selfe was a man of loose life, but he held a respectable position, and it would have been disastrous for him if his private irregularities had come to light. For some time before his death he had been receiving blackmailing letters regarding his relations with a certain married woman, and, very properly, he had put the matter into the hands of the police. They had been pursuing certain clues, and on the afternoon before Selfe's death one of the officers of the Criminal Investigation Department had written to him that everything pointed to his man-servant, who certainly knew of his intrigue, being the culprit. This was a young man named Alfred Wadham: he had only lately entered Selfe's service, and his past history was of the most unsavory sort. They had baited a trap for him, of which details were given, and suggested that Selfe should display it, which, within an hour or two he successfully did. This information and these instructions were conveyed in a letter which, after Selfe's death, was found in a drawer of his writing-table, of which the lock had been tampered with. Only Wadham and his master slept in his flat; and a woman came in every morning to cook breakfast and do the housework, and Selfe lunched and dined at his club, or in the restaurant on the ground floor of this house of flats, and here he dined that night. When the woman came in next morning she found the outer door of the flat open, and Selfe lying dead on the floor of his sitting-room with his throat cut. Wadham had disappeared, but in the slop-pail of his bedroom was water which was stained with human blood. He was caught two days afterward and at his trial elected to give evidence. His story was that he suspected he had fallen into a trap, and that while Mr. Selfe was at dinner he searched his drawers and found the letter sent by the police, which proved that this was the case. He therefore decided to bolt, and he left the flat that evening before his master came back to it after dinner. Being in the witness-box, he was of course subjected to a searching cross-examination, and contradicted himself in several particulars. Then there was that incriminating evidence in his room, and the motive for the crime was clear enough. After a very long deliberation the jury found him guilty, and he was sentenced to death. His appeal which followed was dismissed.

"Wadham was a Catholic, and since it is my office to minister to Catholic prisoners at the jail where he was lying under sentence of death, I had many talks with him, and entreated him for the sake of his immortal soul to confess his guilt. But though he was even eager to confess other misdeeds of his, some of which it was ugly work to speak of, he maintained his innocence on this charge of murder. Nothing shook him, and though as far as I could judge he was sincerely penitent for other misdeeds, he swore to me that the story he told in court was, in spite of the contradictions in which he had involved himself, essentially true, and that if he was hanged, he died unjustly. Up till the last afternoon of his life, when I sat with him for two hours, praying and pleading with him, he stuck to that. Why he should do that, unless indeed he was innocent, when he was eager to search his heart for the confession of other gross wickednesses, was curious; the more I pondered it, the more inexplicable I found it, and during that afternoon, doubt as to his guilt began to grow in me. A terrible thought it was, for he had lived in sin and error, and to-morrow his life was to be broken, like a snapped stick. I was to be at the prison again before six in the morning, and I still had to determine whether I should give him the Sacrament. If he went to his death guilty of murder, but refusing to confess, I had no right to give it him, but if he was innocent, my withholding of it was as

terrible as any miscarriage of justice. Then on my way out
I had a word with one of the warders, which brought my
doubt closer to me.

"'What do you make of Wadham?' I asked.

"He drew aside to let a man pass, who nodded to him:
somehow I knew that he was the hangman.

"'I don't like to think of it, sir,' he said. 'I know he was
found guilty, and that his appeal failed. But if you ask me
whether I believe him to be a murderer, why no, I don't.'

"I spent the evening alone: about ten o'clock as I was
on the point of going to bed, I was told that a man called
Horace Kennion was below, and wanted to see me. He
was a Catholic, and though I had been friends with him
at one time, certain things had come to my knowledge
which made it impossible for me to have anything more to
do with him, and I had told him so. He was wicked—oh,
don't misunderstand me; we all do wicked things constantly: the life of us all is a tissue of misdeeds, but he alone
of all men I had ever met seemed to me to love wickedness for its own sake. I said I could not see him, but the
message came back that his need was urgent, and up he
came. He wanted, he told me, to make his Confession, not
to-morrow, but now, and his Confessor was away. I could
not, as a priest, resist that appeal. And his confession was
that he had killed Gerald Selfe.

"For a moment I thought this was some impious joke,
but he swore he was speaking the truth, and still under
the seal of Confession gave me a detailed account. He had
dined with Selfe that night, and had gone up afterward to
his flat for a game of piquet. Selfe told him with a grin
that he was going to lay his servant by the heels to-morrow for blackmail. 'A smart spry young man to-day,' he
said. 'Perhaps a bit off color to-morrow at this time.' He
rang the bell for him to put out the card-table; then saw
it was ready, and he forgot that his summons remained

unanswered. They played high points and both had drunk a good deal. Selfe lost partie after partie and eventually accused Kennion of cheating. Words ran high, and boiled over into blows, and Kennion, in some rough and tumble of wrestling and hitting, picked up a knife from the table and stabbed Selfe in the throat, through jugular vein and carotid artery. In a few minutes he had bled to death. . . . Then Kennion remembered that unanswered bell, and went tiptoe to Wadham's room. He found it empty; empty, too, were the other rooms in the flat. Had there been any one there, his idea was to say he had come up at Selfe's invitation, and found him dead. But this was better yet: there was no more than a few spots of blood on him, and he washed them in Wadham's room, emptying the water into his slop-pail. Then leaving the door of the flat open, he went downstairs and out.

"He told me this in quite a few sentences, even as I have told it you, and looked up at me with a smiling face.

"'So what's to be done next, Venerable Father?' he said gaily.

"'Ah, thank God you've confessed!' I said. 'We're in time yet to save an innocent man. You must give yourself up to the police at once.' But even as I spoke my heart misgave me.

"He rose, dusting the knees of his trousers.

"'What a quaint notion,' he said. 'But there's nothing further from my thoughts.'

"I jumped up.

"'I shall go myself then,' I said.

"He laughed outright at that.

"'Oh, no, indeed you won't,' he said. 'What about the seal of Confession? Indeed, I rather fancy it's a deadly sin for a priest ever to think of violating it. Really, I'm ashamed of you, my dear Denys. Naughty fellow! But perhaps it was only a joke; you didn't mean it.'

"'I do mean it,' I said. 'You shall see if I mean it.' But even as I spoke, I knew I did not. 'Anything is allowable to save an innocent man from death.'

"He laughed again.

"'Pardon me: you know perfectly well, that it isn't,' he said. 'There's one thing in our creed far worse than death, and that is the damnation of the soul. You've got no intention of damning yours. I took no risk at all when I confessed to you.'

"'But it will be murder, if you don't save this man,' I said.

"'Oh, certainly, but I've got murder on my conscience already,' he said. 'One gets used to it very quickly. And having got used to it, another murder doesn't seem to matter an atom. Poor young Wadham: tomorrow, isn't it? I'm not sure it won't be a sort of rough justice. Blackmail is a disgusting offense.'

"I went to the telephone, and took off the receiver.

"'Really this is most interesting,' he said. 'Walton Street is the nearest police station. You don't need the number: just say Walton Street police. But you can't. You can't say "I have a man with me now, Horace Kennion who has confessed to me that he murdered Selfe." So why bluff! Besides if you could do any such thing, I should merely say that I had done nothing of the kind. Your word, the word of a priest who has broken the most sacred vow, against mine. Childish!'

"'Kennion,' I said, 'for the love of God, and for the fear of hell, give yourself up! What does it matter whether you or I live a few years less, if at the end we pass into the vast infinite with our sins confessed and forgiven? Day and night I will pray for you.'

"'Charming of you,' said he. 'But I've no doubt that now you will give Wadham full absolution. So what does it matter if he goes into—into the vast infinite at eight o'clock to-morrow morning?'

"'Why did you confess to me then,' I asked, 'if you had no intention of saving him, and making atonement?'

"'Well, not long ago you were very nasty to me,' he said. 'You told me no decent man would consort with me. So it struck me, quite suddenly, only to-day, that it would be pleasant to see you in the most awful hole. I daresay I've got Sadic tastes, too, and they are being wonderfully indulged. You're in torment, you know: you would choose any physical agony other than to be in such a torture-chamber of the soul. It's entrancing: I adore it. Thank you very much, Denys.'

"He got up.

"'I kept my taxi waiting,' he said. 'No doubt you'll be busy to-night. Can I give you a lift anywhere? Pentonville?'

"There are no words to describe certain darknesses and ecstasies that come to the soul, and I can only tell you that I can imagine no hell of remorse that could equal the hell that I was in. For in the bitterness of remorse we can see that our suffering is a needful and salutary experience: only through it can our sin be burned away. But here was a torture blank and meaningless. . . . And then my brain stirred a little, and I began to wonder whether without breaking the seal of Confession, I might not be able to effect something. I saw from my window, that the light was burning in the clock tower at Westminster: the House therefore was sitting, and it seemed possible that without violation, I might tell the Home Secretary that a confession had been made me, whereby I knew that Wadham was innocent. He would ask me for any details I could give him, and I could tell him—and then I saw that I could tell him nothing: I could not say that the murderer had gone up with Selfe to his room, for through that information it might be found that Kennion had dined with him. But before I did anything, I must have guidance, and I went to the Cardinal's house by our Cathedral. He had gone to bed, for it was now after midnight, but in answer to the urgency of my request, he came down to see me. I told him without giving any clue, what had happened, and his verdict was what in my heart I knew it would be. Certainly I might see the Home Secretary and tell him that such a confession had been made me, but no word or hint must escape me which could lead to identification. Personally, he did not see how the execution could be postponed on such information as I could give.

"'And whatever you suffer, my son,' he said, 'be sure that you are suffering not from having done wrong, but from having done right. Placed as you are, your temptation to save an innocent man comes from the devil, and whatever you may be called upon to endure for not yielding to it, is of that origin also.'

"I saw the Home Secretary in his room at the House within the hour. But unless I told him more, and he realized that I could not, he was powerless to move.

"'He was found guilty at his trial,' he said, 'and his appeal was dismissed. Without further evidence I can do nothing.'

"He sat thinking a moment; then jumped up.

"'Good God, it's ghastly,' he said. 'I entirely believe, I needn't tell you, that you've heard this confession, but that doesn't prove it's true. Can't you see the man again? Can't you put the fear of God into him? If you can do anything at all, which gives me any justification for acting, up till the moment the drop falls, I will give a reprieve at once. There's my telephone number: ring me up here or at my house at any hour.'

"I was back at the prison before six in the morning. I told Wadham that I believed in his innocence, and I gave him Absolution for all else. He received the Holy and Blessed Sacrament with me, and went without flinching to his death."

Father Denys paused.

"I have been a long time coming to that point in my story," he said, "which concerns that séance you spoke of, but it was necessary for your understanding of what I am going to tell you now, that you should know all this. I said that these messages and communications from the dead come not from them but from some evil and awful power impersonating them. You answered, I remember, 'Why drag in the Devil?' I will tell you.

"When it was over, when the drop on which he stood yawned open, and the rope creaked and jumped, I went home. It was a dark winter's morning, still barely light, and in spite of the tragic scene I had just witnessed. I felt serene and peaceful. I did not think of Kennion at all, only of the boy—he was little more—who had suffered unjustly, and that seemed a pitiful mistake, but no more. I did not touch him, his essential living soul, it was as if he had suffered the sacred expiation of martyrdom. And I was humbly thankful that I had been enabled to act right-ly, and had Kennion now, through my agency, been in the hands of the police and Wadham alive, I should have been branded with the most terrible crime a priest can commit.

"I had been up all night, and after I had said my office, I lay down on my sofa to get a little sleep. And I dreamed that I was in the cell with Wadham and that he knew I had proof of his innocence. It was within a few minutes of the hour of his death, and I heard along the stone-flagged corridor outside the steps of those who were coming. He heard them too, and stood up, pointing at me.

"'You're letting an innocent man die, when you could save him,' he said. 'You can't do it, Father Denys. Father Denys!' he shrieked, and the shriek broke off in a gulp and a gasp as the door opened.

"I woke, knowing that which had roused me was my own name, screamed out from somewhere close at hand,

and I knew whose voice it was. But there I was alone in my quiet empty room, with the dim day peering in. I had been asleep, I saw, for only a few minutes, but now all thought or power of sleep had fled, for somewhere by me, invisible but awfully present was the spirit of the man whom I had allowed to perish. And he called me.

"But presently I convinced myself that this voice coming to me in sleep was no more than a dream, natural enough in the circumstances, and some days passed tranquilly enough. And then one day when I was walking down a sunny crowded street, I felt some definite and dreadful change in what I may call the psychic atmosphere which surrounds us all, and my soul grew black with fear and with evil imaginings. And there was Wadham coming toward me along the pavement, gay and debonair. He looked at me, and his face became a mask of hate. 'We shall meet often I hope, Father Denys,' he said as he passed. Another day I returned home in the twilight, and suddenly, as I entered my room I heard the creak and strain of a rope, and his body, with head covered by the death-cap swung in the window against the sunset. And sometimes when I was at my books, the door opened quietly and closed again, and I knew he was there. The apparition or the token of it did not come often or perhaps my resistance would have been quickened, for I knew it was devilish in origin. But it came when I was off my guard at long intervals, so that I thought I had vanquished it, and then sometimes I felt my faith to reel. But always it was preceded by this sense of evil power bearing down on me, and I have made haste to seek the shelter of the House of Defence which is set very high. And this last Sunday I only—"

He broke off, covering his eyes with his hand, as if shutting out some appalling spectacle.

"I had been preaching," he resumed, "for one of our missions. The church was full, and I do not think there was another thought or desire in my soul, but to further the holy cause for which I was speaking. It was a morning service, and the sun poured in through the stained windows in a glow of colored light. But in the middle of my sermon some bank of cloud drove up, and with it this horrible forewarning of the approach of a tempest of evil. So dark it got that, as I was drawing near the end of my sermon, the lights in the church were switched on, and it leaped into brightness. There was a lamp on the desk in the pulpit, where I had placed my notes, and now when it was kindled it shone full on the pew just below. And there, with his head turned upward toward me, with his face purple and eyes protruding and with the strangling noose round his neck, sat Wadham.

"My voice faltered a second, and I clutched at the pulpit-rail as he stared at me and I at him. A horror of the spirit, black as the eternal night of the lost closed round me, for I had let him go innocent to his death, and my punishment was just. . . . And then like a star shining out through some merciful rent in this soul-storm came again that ray of conviction that as a priest I could not have done otherwise, and with it the sure knowledge that this apparition could not be of God, but of the devil, to be resisted and defied even as we defy with contempt some sweet and insidious temptation. It could not therefore be the spirit of the man at which I gazed, but some diabolical counterfeit. And I looked back from him to my notes, and went on with my sermon, for that alone was my business. That pause had seemed to me eternal: it had the quality of timelessness, but I learned afterward that it had been barely perceptible. And from my own heart I learned that it was no punishment that I was undergoing, but the strengthening of a faith that had faltered."

Suddenly he broke off. There came into his eyes as he fixed them on the door, a look, not of fear at all, but of savage relentless antagonism.

"It's coming," he said to me, "and now if you hear or see anything, despise it, for it is evil."

The door swung open and closed again, and though nothing visible entered, I knew that there was now in the room a living intelligence other than Father Denys's and mine, and it affected my being, my self, just as some horrible odor of putrefaction affects one physically: my soul sickened in it. Then, still seeing nothing, I perceived that the room, warm and comfortable just now, with a fire of coal prospering in the grate, was growing cold, and that some strange eclipse was veiling the light. Close to me on the table stood an electric lamp: the shade of it fluttered in the icy draught that stirred in the air, and the luminous wire was no longer incandescent, but red and dull like the embers in the grate. I scrutinized the dimness, but as yet no material form manifested itself.

Father Denys was sitting very upright in his chair, his eyes fixed and focused on something invisible to me. His lips were moving and muttering, his hands grasped the crucifix he was wearing. And then I saw what I knew he was seeing, too: a face was outlining itself on the air in front of him, a face swollen and purple, with tongue lolling from the mouth, and as it hung there it oscillated to and fro. Clear and clearer it grew, suspended there by the rope that now became visible to me, and though the apparition was of a man hanged by the neck, it was not dead but active and alive, and the spirit that awfully animated it was no human one, but something diabolical.

Suddenly Father Denys rose to his feet, and his face was within an inch or two of that suspended horror. He raised his hands which held the sacred emblem.

"Begone to your torment," he cried, "until the days of it are over, and the mercy of God grants you eternal death."

There rose a wailing in the air: some blast shook the room so that the corners of it quaked, and then the light and the warmth were restored to it, and there was no there but our two selves. Father Denys's face was haggard and dripping with the struggle he had been through, but there shone on it such radiance as I have never seen on human countenance.

"It's over," he said. "I saw it shrivel and wither before the power of His presence. . . . And your eyes tell me you saw it too and you know now that what wore the semblance of humanity was pure evil."

We talked a little longer, and he rose to go.

"Ah, I forgot," he said, "you wanted to know how I could reveal to you what was told me in confession. Horace Kennion died this morning by his own hand. He left with his lawyer a packet to be opened on his death, with instructions that it should be published in the daily press. I saw it in an evening paper, and it was a detailed account of how he killed Gerald Selfe. He wished it to have all possible publicity."

"But why?" I asked.

Father Denys paused.

"He gloried in his wickedness, I think," he said. "He loved it, as I told you, for its own sake, and he wanted every one to know of it, as soon as he was safely away."

Crewe
Walter de la Mare

When misty winter dusk begins to settle on the railway station at Crewe the waiting-room grows steadily more stagnant. Particularly if one is alone in it. The long windows hardly do more than sift the failing light that slopes in on them from the glass roof outside—too feeble to penetrate into the recesses beyond. And the grained-massive, black-leathered furniture becomes less and less inviting. It appears to have been made for a scene of extreme and diabolical violence that has never occurred. One can hardly at any rate imagine it to have been designed by a really good man!

Little things like that of course are apt to get exaggerated in memory, and I may be doing the Company an injustice. But whether this is so or not (and the afternoon I have in mind is now many years distant) I certainly became more acutely conscious of the defects of my surroundings when the few fellow-travellers who had been sharing the faint murk of the room with me had hurried out at the sound of the bell for the down train, leaving me to wait for the up. And nothing and nobody, as I supposed, but a great drowsy fire of cinders in the iron grate for company.

The almost animated talk that had sprung up before we separated, never probably in this world to meet again, had been started by an account in the morning's newspapers of the last voyage of a ship called the *Hesper*. She had arrived the evening before, and some days overdue, from the West Indies, with a cargo of sugar, and was now berthed safely in the Southampton Docks. This must have been something of a relief to those concerned. For even her master had not refused to admit that certain mysterious and tragic events had recently occurred on board, though he preferred not to discuss them with a reporter. And there was little doubt (a) that there had been a full moon at the time, (b) that apart from a heavy swell, the sea was "as calm as a millpond," and (c) that his ship was at present in want of a second mate.

But the *Hesper* is now, of course, an old and familiar tale. Indeed I had myself by that time supped my fill of her mysteries, and had decided to seek the lights and joys and colored bottles of the "refreshment room," when a voice from behind me suddenly broke the hush. It was an unusual voice, rapid, incoherent and internal, like that of a man in his dreams or under the influence of a drug.

I shifted my ungainly chair and turned to look. Evidently the only other occupant of the room had until that moment been as little aware of my presence there as I of his. Indeed from what I could see of him he appeared to have been quite taken aback by the noise I had made—had started up and was positively staring at me from out of the gloom.

"I am sorry," I said, "I thought—"

But he interrupted me, and not as if my company, now that he had recognized me as a fellow-creature, was any the less welcome for being unexpected. "Merely what I was saying, sir," he explained, "is that those gentlemen there who have just left us hadn't no more of a notion of what they were talking about than an infant in its cradle."

This elegant paraphrase, I must confess, bore only the feeblest resemblance to the language I had just overheard.

I looked at him. "How so?" I said, "I am only a landsman myself, and . . ." It seemed unnecessary to finish the sentence, particularly as he too was devoid of any obvious trace of the marine. But then at the moment little else than his flat white face was clearly discernible. He sat on the edge of a vast settee, muffled up in a very respectable overcoat a size or two too large for him, his hands thrust into its pockets.

"You don't have to go to sea for things like that," he went on. "And there is no need to argue about them if you do. But it wasn't my place to interfere. They'll find out all right—all in good time. They go their ways. And talking of that, sir, have you ever heard that there is less risk sitting in a railway carriage at sixty miles an hour than in laying alone, safe, as you might suppose, in your own bed? That's true, too. You know where you are in a spot like this. It's solid, though—" I couldn't catch the words that followed, but they seemed to be uncomplimentary to things in general.

"Yes," I agreed, "it certainly looks solid."

"Ah, looks!" he broke in rather cantankerously, "but what is your 'solid,' come to that? I thought so myself once." He seemed to be pondering over the "once." "But now," he added, "I know different."

Whereupon he sallied out of the obscurity under the high window, and after warming his veined shrunken hands at the heap of smouldering cinders in the grate and his head little more than topped the black marble mantel-piece—he seated himself opposite to me.

In deference to my own none too acute faculties of observation, let me confess at once that I didn't much care for the appearance of this stranger. I fancied at first he was about to solicit a small loan. In spite of his great-coat he looked in need of the barber as well as of medicine and sleep, and that might presently manifest itself in a hankering for alcohol. But I was mistaken. He asked for nothing, not even for sympathy, not even advice. He merely, it seemed, wanted to talk about himself, and perhaps in certain circumstances strangers make better receptacles for such confidences than one's intimates. They tell no tales.

None the less—and, as near as I can, in his own peculiar idiom—I shall attempt to tell his. It impressed me at the time; and I have occasionally speculated since whether his statistics regarding railway travelling proved to him to be just. "Safety first" is a sound principle so far as it goes, but we are all of us outmanoeuvred in the end. And I still wonder what end was his.

He began by asking me if I had ever lived in the country: "in the depps" of the country; but soon discovering that I was more inclined to listen than to talk, he suddenly plunged into his past, and as if it might refresh him to do so.

"I was a gentleman's servant when I began," he set off, "first boot-boy, then washing up and helping at table, then in the pantry and so on. Never married or anything of that; they are nothing but encumbrances in the house; and I must say if you keep yourself *to* yourself, it sees you through—in time. What you have to beware of is those of your own party. That's the same everywhere; nobody's got much past the dog-and-cat stage in that. Not if you look close enough: high or low. I lost one or two nice easy places all through that. And if you don't stay where you are put there's precious little chance of pickings when the funeral's at the door. But that's mostly changed now, so I'm told. High wages and no work being the order of the day. They are all rolling stones, and never mind the moss."

As a philosopher this muffled-up, old white-faced creature certainly tended toward realism, though his reservations on the "solid" had fallen a little short of it. Not

that he seemed to care much about my reality. For though
in the memories he proceeded to share with me he inter-
polated many questions, he very seldom waited for an
answer, and then ignored it. I see now this was not to be
wondered at. We happened to be sharing at the moment
this (for my part) chance resort—the waiting-room on the
between-platform (midway, that is betwixt the worlds of
west and east) at Crewe; and seldom the time and the place
and any sort of listener together.

"The last situation I was in," (he was going on to tell
me), "was with the Reverend W. Somers—with an 'o.' In
the depps of the country, as I say. Just myself and another
manservant, and a woman who came in from the village to
char and cook and get things ready, though I did the best
part of that myself. The finishing touches, I mean. How
long the Reverend hadn't cared for females in the house I
never knew; though parsons get their share of them, I'm
thinking. Not that I'd say he wasn't attached enough to
his sister. They had grown up together, and that covers a
multitude of sins.

"Like *him, she* was, but more of the parrot in appearance; a high face with a beaky nose. Quite a nice lady, too,
except that she was mighty slow in being explained to.
No interference otherwise in spite of her nose. But don't
mistake me; we had to look alive when she came. Oh, yes.
But that, thank God, was seldom. And in the end it made
no difference.

"She didn't like the Vicarage. Who would? Too dark,
too shut in. And in winter freezing cold; lying low maybe.
Trees all in front, everlastings; though open behind, with
a stream and cornfields and hills in the distance; in summer, of course. They went up and down and dim or dark,
according to the weather. You could see for miles from the
corridor windows, small panes that take a lot of clean-
ing. But George did the windows. George had come from

the village, too, if you could call it a village. But he was a permanency. Nothing much but a few cottages, and a farmhouse here and there. What they built a church a mile away from it for I can't say. Give the Roaring Lion a trot, perhaps. The Reverend had private means, of course. I knew that before it came out in the will, but it was a fat living notwithstanding; worked out at ten pounds to the pigsty, I shouldn't wonder, and the Vicarage thrown in. You get what you've got in this world, that's the truth; and some of us a large slice more than we deserve. But the Reverend, I must say, never took advantage of it. Give him his books, and to-morrow like yesterday, and he grumbled no more than a cat in a fish shop.

"Mind you, he liked things as they should be, and he had some of the finest silver I've ever used rouge and shammy on—all the Georges, and furniture to match. I don't mean picked up at sales and from dealers and suchlike, but real old family stuff. That's where the parrot in their noses came from. And everything punctual to the minute and the good things *good*. Soup or fish, a cutlet, a savory, and a glass of sherry or Madeira. No sweets. And I have never seen choicer fruit than was grown in his garden, though it was there that the trouble began. Cherries, gages, peaches, nectarines—old red sunbaked walls nine or ten feet high; a sight like wonder in the spring. I used to go out specially to have a look at it. He had his fancies, mind you, had the Reverend. If we smoked it had to be in the shrubbery with the blackbirds, not under the roof.

"But tobacco's not my trouble. Never was. Keep off what you don't need and you'll never want it when you can't get it. That's my feeling. It was, as I say, an easy place, if you forgot how quiet it was; no company, and not a petticoat to be seen. Good prospects, too, if you could wait. He didn't like change, did the Reverend; made no concealment of it. He told me himself that he had remembered me in his will—'if still in his service'; you know how these lawyers put it. As a matter of fact he gave me to understand that if in the meantime for any reason any of us went elsewhere, the one left was to have the lot. There, as it turned out, I was in error.

"But I'm not complaining of that now; oh, no! I've got enough to see me through however long I'm left. And that might be for a good many years yet."

His intonation suggested a question, but he made no pause for an answer and added argumentatively: "Who *wants* to go, I should like to ask? Early or late. And knowing nothing of what's on the other side?" He lifted his gray eyebrows a little to glance up at me, as he sat stooped up by the fire. But again I couldn't enlighten him.

"Well, there, as I say, I might have stayed to this day if the old gentleman's gardener had cared to stay too. *He* began it. Him gone we all went. Like ninepins. You might hardly credit it, sir, but I am the only one left of that complete establishment. Gutted. And that's where these gentlemen here were talking round their hats. What I say is, keep on this side of the tomb as long as you can. Don't meddle with that hole. Why? Because while some fine day you will have to go down into it, you can never be quite sure what mayn't come back out of it.

"*There'll be no partings there*—I have heard them singing the tune out like missel thrushes in the spring. But they seem to forget there may be some mighty unpleasant *meetings*. They talk of the further shore as if once there, friend or foe, there's no returning. But it's my belief there is some kind of a ferry plying on that river. All depends on your want to get back.

"Anyhow the Vicarage reeked of it. A low old house, with lots of little windows and much too many doors; and, as I say, the trees too close up on one side, almost brushing the panes. No wonder they said it was what they call haunted. You could feel that with your eyes shut; and like breeds like. The Vicar—two or three I mean, before my own, my last gentleman—had even gone to the trouble of having the place exorcised. Candles and holy water, that kind of thing. Sheer flummummery *I* call it. But if what I've heard—and long before that gowk of a George came to work in the house—was anything more than mere age and owls and birds in the ivy, it must badly have needed it. And when you get accustomed to noises, you can tell which from which. By usual, I mean. Though more and more I'm getting to ask myself if anything's anything much more than what you think it is—for the time being.

"Same with noises, of course. What's this voice of conscience that they talk about but something you needn't hear if you don't like? I am not complaining of that. If at the beginning there was anything in that house that was better out than in, it never troubled me; at least, not at first. And the Reverend, even though you could often count his congregation on your ten fingers, except at Harvest Festival, was so wove up in his books that I doubt if he'd have been roused up out of 'em even by the Last Trump. It's my belief that in those last few months, when I stepped in to see to the fire, as often as not he'd been sitting asleep over them.

"No, I'm not complaining. Live at peace with who you can, I say. But when it comes to as crusty a customer, and a Scotchman at that, as was the Reverend's gardener, then there's a limit. Mengus he called himself, though I can't see how, if you spell it with a 'z.' When I first came into the place it was all gold that glitters. I'm not the man for contentiousness, left alone. But afterward, when the rift came, I don't suppose we ever hardly exchanged the time of day but what there came words of it. A long-legged man, he was—this Mr. Menzies; too long I should have thought for strict comfort in grubbing and hoeing and weeding. He had ginger hair, scanty, and the same on his face, whiskers—and a stoop. He lived down at the lodge; and his widowed daughter kept house for him, with one little boy as fair as she was dark. Harmless enough as children go, but noisy, and not for the house.

"Now why, I ask you, shouldn't I gather a little of this gentleman's fruit or a cucumber for a salad, if need be, and him not there? What if I wanted a few grapes for dessert or a nice apricot tart for the Reverend's luncheon, and our Mr. Menzies gone home or busy with the frames? I don't hold with all these hard and fast restrictions, at least outside the house. Not he, though! We wrangled about it week in, week out. And he with a temper when roused that was past all Masoning.

"Not that I ever took much notice of him until it came to a point past bearing. I let him rave. But duty is duty, there's no getting away from it. And when, besides all that fuss about his fruit, a man takes advantage of what is meant in pure friendliness, well one's bound to make a move.

"What I mean to say is, I used occasionally—window wide open and all that, the pantry being on the other side of the house and away from the old gentleman's study—I say I used occasionally and all in the way of friendliness to offer our friend a drink. Like as with many of Old Adam's trade, drink was a little weakness of his, though I don't mean I hold with it because of that. But peace and quietness is the first thing, and to keep an easy face to all appearance, even if you do find it a little hard at times to forgive and forget.

"When he was civil, as I say, and as things should be, he could have a drink, and welcome. When not, not. It came to a kind of habit; and to be expected; which is always a bad condition of things. Oh, it was a thousand pities! There was the Reverend, growing feeble as you could see, and him believing all the while that everything around him was calm and sweet as the new Jerusalem, while there was nothing but strife and acrimony, as they call it, underneath. There's many a house looks as snug and cosey as a nut. But crack it and look inside! Mildew.

"Well, there came along at last a mighty hot summer; two years ago, you may remember. Two years ago, next August, an extraordinary hot summer. And see the stones in the stubble fields shivering in the sun. And gardening is thirsty work, I will say that for it. Which being so, better surely virgin water from the tap or a drop of cider, same as the harvesters have, than ardent spirits; whether it is what you are bred up to or not. It stands to reason.

"Besides, we had had words again, and though I can stretch a point with a friend and no harm done, I'm not a man to come coneying and currying favor. Let him get his own drinks, was my feeling in the matter. And you can hardly call me to blame if he did. *There* was the pantry window hanging wide open in the shade of the trees—and day after day of scorching sun and not a breath to breathe. And there was the ruin of him within arm's reach from outside, and a water tap handy too. Very inviting, I'll allow.

"I'm not attesting, mind you, that he was confirmed at it, no more than I'm a man to be measuring what's given me to take charge of by tenths of inches. It's the principle of the thing. You might have thought too, that a simple honest pride would have kept him back. Nothing of the sort; and no matter, wine or spirits. I'd watch him there, though he couldn't see me, being behind the door. And practices like that, sir, as you will agree with me, can't go on. They couldn't go on, Vicarage or no Vicarage. Besides from being secret it began to be open. It had gone too far. Brazen it out; that was the lay. I came down one fine morning to find one of my best decanters smashed to smithereens on the stone floor, Irish glass and all. Cats and sherry, who ever heard of it? And out of revenge he filled the pantry with wasps by bringing in over-ripe plums, petty waste of time like that; and some of the greenhouses thick with blight!

"And so things went, from bad to worse, and at such a pace as I couldn't have credited. A widower, too; with a married daughter dependent on him; which is worse even than a wife, who *expects* to take the bad with the good. No, sir, I had to call halt to it. A friendly word in his ear, or keeping everything out of his reach, you may be thinking, might have been of use. Believe me, not from me. And how can you foster such a weakness by taking steps out of the usual to prevent it? It wouldn't be proper to your self-respect. Then I thought of George, not demeaning myself in any way, of course, in so doing. George had a face half as long as your arm, pale and solemn, enough to make a cat laugh. Dress him in a surplice and so on, he might have been the Reverend's curate. Strange that, for a youth born in the country. But curate or no curate, he had eyes in his head and must have seen what there was to be seen.

"I said to him one day, and I remember him standing there, in his black coat, against the white of the cupboard paint, I said to him: 'George, a word in time saves nine, but it would come better from you than from me. You take me? Hold your time till our friend's sober again and can listen to reason. Then hand it over to him—a word of warning, I mean. Say we are muffling things up as well as we can from the old gentleman, but that if he should happen to hear of it there'd be fat in the fire; and no mistake. He would take it easier from you, George, the responsibility being mine.'

"Lor', how I remember George! He had a way of looking at you as if he couldn't say Boo to a goose; swollen hands and bolting blue eyes, as simple as an infant's. But he wasn't stupid, oh no, and now I reflect, I think he knew that our little plan wouldn't carry very far. But as whatever he might be thinking, he was so awkward with his tongue that he could never find anything to say until it was too late, I left it at that. Besides I had come to know he was with all his faults a young man you could trust for doing what he was told to do. So, as I say, I left it at that.

"What he actually said I never knew. But as for its being of any use, it was more like pouring paraffin on a bonfire. The very afternoon our friend came to the pantry window and stood looking in—swaying he was, on his feet, and I can see the midges behind him, floating in a patch of sunshine as though they were here before my eyes. He was so bad that he had to lay hold of the sill to keep himself from falling. Not thirst this time, but just fury. And then, seeing that mere flaunting of fine feathers wasn't going to inveigle me into a cockfight, he began to talk. No bad language, mind you—*that's* easy to shut your ears to—but cold reasonable abuse, which isn't. At first I took no notice, went on humming and polishing at my leisure, and no hurry. What's the use of arguing with a man, and a Scotchman to boot, that's beside himself with rage? Besides I wanted peace in the house, if only for the old gentleman's sake, who I thought was definitely under the weather and had been coming on very poorly of late.

"'Where's that George of yours,' he said to me at last—with additions. 'Where's that George? Fetch him out, and I'll teach him to come playing holy Moses to my own daughter. Fetch him out, I say, and we'll finish it here and now.' And all pitched high, and half his words no more English than the mewing of a cat.

'But I kept my temper and answered him quite pleasant, as pleasantly as I knew how. 'I don't want to meddle in anybody's quarrels,' I said. 'So long as George so does his work in this house as it'll satisfy *my* eye, I am not responsible for his actions in his off-time and out of bounds.'

"How was I to know, may I ask, if it was *not* our Mr. 'Mengus' who had smashed one of my best decanters? What proof was there? What *reason* had I for thinking else?

"'George is a quiet, unbeseeming young fellow,' I said, 'and if he thinks it's his duty to report any misgoings-on either to me or to the Reverend, it doesn't concern anybody else.'

"That seemed to sober my fine gentleman. Mind you, I'm not saying that there was anything unremidibly wrong with him. He was a first-class gardener, but then he had an uncommonly good place to match—first-class wages; and no milk, wood, coals or house rent to worry about. But making fusses like that, and the Reverend poorly; that's not what he thought of when he put us all down in his will. I'll be bound of that. Well, there he stood looking in at the window, and me behind the table in my green baize apron as calm as if his wrangling meant no more to me than the wind in the chimenney. It was the word 'report,' I fancy, that took the wind out of his sails. It had brought him up like a station buffer. And he was still looking at me, and chewing it over, as though he had the taste of poison on his tongue.

"Then he said very quiet, 'So that's his little game is it? You are just a pair, then.'

"'If by pair you're meaning me,' I said, 'well, I'm ready to take on my share of the burden when it's ready to fit my back. But not before. George may have gone a bit beyond himself, but he meant well, and you know it.'

"'What I am asking is this,' says our friend, 'have you ever seen me the worse for liquor? Answer me that!'

"'If I liked your tone better,' I said, 'I wouldn't say as I don't see why it would be necessarily the *worse.*'

"'Eh? You mean, Yes, then?' he said.

"'I meant no more than what I said,' I answered him, looking at him over the cruet as straight as I'm looking at you now. 'I don't want to meddle with your private affairs, and I don't want you to come meddling with mine.' He seemed taken aback by that and I noticed he was looking a bit pinched, and hollow under the eyes.

"But how was *I* to know this grandson of his was out of sorts with a bad throat and that, seeing that he hadn't mentioned it till a minute before? I ask you.

"'The best thing you and George can do,' I went on, 'is to bury the hatchet; and out of hearing of the house, too.'

"With that I turned away and went off into it myself, leaving him there to think things over at his leisure. I am asking you, sir, as a free witness, what else could I have done? . . ."

There was very little light of day left in our waiting-room by this time. Only the dulling glow of the fire and the faint phosphorescence caused by a tiny bead of gas in the incandescent mantles of the great iron bracket over our heads. My realist seemed to be positively in want of an answer to this last question, but as I sat looking back into his intent white face nothing that could be described as of a helpful nature offered itself.

"It may be this anxiety over his grandson had shortened his temper," I said at last. "But I should like to hear what came after."

"What came after, now," the little man repeated, drawing his right hand gingerly out of the depths of his pocket, and smoothing down his face with it as if he were tired. "Well, a good deal came after, but not quite what I expected. And you'd hardly say perhaps that anxiety over his grandson would excuse him for little short of manslaughter, and him a good six inches to the good at that? Keeping facts as facts, if you'll excuse me, our friend waylaid George by the stables that very evening, and a wonderful peaceful evening it was, shepherd's delight and all that. But to judge from the looks of the young fellow's face when he came into the house there hadn't been much of that in the quarter of an hour they had had together.

"I said, 'Sponge it down, George, sponge it down. And perhaps the old gentleman won't notice anything wrong.' It wasn't to reason I could let him off his duties and enter into long prevarications which in the long run would only make things worse. And it's that you have to think of. But as for the Reverend's not noticing it, there, as luck would have it, I was wrong myself.

"For when him and me were leaving the dining-room that evening after the table had been cleared and the dessert put on, he looked up from round the candles and told George to stay behind. Some quarter of an hour after that George came along to me snuffling as if he'd been crying. But I asked no questions, not me; and, as I say, he was always pretty slow with his tongue. All that I could get out of him was that he had decocted a cock-and-bull story to account for his looks the like of which nobody in his senses could credit, let alone such a power of questioning as the old gentleman could bring to bear when roused and apart from what comes, I suppose, from reading books. So the fat *was* in the fire and no mistake. And the next thing I heard, after coming back late next evening, was that our Mr. Menzies had been called into the house and given the sack there and then, with a quarter's wages in lieu of notice. Which, after all, mind you, was as good as three-quarters a gift. Not that I'm saying this was letting him off light, and I agree money isn't necessarily everything when there's what's called character to take into account. But if ever there was one of the quality fair and upright in all his dealings, as the saying goes, then that was the Reverend Somers. He couldn't abide drink topped with insolence. That's all.

"Well, our friend came rapping at the back door that evening, shaken to the marrow if ever man was, and just livid. I told him, and I meant it too, that I was sorry for what had occurred. 'It's a bad ending,' I said, 'to a tale that ought never to have been told.' I said to him the only thing left now was to let bygones be bygones; that he had already had his fingers on George, and better go no further. Not he. He said, and he was sober enough then in all conscience, that, come what come may, he'd be even with him. Ay, and he made mention of me also, but not so rabid. A respectable man, too. Never a word against him till then; and not far short of sixty. And by rabid I don't mean violent. He spoke as low and quiet as if there was a judge on the bench there to hear him, sentence said and everything over. And then . . ."

The old creature paused until a passing train had gone roaring on its way. "And then he must have gone straight out—and good-by said to nobody; though he wasn't found till morning. He must, I say, have gone straight out to the old barn and hung himself. The mid-most rafter, sir, and a drop that would have sufficed for a Giant Goliath. And it's my belief, good-by or no good-by, that it wasn't so much the *disgrace* of the affair but his daughter—Mrs. Shaw by name—and his grandson that were preying on his mind. Yet—why, he never so much as asked me to say a good word for him. Not one.

"Well, that was the end of that. So far. And it's a very curious thing to me—though they say the Cartholics aren't above making use of it—how, going back over the past clears it all up like; just for the time being. But it's what you were saying about what's *solid* that set me thinking and keeps repeating itself in my mind. Solid was the word you used. And they seem it, I agree." He deliberately twisted his head and took a prolonged look at the bench on which he was seated. "But it doesn't follow there's much comfort in them because of that. Even if they are solid, they go when all is said to what's little else but gas and ashes once they're fallen to pieces and put on the fire. Which holds good, and even more so, for them that sit on them. Peculiar habit that too! Yes, I've been told, sir, that whittle us down, and all the moisture of us gone up in steam, what's left would scarcely turn the scales by a single hounce!"

If sitting *is* a peculiar habit, it was even more peculiar how etherializing the effect of my new acquaintance's misplaced aspirate had been—his one and only example throughout this interminable monologue.

"They say that we'd amount to no more than what you could squeeze into a walnut. And my point *is*, sir," he was emphasizing, "that if *that's* all the solid there is to you and me, we shouldn't need much of the substantial for what you might call the mere sole look of things, if you follow me, *if* we chose or chanced, I mean, to come back when gone. Just enough, I suppose, to be obnoxious, as the Reverend used to say, to the naked eye.

"But all that being as it may be, the whole thing had tided over, and George pretty nearly himself again, and another gardener advertised for—and I must say the Reverend, though after this horrible affair he was never the same man again, treated the young woman I mentioned very handsomely—I say, the whole thing had tided over, and the house was as silent as a tomb again, ay, as the sepulchre itself, when I began to notice something peculiar.

"At first maybe, little more *than* the silence. What in the contrast, as a matter of fact, I took for peace. But afterward not so. There was a strain, so to speak, as you went about quite naturally. A strain. And especially after dark. It may have been only in one's head. I can't say. But it was there; and I could see without watching that even George had noticed it; and *he'd* hardly notice a black-beetle on a pancake.

"But at last there came something you could put word
to, catch in the act, so to speak. I had gone out toward the
cool of the evening after a broiling hot day, to get a little
air. There was a copse of beeches, which is a very pleasant
tree for shade, sir, as perhaps you may know, a little under
the mile from the back of the Vicarage. And I sat there
quiet a bit, with the birds and all—they were beginning
to sing again, I remember. And—you know how memory
strays back, though sometimes it's more like a goat teth-
ered to a peg on a common—I was thinking over what a
curious thing it is how one man's poison is another man's
meat. For the funeral over, and all that, the old gentleman
had thanked me for what I had done. You see it had been
a hard break in his trust of a man, and he looked up from
his bed at me almost with tears in his eyes. He said he
wouldn't forget it. I ought to have mentioned pr'aps that
he was taken ill the night of the inquest; a sort of stroke,
the doctor called it, though he came round remarkably
well considering his age.

"Well, I had been thinking over all this in the woods
there, and was on my way back again to the house by the
field-path, when I looked up sudden-like and saw what I
take my oath I never remembered to have noticed there
before—a scarecrow; and right in the middle of the corn-
field that lay beyond the stream with the bulrushes at the
back of the house. Nothing funny in that, you may say.
But mark me, this was early September, and the stubble all
bleaching in the sun, and it didn't look an *old* scarecrow,
neither. It stood up with its arms out, and a hat down over
its eyes, bang in the middle of the field, its back to me,
and its front to the house. I knew that field like my own
face in the looking-glass. Then how could I have missed
it? What else then but that I stood still and had a good
long stare at it, first because, as I say, I had never seen it
before, and next because—but I'll be coming to that later.

"That done, and *not* to my satisfaction, I turned back a little and came along on the other side of the hedge, and so indoors, and went up to the upper storey to have a look at it from the windows. For you never know with these country people what they are up to, though they may seem stupid enough. Looked at from there, it wasn't so much in the middle of the field as I had fancied, seeing it from the other side. But how, thought I to myself, could you have escaped me, my friend, if you had been there all summer? I don't see how it could; that's flat. But if not, then it must have been put up more recent.

"I had all but forgotten about it next morning, but as afternoon came on I went upstairs and had another look. There was less heat-haze or something, and I could see it clearer and nearer, so to speak, but not quite clear enough. So I whipped along to the Reverend's study, him being still, poor gentleman, confined to his bed—in fact he never got up from it—I whipped along, I say, to the study to fetch his glasses, his binoculars, and I fastened them on that scarecrow like a microscope on a fly. Perhaps you will hardly credit me, sir, when I say that what seemed to me most different about it—from what you might expect—was that it didn't look in any ordinary manner of speaking, quite real.

"I could watch it with the glasses as plain as if it had been in touch of my hand, even to the buttons and the hatband. It didn't seem the first time I had set eyes on the *clothes,* either, though I couldn't have laid name to them. Yet there was something in the appearance of the thing, something in the way it bore itself up, so to speak, with its arms thrown up at the sky, and its empty face, which wasn't what you'd expect of mere sticks and rags. Not, I mean, if they were nothing but just real—real like that chair, I mean, you are sitting in now.

"I called George. I said: 'George, lay your eye to these glasses'—and his face was still a bit discolored, though his little affair in the stableyard was now three weeks old. 'Take a squint through these, George,' I said, 'and tell me what you think of *that* over there.'

"George was a slow dawdling mug if ever there was one—clumsy-fingered. But he fixed them at last, and took a good long look. Then he gave them back into my hand. 'Well,' I said, watching his face.

"'Why, Mr. Blake,' he said—meaning me, 'it's a scare-crow.'

"'How would you like it a bit nearer?' I said; just off-hand, like that.

"He looked at me. 'It's near enough in *them*,' he said.

"'Does the air round it strike you as funny at all?' I asked him. 'Out-of-the-way funny—quivering-like?'

"'That's the heat,' he said, but his mouth was trembling.

"'Well, George,' I said, 'heat or no heat, you or me must go and have a look at that thing closer some time. But not this afternoon. It's too late.'

"But we didn't; neither me *nor* him, though I fancy he went on thinking about it on his own account in between. And, lo and behold! when I got up next morning, and slid out of my bedroom, and just as I was, into the corridor to have another look at it—and Lor', as you looked out, the country was all as still as a map—it wasn't there. It wasn't there. It was vanished. Nor could I get a glimpse of it from downstairs through the bushes this side of the stream. And all so still and early you could hear the water moving. Now who, thinks I to myself, is answerable for *this* jiggery-pokery.

"But it's no good in this world, sir, putting reasons to a thing more far-fetched than are necessary to account for it. That you *will* agree. Some farmer's lout, I thought to myself, must have come and moved the thing overnight. But, that being so, what did he ever put it up for; harvest

done, mind you, and the crows, one would think, as welcome to what they could pick up in the stubble—if they
hadn't picked it up already—as robins to house crumbs?

"I didn't go out next day, not at all; and there being
only George and me in the Vicarage, and the Reverend
shut off in his room, I never knew such a holy quiet. The
heavens like a vault. Eighty-four in the shade by the glass
in the verandah, and this the fourth of September. All
day long, and I'll vouch for it, the whole twenty acres of
that field, but for the peewits and rooks lay empty. And
when with the sun going down the harvest moon came up
that evening—and that summer it showed up punctual as a
clock the whole month round—you could see right across
the flat country to the hills. And the nightjars croaking
too. You could cut the heat with a knife.

"That time the old gentleman's gruel was gone up and
George out of the way, I took yet another squint through
the glasses from the upper windows. And I am ready to
own that something inside of me gave a sort of a *hump*
when, large as life, I saw that the scarecrow was come back
again; though this, sir, is where you'll have, if you please,
to go careful with me. What I saw the instant before I
began to look, and to that I'd lay my affidavit, was something moving, and pretty rapid too, and it was only at the
very moment I clapped the glasses on to it that it suddenly
fixed itself into what I already *supposed* I should find it
to be. I've noticed that—though in little things not mat-
tering much—before. It's your own mind that learns you
when what you look for turns out to be what you expect.

"You might be suggesting that both shape and scarecrow too were all my eye and Betty Martin. But we'll see
later on about that. And what about George? You don't
mean to infer that he could borrow a mere fancy clean out
of my head to order, and turn it into a scarecrow in the
middle of a field and in broad daylight too? That would

be the long bow, and no mistake. Yet, as I say, even when I first cast eyes on it, it looked too real to be real. So there's the two on the one side, and the two on the other, and they don't make four.

"Well, sir, I must say that from that moment on I didn't like the look of things, and never have I shared a meal so mum as when George and me sat to supper that evening. From being a hearty eater his appetite was fallen almost to a cipher. He munched and couldn't swallow. I doubt if his vittles had a taste of them left. And we both of us knew as though it had been printed on the tablecloth what the other was thinking about.

"And it was while we sat there, him and me alone, George on the right and the window opposite, and me on the cupboard side in what was called the servants' hall, that we heard some words said. Not what you could understand, but still, words. I couldn't tell from where, except that it wasn't from the Reverend, and I couldn't tell what, but they dropped upon us and between us as if there had been a parrot in the room, clapping its horny bill, so to say, motionless in the air. At this George stopped munching for good, his face little short of green. But, except for a cockling up inside of me, I didn't make any sign I'd heard. After all, it was nothing that made any difference to *me,* though what was going on was, to say the least of it, not all as it should be. And if you knew the old Vicarage, you'd agree.

"Lock-up time came at last. And George took his candle and went up to bed. Not quite as willing as usual, I fancied; though he had always been a glutton for his full meed of sleep. You could notice by the sound of his feet on the stairs that he was pushing himself on. As for myself, it had always been my way to sit up after him reading a bit with the Reverend's *Times,* but that night I went off early. I gave a last look in on the old gentleman, and I might as well mention a nurse had been sent for, and his sister expected any day from Scotland; then coming back along the corridor I blew out my candle and stood waiting. The candle out, the moon came streaming in, and the outside from the window lay almost as bright as day. I looked this ways and that ways, back and front; but nothing to be seen, nor heard neither. Yet it seemed no more than one deep breath after I had closed my eyes in sleep that I was stark wide awake again, trying to make sense of some sound I'd heard.

"Old houses—I'm used to them. The timbers crinkle like a beehive in the dead of night. But this wasn't timbers, oh no! It might maybe have been wind, you'll say. But what chance of wind with not a hand's-breadth of cloud moving in the sky, and such a blare of moonlight as would keep a field mouse from so much as weeping out of its hole. What's more, not to know whether what you are listening to is in or out of your head isn't much help to a good night's rest. Still I fell off at last, unnoticing.

"Next morning, as George came back from taking up the breakfast tray, I had a good look at him in the sunlight, but you couldn't tell whether the marks round his eyes were natural—from what had gone before with the other, I mean—or from *insommia*. Best not to meddle, I thought, just wait. So I gave him good morning, and poured out the coffee and we sat to it as usual, the wasps coming in over the marmalade as if nothing had happened.

"All quiet that day, only rather more so, as it always is in a sick-room house. Doctor come and gone, but no nurse yet; and the old gentleman I thought looking very ailing. But he spoke to me quite cheerful. Just like his old self, too, to be sympathizing with me for the double-duty I'd been doing in the house. He asked after the garden, too, though there was as fine a bunch of black grapes on his green plate as any out of Canaan. It was the drought was in his mind. And just as I was leaving the room, my hand on the door, he mentioned one or two nice things about my having stayed on with him so long. 'You can't pay for that out of any bank,' he said to me, smiling at me almost merry-like, his beard over the sheet.

"'I hope and trust, sir,' I said, 'while I am with you, there will be no further fuss.' But I had a surety even as I said the words that he hadn't far to go, so that fusses now didn't really much matter to him. I don't see how you would be likely to notice them when things are coming to a conclusion; though I am thankful to say that what did occur was kept from him to the end.

"That night there came something sounding about the house that wasn't natural, and no mistake. I had scarcely slept a wink, and as soon as I heard it I was on with my tailcoat over my nightshirt in a jiffy, though there was no need for light. I had fetched along my winter coat, too, one the Reverend himself had passed on to me—this very coat on my back—and with that over my arm, I pushed open the door and looked in on George. Maybe he had heard my coming, or the other, I couldn't tell which; but there he was, sitting up in bed—the moon-light flooding in on his long face and tousled hair—and his trousers and braces thrown on the chair beside it.

"I said to him, 'What's wrong, George? Did you hear anything? A voice or anything?'

"He sat looking at me with his mouth open as if he couldn't shut it, and I could see he was shaken to the very roots. Now mind you, here I was, in the same quandary, as they call it, as before. What I'd heard might be real, some animal, fox or the like, prowling round outside, or it might not. If not, and the house being exorcised, as I said, though a long way back, and the Reverend gentleman still in this world himself, I had a kind of trust that what was there, if it was anything, couldn't get in. But naturally I was in something of a fever to make sure.

"'George,' I said, 'you mustn't risk a chill or anything of that sort'—and it had grown a bit cold in the small hours—'but it's up to us, with the Reverend ill and all, to know what's what. So if *you'll* take a look round on the outside, I'll have a search through on the in. What we must be cautious about is that the old gentleman isn't disturbed.'

"George went on looking at me, though he had by this time shuffled out of bed and into the overcoat I had handed him. He stood there, with his boots in his hand, shivering, but more maybe because he felt cold after the warmth of his sheets than because he had quite taken in what I had said.

"'Do you think, Mr. Blake,' he asked me, sitting down again on his bed, 'you don't think he is come back?'

"'Who's, George, come back?' I asked him.

"'Why, what we looked through the glasses at in the field,' he said. 'It had his look.'

"'Why, George,' I said, speaking as quiet as you might to a child, 'we know as how dead men tell no tales. Let alone scarecrows, then. All we've got to do is just to make sure *sure*. You do then as you're bid, lad; you go your way, and I'll go mine. There's never any harm can befall a man if his conscience is easy.'

"But that didn't seem to satisfy him. He gave a gulp and stood up again, still looking at me. Stupid or not, he was always one for doing his duty, was George. And I must say that what I call courage is facing what you're afraid of in your very bones, and not mere crashing into danger, eyes shut.

"'I'd lief as not go down, Mr. Blake,' he said; 'leastways, not alone.'

"'What have you to fear, George, my lad,' I said, 'man or spectre, the fault was none of yours.'

"He buttoned the coat up, same as I am wearing it now, and he gave me just one look more. It's hard to say all that's in a fellow creature's eyes, sir, when they are full of what no tongue in him could tell; but he had shut his mouth at last, and the moon on his face gave him a queer look, far-away-like, as if all that there was of him, this world or the next, had come to keep him company.

"And when the hush that had come down on the house was broken again, and this time it *was* the wind, though away high up over the roof, he didn't look at me any more. It was the last between us. He turned his back on me and went off out into the passage and down the stairs, and I listened until I could hear him in the distance taking down the bar at the back. It was one of those old-fashioned doors, sir, you must understand, loaded with locks and bolts, like in all old places.

"As for myself, I didn't move for a bit—there wasn't any hurry that I could see—except that I sat down on the bed in the place where George had sat; and waited. And you may depend upon it I stayed pretty quick there—with all that responsibility, not knowing what might happen next. And then presently what I heard was as though a voice had said something, very sharp and bitter; then said no more. There was a sort of moan, and then no more again. But by that time I was on my way on my rounds inside the house as I'd promised, and when I got back to my bedroom everything was still and quiet. And I took it of course that George had got back to his . . ."

Though the fire had faded and the day was gone, the fish-like phosphorescence of the gas mantles seemed to have grown brighter, and this elderly man, whose name was Blake I understood, was looking at me out of his white,

almost leper-like face in this faint gloom as steadily almost
as George must have been looking at him a few minutes
before he had descended the back stairs of the Vicarage,
never, I gathered, to set foot on them again.

"Did you manage to get any more sleep that night?" I
said.

Mr. Blake seemed to be pleasingly surprised at so easy
a question.

"That was the mistake of it," he said. "He wasn't found
till morning—cold for hours, and precious little to show
why."

"So you did manage to get some sleep," I persisted. But
this time he made no answer.

"Your share, I suppose, was quite a substantial one?"

"Share?" he said.

"In the will . . . ?"

"Now, didn't I myself tell you," he protested with some
warmth, "that that, as it turned out, wasn't so; though
why, it would take half a dozen or more of these lawyers
to explain. And even at that, I don't know as what I did
get has brought me anything much to boast about. I'm a
free man; that's true. But for how long? Nobody can stay
in this world here for ever, can he?"

With a peculiar rocking movement of his small head he
peered round and out of the door. "And though," he went
on, "you may have not one *iota* of harm to blame yourself
for to yourself, there may be misunderstandings and them
that hold them waiting for you in the next. So when it
comes to what that captain of the *Hesper* . . ."

But at that moment our prolonged *tête-à-tête* was
interrupted by a thick-set vigorous young porter carrying a bucket of coals in one hand and a stumpy torch
of smouldering brown paper in the other. He mounted a
chair and with a tug of finger and thumb instantly flooded
our dingy quarters with an almost intolerable gassy glare.

That done, he raked out the ash-gray fire with a lump of iron that may once have been a poker, and flung all but the complete contents of his bucket of coal on to it. Then he glanced round and saw who was sitting there. Me he passed over. I was merely a bird of passage. But he greeted my companion as if he were an old acquaintance.

"Good evening, sir," he said, and in that slightly cosseting voice which suggests past favors. "Let in a little light on the scene! I didn't notice you when I came in, and was beginning to wonder where you had got to."

His patron smirked back at him as if any such trifling little human attention was a peculiar solace. This time the porter deliberately caught my eye, as if—strangers though we were—there were some little privy and amused understanding between us in which this third party was unlikely to share. I ignored it, rose to my feet and clutched my bag. A train had come hooting into the station, its gliding lighted windows patterning the platform planks. Alas, yet again it wasn't mine. Still, such is humanity, I preferred my own company only, just then.

When I reached the door I glanced back at Mr. Blake, sitting there in the overcoat beside the apparently extinguished fire. In a sort of lost-dog fashion he was gazing after me, as though he deplored the withdrawal even of my tepid companionship. But in that dreadful luminosity there was nothing, so far as I could see, that any mortal man could be afraid of, alive or dead. So I left him to the porter, and set out hurriedly for the more comfortable lights and joys and colored bottles of the refreshment room. And as yet we have not met again.

The Cosy Room
Arthur Machen

I

And he found to his astonishment that he came to the appointed place with a sense of profound relief. It was true that the window was somewhat high up in the wall, and that, in case of fire, it might be difficult, for many reasons, to get out that way; it was barred like the basement windows that one sees now and then in London houses but as for the rest it was an extremely snug room. There was a gay flowery paper on the walls, a hanging bookshelf—his stomach sickened for an instant—a little table under the window with a board and draughtsmen on it, two or three good pictures, religious and ordinary, and the man who looked after him was arranging the tea things on the table in the middle of the room. And there was a nice wicker chair by a bright fire. It was a thoroughly pleasant room; snug you would call it. And, thank God, it was all over, anyhow.

II

It had been a horrible time for the last three months, up to an hour ago. First of all there was the trouble; all over in a minute, that was, and couldn't be helped, though it was a pity, and the girl wasn't worth it. But then there was the getting out of the town. He thought at first of just going about his ordinary business and knowing nothing about it; he didn't think that anybody had seen him following Joe down to the river. Why not loaf about as usual, and say nothing, and go into the Ringland Arms for a pint. It might be days before they found the body under the alders; and there would be an inquest, and all that. Would it be the best plan just to stick it out, and hold his tongue if the police came asking him questions. But then, how could he account for himself and his doings that evening? He might say he went for a stroll in Bleadon Woods, and home again without meeting anybody. There was nobody who could contradict him that he could think of.

And now, sitting in the snug room with the bright wall paper, sitting in the cosy chair by the fire—all so different from the tales they told of such places—he wished he had stuck it out and faced it out, and let them come on and find out what they could. But, then, he had got frightened. Lots of men had heard him swearing it would be outing does for Joe if he didn't leave the girl alone. And he had shown his revolver to Dick Haddon, and "Lobster" Carey, and Finniman, and others, and then they would be fitting the bullet into the revolver, and it would be all up. He got into a panic, and shook with terror, and knew he could never stay in Ledham, not another hour.

III

Mrs. Evans, his landlady, was spending the evening with her married daughter at the other side of the town, and would not be back till eleven. He shaved off his stubbly black beard and mustache, and slunk out of the town in the dark and walked all through the night by a lonely bye-road, and got to Darnley twenty miles away in the morning in time to catch the London excursion. There was a great crowd of people, and so far as he could see, nobody that he knew, and the carriages packed full of Darnleyites

and Lockwood weavers, all in high spirits and taking no
notice of him. They all got out at King's Cross, and he
strolled about with the rest, and looked round here and
there as they did and had a glass of beer at a crowded bar.
He didn't see how anybody was to find out where he had
gone.

IV

He got a back room in a quiet street off the Caledonian
Road, and waited. There was something in the evening
paper that night, something that you couldn't very well
make out. By the next day Joe's body was found, and they
got to Murder—the doctor said it couldn't be suicide. Then
his own name came in, and he was missing, and was asked
to come forward. And then, he read that he was supposed
to have gone to London: and he went sick with fear. He
went hot and he went cold. Something rose in his throat
and choked him. His hands shook as he held the paper,
his head whirled with terror. He was afraid to go home to
his room, because he knew he could not stay still in it; he
would be tramping up and down, like a wild beast, and
the landlady would wonder. And he was afraid to be in
the streets, for fear a policeman would come behind him
and put a hand on his shoulder. There was a kind of small
square round the corner and he sat down on one of the
benches there, and held up the paper before his face, with
the children yelling and howling and playing all about
him on the asphalt paths. They took no notice of him, and
yet they were company of a sort: it was not like being all
alone in that little, quiet room. But it soon got dark and
the man came to shut the gates.

V

And after that night; nights and days of horrors and sick
terrors that he never had known a man could suffer and

live. He had brought enough money to keep him for a while, but every time he changed a note he shook with fear, wondering whether it would be traced. What could he do; where could he go? Could he get out of the country? But there were passports and papers of all sorts; that would never do. He read that the police held a clue to the Ledham Murder Mystery; and he trembled to his lodgings and locked himself in and moaned in his agony, and then found himself chattering words and phrases at random, without meaning or relevance; strings of gibbering words: "all right, all right, all right . . . yes, yes, yes, yes . . . there, there, there . . . well, well, well, well . . ." just because he must utter something, because he could not bear to sit still and silent, with that anguish tearing his heart, with that sick horror choking him, with that weight of terror pressing on his breast. And then, nothing happened; and a little, faint, trembling hope fluttered in his breast for a while, and for a day or two he felt he might have a chance after all. One night he was in such a happier state, that he ventured round to the little public house at the corner, and drank a bottle of Old Brown Ale with some enjoyment, and began to think of what life might be again, if by a miracle—he recognized, even then, that it would be a miracle—all this horror passed away, and he was once more just like other men, with nothing to be afraid of. He was relishing the Brown Ale, and quite plucking up a spirit, when a chance phrase from the bar caught him: "looking for him not far from here, so they say." He left the glass of beer half full, and went out wondering whether he had the courage to kill himself that night. As a matter of fact the men at the bar were talking about a recent and sensational cat burglar; but every such word was doom to this wretch. And ever and again, he would check himself in his horrors, in his mutterings and gibberings, and wonder with amazement that the heart of a man could suffer such bitter agony, such rending torment. It was as if he had found out and discovered, he alone of all men living, a new world of which no man before had ever dreamed, in which no man could believe, if he were told the story of it. He had woke up in his past life from such nightmares, now and again, as most men suffer. They were terrible, so terrible that he remembered two or three of them that had oppressed him years before; but they were pure delight to what he now endured. Not endured, but writhed under as a worm twisting amidst red, burning coals.

He went out into the streets, some noisy, some dull and empty, and considered in his panic-stricken confusion which he should choose. They were looking for him in that part of London; there was deadly peril in every step. The streets where people went to and fro and laughed and chattered might be the safer; he could walk with the others and seem to be of them, and so be less likely to be noticed by those who were hunting on his track. But then, on the other hand, the great electric lamps made these streets almost as bright as day, and every feature of the passers-by was clearly seen. True, he was clean shaven now, and the pictures of him in the papers showed a bearded man, and his own face in the glass still looked strange to him. Still, there were sharp eyes that could penetrate such disguises; and they might have brought down some man from Ledham who knew him well, and knew the way he walked; and so he might be hailed and held at any moment. He dared not walk under the clear blaze of the electric lamps. He would be safer in the dark, quiet bye-ways.

He was turning aside, making for a very quiet street close by, when he hesitated. This street, indeed, was still enough after dark, and not over well lighted. It was a street of low, two-storied houses of gray brick that had grimed, with three or four families in each house. Tired men came home here after working hard all day, and people drew their blinds early and stirred very little abroad, and went early to bed; footsteps were rare in this street and in other streets into which it led, and the lamps were few and dim compared with those in the big thoroughfare. And yet, the very fact that few people were about made such as were all the more noticeable and conspicuous. And the police went slowly on their beats in the dark streets as in the bright, and with few people to look at, no doubt they looked all the more keenly at such as passed on the pavement. In his world, that dreadful world that he had discovered and dwelt in alone, the darkness was brighter than the daylight, and solitude more dangerous than a multitude of men. He dared not go into the light, he feared the shadows, and went trembling to his room and shuddered there as the hours of the night went by; shuddered and gabbled to himself his infernal Rosary: "all right, all right, all right . . . splendid, splendid . . . that's the way, that's the way, that's the way, that's the way . . . yes, yes, yes . . . first rate, first rate . . . all right . . . one, one, one, one:" gabbled in a low mutter to keep himself from howling like a wild beast.

VI

It was somewhat in the manner of a wild beast that he beat and tore against the cage of his fate. Now and again, it struck him as incredible. He would not believe that it was so. It was something that he would wake from, as he had waked from those nightmares that he remembered, for things did not really happen so. He could not believe it, he would not believe it. Or, if it were so indeed, then all these horrors must be happening to some other man into whose torments he had mysteriously entered. Or, he had got into a book, into a tale which one read and shuddered at, but did not for one moment credit; all make-believe, it must be, and presumably everything would be all right again. And then the truth came down on him like a heavy hammer, and beat him down, and held him down—on the burning coals of his anguish.

Now and then, he tried to reason with himself. He forced himself to be sensible as he put it; not to give way, to think of his chances. After all, it was three weeks since he had got into the excursion train at Darnley, and he was still a free man, and every day of freedom made his chances better. These things often die down. There were lots of cases in which the police never got the man they were after. He lit his pipe and began to think things over quietly. It might be a good plan to give his landlady notice, and leave at the end of the week, and make for somewhere in south London, and try to get a job of some sort: that would help to put them off his track. He got up, and looked thoughtfully out of the window; and caught his breath. There, outside the little newspaper shop opposite, was the bill of the evening paper: New Clue in Ledham Murder Mystery.

VII

The moment came at last. He never knew the exact means by which he was hunted down. As a matter of fact, a woman who knew him well happened to be standing outside Darnley station on the Excursion Day morning, and she had recognized him, in spite of his beardless chin. And then, at the other end, his landlady on her way upstairs, had heard his mutterings and gabblings, though the voice was low. She was interested, and curious, and a little frightened, and wondered whether her lodger might be dangerous, and naturally, she talked to her friends. So the story trickled down to the ears of the police, and the police asked about the date of the lodger's arrival. And there you were. And there was our nameless friend, drinking a good, hot cup of tea, and polishing off the bacon and eggs with rare appetite; in the cosy room with the cheerful paper; otherwise, the Condemned Cell.

The Snow
Hugh Walpole

The second Mrs. Ryder was a young woman not easily frightened, but now she stood in the dusk of the passage leaning back against the wall, her hand on her heart, looking at the gray-faced window beyond which the snow was steadily falling against the lamplight.

The passage where she was led from the study to the dining-room and the window looked out onto the little paved path that ran at the edge of the Cathedral green. As she stared down the passage she couldn't be sure whether the woman were there or no. How absurd of her! She knew the woman was not there. But if the woman was not, how was it that she could discern so clearly the old-fashioned gray cloak, the untidy gray hair and the sharp outline of the pale cheek and pointed chin? Yes, and more than that, the long sweep of the gray dress, falling in folds to the ground, the flash of a gold ring on the white hand. No. No. NO. This was madness. There was no one and nothing there. Hallucination . . .

Very faintly a voice seemed to come to her: "I warned you. This is for the last time. . . ."

The nonsense! How far now was her imagination to carry her? Tiny sounds about the house, the running of a tap somewhere, a faint voice from the kitchen, these and

something more had translated themselves into an imagined voice. "The last time . . ."

But her terror was real. She was not normally frightened by anything. She was young and healthy and bold,
fond of sport, hunting, shooting, taking any risk. Now she
was truly *stiffened* with terror—she could not move, could
not advance down the passage as she wanted to and find
light, warmth, safety in the dining-room. All the time the
snow fell steadily, stealthily, with its own secret purpose,
maliciously, beyond the window in the pale glow of the
lamplight.

Then unexpectedly there was noise from the hall, opening of doors, a rush of feet, a pause and then in clear
beautiful voices the well-known strains of "Good King
Wenceslas." It was the Cathedral choir boys on their regular Christmas round. This was Christmas Eve. They always
came just at this hour on Christmas Eve.

With an intense, almost incredible relief she turned
back into the hall. At the same moment her husband came
out of the study. They stood together smiling at the little
group of mufflered becoated boys who were singing, heart
and soul in the job, so that the old house simply rang with
their melody.

Reassured by the warmth and human company she lost
her terror. It had been her imagination. Of late she had
been none too well. That was why she had been so irri-
table. Old Doctor Bernard was no good: he didn't understand her case at all. After Christmas she would go to London and have the very best advice . . .

Had she been well she could not, half an hour ago,
have shown such miserable temper over nothing. She knew
that it was over nothing and yet that knowledge did not
make it any easier for her to restrain herself. After every
bout of temper she told herself that there should never be
another—and then Herbert said something irritating, one

of his silly muddle-headed stupidities, and she was off again!

She could see now as she stood beside him at the bottom of the staircase, that he was still feeling it. She had certainly half an hour ago said some abominably rude personal things—things that she had not at all meant—and he had taken them in his meek quiet way. Were he not so meek and quiet, did he only pay her back in her own coin, she would never lose her temper. Of that she was sure. But who wouldn't be irritated by that meekness and by the only reproachful thing that he ever said to her: "Elinor understood me better, my dear." To throw the first wife up against the second! Wasn't that the most tactless thing that a man could possibly do? And Elinor, that old, worn elderly woman, the very opposite of her own gay bright amusing self? That was why Herbert had loved her, because she was gay and bright and young. It was true that Elinor had been devoted, that she had been so utterly wrapped up in Herbert that she lived only for him. People were always recalling her devotion, which was sufficiently rude and tactless of them.

Well, she could not give any one that kind of old-fashioned sugary devotion; it wasn't in her, and Herbert knew it by this time.

Nevertheless she loved Herbert in her own way, as he must know, know it so well that he ought to pay no attention to the bursts of temper. She wasn't well. She would see a doctor in London . . .

The little boys finished their carols, were properly rewarded and tumbled like feathery birds out into the snow again. They went into the study, the two of them, and stood beside the big open log-fire. She put her hand up and stroked his thin beautiful cheek.

"I'm so sorry to have been cross just now, Bertie. I didn't mean half I said, you know."

But he didn't, as he usually did, kiss her and tell her that it didn't matter. Looking straight in front of him he answered:

"Well, Alice, I do wish you wouldn't. It hurts, horribly. It upsets me more than you think. And it's growing on you. You make me miserable. I don't know what to do about it. And it's all about nothing."

Irritated at not receiving the usual commendation for her sweetness in making it up again she withdrew a little and answered:

"Oh, all right. I've said I'm sorry. I can't do any more."

"But tell me," he insisted, "I want to know. What makes you so angry, so suddenly?—and about nothing at all."

She was about to let her anger rise, her anger at his obtuseness, obstinacy, when some fear checked her, a strange unanalyzed fear, as though some one had whispered to her 'Look out! This is the last time!'

"It's not altogether my own fault," she answered and left the room.

She stood in the cold hall, wondering where to go. She could feel the snow falling outside the house and shivered. She hated the snow, she hated the winter, this beastly, cold, dark, English winter that went on and on only at last to change into a damp, foggy English spring.

It had been snowing all day. In Polchester it was unusual to have so heavy a snowfall. This was the hardest winter that they had known for many years.

When she urged Herbert to winter abroad—which he could quite easily do—he answered her impatiently; he had the strongest affection for this poky dead and alive Cathedral town. The Cathedral seemed to be precious to him; he wasn't happy if he didn't go and see it every day! She wouldn't wonder if he didn't think more of the Cathedral than he did of herself. Elinor had been the same; she had even written a little book about the Cathedral,

about the Black Bishop's Tomb and the stained glass and
the rest . . .

What was the Cathedral after all? Only a building!

She was standing in the drawing-room looking out over
the dusky ghostly snow to the great hulk of the Cathedral
that Herbert said was like a flying ship, but to herself was
more like a crouching beast licking its lips over the miserable sinners that it was forever devouring.

As she looked and shivered, feeling that in spite of
herself her temper and misery were rising so that they
threatened to choke her, it seemed to her that her bright
and cheerful fire-lit drawing-room was suddenly open to
the snow. It was exactly as though cracks had appeared
everywhere, in the ceiling, the walls, the windows, and
that through these cracks the snow was filtering, drib-
bling in little tracks of wet down the walls, already perhaps making pools of water on the carpet.

This was of course imagination, but it was a fact that
the room was most dreadfully cold although a great fire
was burning and it was the cosiest room in the house.

Then, turning, she saw the figure standing by the door.
This time there could be no mistake. It was a gray shadow, and yet a shadow with form and outline—the untidy
gray hair, the pale face like a moon-lit leaf, the long gray
clothes and something obstinate, vindictive, terribly menacing in its pose.

She moved and the figure was gone; there was nothing
there and the room was warm again, quite hot in fact. But
young Mrs. Ryder, who had never feared anything in all
her life save the vanishing of her youth, was trembling so
that she had to sit down, and even then her trembling did
not cease. Her hand shook on the arm of her chair.

She had created this thing out of her imagination of
Elinor's hatred of her and her own hatred of Elinor. It
was true that they had never met but who knew not that

the spiritualists were right, and Elinor's spirit, jealous of
Herbert's love for her, had been there driving them apart,
forcing her to lose her temper and then hating her for losing it. Such things might be! But she had not much time
for speculation. She was preoccupied with her fear. It was
a definite, positive fear, the kind of fear that one has just
before one goes into an operation. Some one or something
was threatening her. She clung to her chair as though to
leave it was to plunge into disaster. She looked around
her everywhere; all the familiar things, the pictures, the
books, the little tables, the piano were different now, iso-
lated, strange, hostile, as though they had been won over
by some enemy power.

She longed for Herbert to come and protect her; she
felt most kindly to him. She would never lose her temper
with him again—and at that same moment some cold voice
seemed to whisper in her ear: "You had better not. It will
be for the last time."

At length she found courage to rise, cross the room and
go up to dress for dinner. In her bedroom courage came to
her once more. It was certainly very cold, and the snow, as
she could see when she looked between her curtains, was
falling more heavily than ever, but she had a warm bath,
sat in front of her fire and was sensible again.

For many months this odd sense that she was watched
and accompanied by some one hostile to her had been growing. It was the stronger perhaps because of the things that
Herbert told her about Elinor; she was the kind of woman
he said, who, once she loved any one, would never relin-
quish her grasp; she was utterly faithful. He implied that
her tenacious fidelity had been at times a little difficult.

"She always said," he added once, "that she would watch
over me until I rejoined her in the next world. Poor Elinor!" he sighed. "She had a fine religious faith, stronger
than mine, I fear."

It was always after one of her tantrums that young Mrs. Ryder had been most conscious of this hallucination, this dreadful discomfort of feeling that some one was near you who hated you—but it was only during the last week that she began to fancy that she actually saw any one, and with every day her sense of this figure had grown stronger.

It was of course only nerves, but it was one of those nervous afflictions that became tiresome indeed if you did not rid yourself of it. Mrs. Ryder, secure now in the warmth and intimacy of her bedroom, determined that henceforth everything should be sweetness and light. No more tempers! Those were the things that did her harm.

Even though Herbert were a little trying, was not that the case with every husband in the world? And was it not Christmas time? Peace and Good will to men! Peace and Good will to Herbert!

They sat down opposite one another in the pretty little dining-room hung with Chinese woodcuts, the table gleaming and the amber curtains richly dark in the firelight.

But Herbert was not himself. He was still brooding, she supposed, over their quarrel of the afternoon. Weren't men children? Incredible the children that they were!

So when the maid was out of the room she went over to him, bent down and kissed his forehead.

"Darling . . . you're still cross, I can see you are. You mustn't be. Really you mustn't. It's Christmas time and, if I forgive you, you must forgive me."

"You forgive me?" he asked, looking at her in his most aggravating way. "What have you to forgive me for?"

Well, that was really too much. When she had taken all the steps, humbled her pride.

She went back to her seat, but for a while could not answer him because the maid was there. When they were alone again she said, summoning all her patience:

"Bertie dear, do you really think that there's anything to be gained by sulking like this? It isn't worthy of you. It isn't really."

He answered her quietly.

"Sulking? No, that's not the right word. But I've got to keep quiet. If I don't I shall say something I'm sorry for." Then, after a pause, in a low voice, as though to himself: "These constant rows are awful."

Her temper was rising again; another self that had nothing to do with her real self, a stranger to her and yet a very old familiar friend.

"Don't be so self-righteous," she answered, her voice trembling a little. "These quarrels are entirely my own fault, aren't they?"

"Elinor and I never quarrelled," he said, so softly that she scarcely heard him.

"No! Because Elinor thought you perfect. She adored you. You've often told me. I don't think you perfect. I'm not perfect either. But we've both got faults. I'm not the only one to blame."

"We'd better separate," he said, suddenly looking up. "We don't get on now. We used to. I don't know what's changed everything. But, as things are, we'd better separate."

She looked at him and knew that she loved him more than ever, but because she loved him so much she wanted to hurt him, and because he had said that he thought he could get on without her she was so angry that she forgot all caution. Her love and her anger helped one another. The more angry she became the more she loved him.

"I know why you want to separate," she said. "It's because you're in love with some one else." ("How funny," something inside her said. "You don't mean a word of this.") "You've treated me as you have, and then you leave me."

"I'm not in love with any one else," he answered her steadily, "and you know it. But we are so unhappy together that it's silly to go on . . . silly. . . . The whole thing has failed."

There was so much unhappiness, so much bitterness in his voice that she realized that at last she had truly gone too far. She had lost him. She had not meant this. She was frightened and her fear made her so angry that she went across to him.

"Very well then . . . I'll tell every one . . . what you've been. How you've treated me."

"Not another scene," he answered wearily. "I can't stand any more. Let's wait. To-morrow is Christmas Day . . ."

He was so unhappy that her anger with herself maddened her. She couldn't bear his sad hopeless disappointment with herself, their life together, everything.

In a fury of blind temper she struck him; it was as though she were striking herself. He got up and without a word left the room. There was a pause and then she heard the hall door close. He had left the house.

She stood there, slowly coming to her control again. When she lost her temper it was as though she sank under water. When it was all over she came once more to the surface of life, wondering where she'd been and what she had been doing. Now she stood there, bewildered, and then at once she was aware of two things, one that the room was bitterly cold and the other that some one was in the room with her.

This time she did not need to look around her. She did not turn at all but only stared straight at the curtained windows, seeing them very carefully, as though she were summing them up for some future analysis, with their thick green folds, gold rod, white lines—and beyond them the snow was falling.

She did not need to turn but, with a shiver of terror, she was aware that that gray figure who had, all these last weeks, been approaching ever more closely, was almost at her very elbow. She heard quite clearly: "I warned you. That was the last time."

At the same moment Onslow the butler came in. Onslow was broad, fat and rubicund—a good faithful butler with a passion for church music. He was a bachelor and it was said disappointed of women. He had an old mother in Liverpool to whom he was greatly attached.

In a flash of consciousness she thought of all these things when he came in. She expected him also to see the gray figure at her side. But he was undisturbed, his ceremonial complacency clothed him securely.

"Mr. Fairfax has gone out," she said firmly. Oh, surely he must see something, feel something.

"Yes, Madame!" Then, smiling rather grandly: "It's snowing hard. Never seen it harder here. Shall I build up the fire in the drawing-room, Madame?"

"No, thank you. But Mr. Fairfax's study . . ."

"Yes, Madame. I only thought that as this room was so warm you might find it chilly in the drawing-room."

This room warm, when she was shivering from head to foot; but holding herself lest he should see . . . She longed to keep him there, to implore him to remain; but in a moment he was gone, softly closing the door behind him.

Then a mad longing for flight seized her, and she could not move. She was rooted there to the floor, and even as wildly, trying to cry, to scream, to shriek the house down she found that only a little whisper would come, she felt the cold touch of a hand on hers.

She did not turn her head: her whole personality, all her past life, her poor little courage, her miserable fortitude was summoned to meet this sense of approaching death which was as unmistakable as a certain smell, or the familiar ringing of a gong. She had dreamt in nightmares of approaching death and it had always been like this, a fearful constriction of the heart, a paralysis of the limbs, a choking sense of disaster like an anaesthetic.

"You were warned," something said to her again.

She knew that if she turned she would see Elinor's face, set, white, remorseless. The woman had always hated her, been vilely jealous of her, protecting her wretched Herbert.

A certain vindictiveness seemed to release her. She found that she could move, her limbs were free.

She passed to the door, ran down the passage, into the hall. Where would she be safe? She thought of the Cathedral where to-night there was a carol service. She opened the hall door and just as she was, meeting the thick involving muffling snow, she ran out.

She started across the green toward the Cathedral door. Her thin black slippers sank in the snow. Snow was everywhere—in her hair, her eyes, her nostrils, her mouth, on her bare neck, between her breasts.

"Help! Help! Help!" she wanted to cry, but the snow choked her. Lights whirled about her. The Cathedral rose like a huge black eagle and flew toward her.

She fell forward and even as she fell a hand, far colder than the snow, caught her neck. She lay struggling in the snow and as she struggled there two hands of an icy fleshless chill closed about her throat.

Her last impression was of the hard outline of a ring pressing into her neck. Then she lay still, her face in the snow and the flakes eagerly, savagely, covered her.

The Cat Jumps
Elizabeth Bowen

After the Bentley murder, Rose Hill stood empty two years. Lawns mounted to meadows, white paint peeled from the balconies; the sun, looking more constantly, less fearfully in than sightseers' eyes through the naked windows, bleached the floral wallpapers. The week after the execution, Harold Bentley's legatees had placed the house on the books of the principal agents, London and local. But though sunny, modern and convenient, though so delightfully situate over the Thames valley (above flood level) within easy reach of a golf course, Rose Hill, while frequently viewed, remained unpurchased. Dreadful associations apart, the privacy of the place had been violated: With its terraced garden, lily pond and pergola cheerfully rose-encrusted the public had been made too familiar. On the domestic scene, too many eyes had burnt the impress of their horror. Moreover, that pearly bathroom, bedroom with wide outlook over a loop of the Thames . . . "The Rose Hill Horror": headlines flashed up at the very sound of the name. "Oh, *no,* dear!" many wives had exclaimed drawing their husbands from the gate. "Come away!" they urged, crumpling the agent's order to view as though the house were advancing on them. And husbands came away—with a backward glance at the garage. Funny to think: a chap who was hanged had kept his car there.

The Harold Wrights, however, were not deterred. They had light, bright, shadowless, thoroughly disinfected minds. They believed that they disbelieved in most things but were unprejudiced; they enjoyed frank discussions. They dreaded nothing but inhibitions: they had no inhibitions. They were pious agnostics, earnest for social reform; they explained everything to their children and were annoyed to find their children could not sleep at nights because they thought there was a complex under the bed. They knew all crime to be pathological, and read their murders only in scientific books. They had Vita Glass put into all their windows. No family, in fact, could have been more unlike the mistaken Harold Bentleys.

Rose Hill, from the first glance, suited the Wrights admirably. They were in search of a cheerful week-end house with a nice atmosphere where their friends could join them for frank discussions, and their own and their friends' children "run wild" during the summer months. Harold Wright, who had a good head, got the agent to knock six hundred off the quoted price of the house. "That unfortunate affair," he murmured. Jocelyn commended his inspiration. Otherwise, they did not give the Bentleys another thought.

The Wrights had the floral wallpapers all stripped off and the walls cream-washed; they removed some disagreeably thick pink shades from the electricity, and had the paint renewed inside and out. (The front of the house was bracketed over with balconies, like an overmantel.) Their bedroom mantelpiece, stained by the late Mrs. Bentley's cosmetics, had to be scrubbed with chemicals. Also, they had removed from the rock-garden Mrs. Bentley's little dog's memorial tablet, with a quotation on it from "Indian Love Lyrics." Jocelyn Wright, looking into the unfortunate bath, *the* bath, so square and opulent with its surround of nacreous tiles, said, laughing lightly, she supposed any one *else* would have had that bath changed. "Not that that would be possible," she added, "the bath's built in . . . I've always wanted a built-in bath."

Harold and Jocelyn turned from the bath to look down at the cheerful river shimmering under a spring haze. All the way down the slope cherry trees were in blossom. Life should be simplified for the Wrights—they were fortunate in their mentality.

After an experimental week-end, without guests or children, only one thing troubled them: a resolute stuffiness, upstairs and down—due, presumably, to the house's having been so long shut up—a smell of unsavory habitation, of rich cigarette smoke stale in the folds of unaired curtains, of scent spilled on unbrushed a carpets; an alcoholic smell—persistent in their perhaps too sensitive nostrils after days of airing, doors and windows open, in rooms drenched thoroughly with sun and wind. They told each other it came from the parquet—they didn't like it, somehow. They had the parquet taken up—at great expense—and put down plain oak floors.

In their practical way, the Wrights now set out to expel, live out, live down, almost (had the word had place in their vocabulary) to 'lay' the Bentleys. Deferred by trouble over the parquet, their occupation of Rose Hill (which should have dated from mid-April) did not begin till the end of May. Throughout a week, Jocelyn had motored from town daily, so that the final installation of themselves and the children was able to coincide with their first week-end party—they asked down five of their friends to warm the house.

That first Friday, everything was auspicious; afternoon sky blue as the garden irises; later, a full moon pendant over the river; a night so warm that, after midnight, their enlightened friends, in pyjamas, could run on the blanched lawns in a state of high though rational excitement. Jane, John, and Janet, their admirably spaced-out children, kept awake by the moonlight, hailed their elders out of the nursery skylight. Jocelyn waved to them: they never had been repressed.

The girl Muriel Barker was found looking up the terraces at the house, a shade doubtfully. "You know," she said, "I do rather wonder they don't feel . . . *sometimes* . . . You know what I mean?"

"No," replied her companion, a young scientist.

Muriel sighed. "No one would mind if it had been just a short sharp shooting. But, it was so . . . prolonged. It went on all over the house. Do you remember?" she said timidly.

"No," replied Mr. Cartaret, "it didn't interest me."

"Oh, nor me either!" agreed Muriel quickly, but added: "How he must have hated her . . ."

The scientist, sleepy, yawned frankly and referred her to Krafft Ebing. But Muriel went to bed with "Alice in Wonderland"; she went to sleep with the lights on. She was not, as Jocelyn realized later, the sort of girl to have asked at all.

Next morning was overcast; in the afternoon it rained, suddenly and heavily, interrupting for some, tennis, for others, a pleasant discussion, in a punt, on marriage under the Soviet. Defeated, they all rushed in. Jocelyn went round from room to room, shutting tightly the rain-lashed casements along the front of the house: these continued to rattle; the balconies creaked. An early dusk set in; an oppressive, almost visible moisture, up from the darkening river, pressed on the panes like a presence and slid through the house. The party gathered in the library, round an expansive but thinly-burning fire. Harold circulated photographs of modern architecture; they discussed these tendencies. Then Mrs. Monkhouse, sniffing, exclaimed: "Who uses 'Trefle Incarnat'?"

"Now *who* ever would"—her hostess began scornfully. Then from the hall came a howl, a scuffle, a thin shriek. They sat too still; in the dusky library Mr. Cartaret laughed out loud. Harold Wright, indignantly throwing open the door, revealed Jane and Jacob rolling at the foot of the stairs biting each other, their faces dark with uninhibited passion. Bumping alternate heads against the foot of the banisters, they shrieked in concord.

"Extraordinary," said Harold, "they've never done that before. They have always understood each other so well."

"I wouldn't do that," advised Jocelyn, raising her voice slightly, "you'll hurt your teeth. Other teeth won't grow at once, you know."

"You should let them find that out for themselves," disapproved Edward Cartaret, taking up the *New Statesman*. Harold, in perplexity, shut the door on his children who soon stunned each other to silence.

Meanwhile, Sara and Talbot Monkhouse, Muriel Barker and Theodora Smith had drawn together over the fire in a tight little knot. Their voices twanged with excitement. By that shock just now, something seemed to have been released. Even Cartaret gave them half his attention. They were discussing *crime passionel*.

"Of course, if that's what they really want to discuss . . ." thought Jocelyn. But it did seem unfortunate. Partly from an innocent desire to annoy her visitors, partly because the room felt awful—you would have thought fifty people had been there for a week—she went across and opened one of the windows, admitting a pounce of damp wind. They all turned, startled, to hear rain crash on the lead of an upstairs balcony. Muriel's voice was left in forlorn solo: "Dragged herself . . . whining 'Harold' . . ."

Harold Wright looked remarkably conscious. Jocelyn said brightly "Whatever *are* you talking about?" But unfortunately, Harold, on almost the same breath suggested: "Let's leave that family alone, shall we?" Their friends all felt they might not be asked again. Though they did feel, plaintively, that they had been being natural. However, they discovered Muriel, who getting up abruptly, said she thought she'd like to go for a walk in the rain before dinner. Nobody accompanied her.

Later, overtaking Mrs. Monkhouse on the stairs, Muriel confided: absolutely, she could not stand Edward Cartaret. She could hardly bear to be in the room with him. He seemed so . . . cruel. Cold-blooded? No, she meant cruel. Sara Monkhouse, going into Jocelyn's room for a chat (at her entrance Jocelyn started violently) told Jocelyn that Muriel could not stand Edward, could hardly bear to be in a room with him. "Pity," said Jocelyn, "I had thought they might do for each other." Jocelyn and Sara agreed that Muriel was unrealized: what she ought to have was a baby. But when Sara, dressing, told Talbot Monkhouse that Muriel could not stand Edward, and Talbot said Muriel was unrealized, Sara was furious. The Monkhouses, who never did quarrel, quarrelled bitterly and were late for dinner. They would have been later if the meal itself had not been delayed by an outburst of sex-antagonism between the nice Jacksons, a couple imported from London to run the house. Mrs. Jackson, putting everything in the oven, had locked herself into her room.

"Curious," said Harold, "the Jacksons' relations to each other always seemed so modern. They have the most intelligent discussions."

Theodora said she had been re-reading Shakespeare—this brought them point-blank up against Othello. Harold, with Titanic force, wrenched round the conversation to Relativity: about this no one seemed to have anything

to say but Edward Cartaret. And Muriel, who by some
mischance had again been placed beside him, sat deathly,
turning down her dark-rimmed eyes. In fact, on the intelligent sharp-featured faces all round the table, something, perhaps simply a clearness, seemed to be lacking, as
though these were wax faces for one fatal instant exposed
to a furnace. Voices came out from some dark interiority;
in each conversational interchange a mutual vote of no
confidence was implicit. You would have said that each
personality had been attacked by some kind of decompo-
sition.

"No moon to-night," complained Sara Monkhouse.
Never mind, they would have a cozy evening, they would
play paper games, Jocelyn promised.

"If you can see," said Harold. "Something seems to be
going wrong with the light."

Did Harold think so? They had all noticed the light
seemed to be losing quality, as though a film, smoke-like,
were creeping over the bulbs. The light, thinning, darkening, seemed to contract round each lamp into a blurred
aura. They had noticed but, each with a proper dread of
his own subjectivity, had not spoken.

"Funny stuff," Harold said, "electricity."

Mr. Cartaret could not agree with him.

Though it was late, though they yawned and would not
play paper games, they were reluctant to go to bed. You
would have supposed a delightful evening. Jocelyn was not
gratified.

The library stools, rugs, and divans were strewn with
Krafft Ebing, Freud, Forel, Weiniger and the heterosexual
volume of Havelock Ellis. (Harold had thought it right
to instal his reference library; his friends hated to discuss
without basis.) The volumes were pressed open with paper-
knives and small pieces of modern statuary; stooping from

one to another, purposeful as a bee, Edward Cartaret read
extracts aloud to Harold, to Talbot Monkhouse and to
Theodora Smith who stitched *gros point* with resolution.
At the far end of the library, under a sallow drip from a
group of electric candles, Mrs. Monkhouse and Miss Barker shared an ottoman, spines pressed rigid against the wall.
Tensely, one spoke, one listened.

"And these," thought Jocelyn, leaning back with her
eyes shut between the two groups, "are friends I liked to
have in my life. Pellucid, sane . . ."

It was remarkable how much Muriel knew. Sara, very
much shocked, edged up till their thighs touched. You
would have thought the Harold Bentleys had been Muriel's relatives. Surely, Sara attempted, in one's large, bright
world one did not think of these things? Practically they
did not exist! Surely Muriel should not. . . . But Muriel
looked at her strangely.

"Did you know," she said, "that one of Mrs. Bentley's
hands was found in the library?"

Sara, smiling a little awkwardly, licked her lip. "Oh,"
she said.

"But the fingers were in the dining-room. He began
there."

"Why isn't he in Broadmoor?"

"That defense failed. He didn't really subscribe to it.
He said, having done what he wanted was worth anything."

"Oh!"

"Yes, he was nearly lynched. . . . She dragged herself upstairs. She couldn't lock any doors—naturally. One maid,
her maid, got shut into the house with them: he'd sent
all the others away. For a long time, everything seemed
so quiet: the maid crept out and saw Harold Bentley sitting halfway upstairs, finishing a cigarette. All the lights
were full on. He nodded to her and dropped the cigarette
through the banisters. Then she saw the . . . state of the

hall. He went upstairs after Mrs. Bentley saying: 'Lucinda!' He looked into room after room, whistling, then he said, 'Here we are,' and shut a door after him.

"The maid fainted. When she came to it was still going on, upstairs. . . . Harold Bentley had locked all the garden doors, there were locks even on the French windows. The maid couldn't get out. Everything she touched was . . . sticky. At last she broke a pane and got through. As she ran down the garden—the lights were on all over the house—she saw Harold Bentley moving about in the bathroom. She fell right over the edge of the terrace and one of the tradesmen picked her up next day.

"Doesn't it seem odd, Sara, to think of Jocelyn in that bath?"

Finishing her recital Muriel turned on Sara an ecstatic and brooding look that made her almost beautiful. Sara fumbled with a cigarette, match after match failed her. "Muriel, you should see a specialist."

Muriel held out her hand for a cigarette. "He put her heart in her hat-box. He said it belonged there."

"You had no right to come here. It was most unfair on Jocelyn. Most . . . indelicate."

Muriel, to whom the word was, properly, unfamiliar, eyed incredulously Sara's lips.

"How dared you come?"

"I thought I might like it. I thought I ought to fulfil myself. I'd never had any experience of these things."

"*Muriel . . .*"

"Besides, I wanted to meet Edward Cartaret. Several people said we were made for each other. Now, of course, I shall never marry. Look what comes of it. . . . I must say, Sara, I wouldn't be you or Jocelyn. Shut up all night with a man all alone—I don't know how you dare sleep. I've arranged to sleep with Theodora, and we shall barricade the door. I noticed something about Edward Cartaret the moment I arrived; a kind of insane glitter. He is utterly pathological. He's got instruments in his room, in that black bag. Yes, I looked. Did you notice the way he went on and on about cutting up that cat, and the way Talbot and Harold listened?"

Sara, looking furtively round the room, saw Mr. Cartaret making passes over the head of Theodora Smith with a paper-knife. Both appeared to laugh heartily, but in silence.

"Here we are," said Harold, showing his teeth, smiling.

He stood over Muriel with a syphon in one hand, glass in the other.

At this point Jocelyn, rising, said she, for one, intended to go to bed.

Jocelyn's bedroom curtains swelled a little over the noisy window. The room was stuffy and—insupportable, so that she did not know where to turn. The house, fingered outwardly by the wind that dragged unceasingly past the walls was, within, a solid silence: silence heavy as flesh. Jocelyn dropped her wrap to the floor then watched how its feathered edges crept a little—a draught came in, under her bathroom door.

Jocelyn turned in despair and hostility from the strained, pale woman looking at her from her oblong glass. She said aloud: "There is no fear," then within herself, heard this taken up: "But the death fear, that one is not there to relate! If the spirit, dismembered in agony, dies before the body! If the spirit, in the whole knowledge of its dissolution, drags from chamber to chamber, drops from plane to plane of awareness (as from knife to knife down an oubliette) shedding, receiving agony! Till, long afterward, death with its little pain is established in the indifferent body." There was no comfort: death (now at

every turn and instant claiming her) was in its every possible manifestation, violent death: ultimately, she was to
be given up to terror.

Undressing, shocked by the iteration of her reflected
movements, she flung a towel over the glass. With what
desperate eyes of appeal, at Sara's door, she and Sara had
looked at each other, clung with their looks—and parted.
She could have sworn she heard Sara's bolt slide softly to.
But what then, subsequently, of Talbot? And what—she
eyed her own bolt, so bright (and for the late Mrs. Bentley, so ineffective) what of Harold?

"It's atavistic!" she said aloud, in the dark-lit room,
and, kicking her slippers away, got into bed. She took
Erewhon from the rack but lay rigid, listening. As though
snatched by a movement, the towel slipped from the
mirror beyond her bed-end. She faced the two eyes of an
animal in extremity, eyes black, mindless. The clock struck
two: she had been waiting an hour.

On the floor, her feathered wrap shivered again all over.
She heard the other door of the bathroom very stealthily
open, then shut. Harold moved in softly, heavily, knocked
against the side of the bath and stood still. He was quietly
whistling.

"Why didn't I understand? He must always have hated
me. It's to-night he's been waiting for . . . *He wanted this
house*. His look, as we went upstairs . . ."

She shrieked: "Harold!"

Harold, so softly whistling, remained behind the imperturbable door, remained quite still . . . "he's *listening*
for me . . ." One pin-point of hope at the tunnel end: to
get to Sara, to Theodora, to Muriel. Unmasked, incau-
tious, with a long tearing sound of displaced air, Jocelyn
leapt from bed to the door.

But her door had been locked from the outside.

With a strange rueful smile, like an actress, Jocelyn, skirting the foot of the two beds, approached the door of the bathroom. "At least I have still . . . my feet." For, for some time the heavy body of Mrs. Bentley, tenacious of life, had been dragging itself from room to room. *"Harold!"* she said to the silence, face close to the door.

The door opened on Harold, looking more dreadfully at her than she had imagined. With a quick, vague movement he roused himself from his meditation. Therein he had assumed the entire burden of Harold Bentley. Forces he did not know of assembling darkly, he had faced for untold ages the imperturbable door to his wife's room. She would be there, densely, smotheringly there. She lay like a great cat, always, over the mouth of his life.

The Harolds, superimposed on each other, stood searching the bedroom strangely. Taking a step forward, shutting the door behind him:

"Here we are," said Harold.

Jocelyn went down heavily. Harold watched.

Harold Wright was appalled. Jocelyn had fainted: Jocelyn never had fainted before. He shook, he fanned, he applied restoratives. His perplexed thoughts fled to Sara—oh, Sara certainly. "Hi!" he cried, "Sara!" and successively fled from each to each of the locked passage doors. There was no way out.

Across the passage, a door throbbed to the maniac drumming of Sara Monkhouse. She had been locked in. For Talbot, agonized with solicitude, it was equally impossible to emerge from his dressing-room. Farther down the passage, Edward Cartaret, interested by this nocturnal manifestation, wrenched and rattled his door handle in vain.

Muriel, on her way through the house to Theodora's bedroom, had turned all the keys on the outside, impartially. She did not know which door was Edward Cartaret's. Muriel was a woman who took no chances.

Rats

M. R. James

"And if you was to walk through the bedrooms now, you'd see the ragged, mouldy bedclothes a-heaving and a-heaving like seas." "And a-heaving and a-heaving with what?" he says. "Why, with the rats under 'em."

But was it with the rats? I ask, because in another case it was not. I cannot put a date to the story, but I was young when I heard it, and the teller was old. It is an ill-proportioned tale, but that is my fault, not his.

It happened in Suffolk, near the coast. In a place where the road makes a sudden dip and then a sudden rise; as you go northward, at the top of that rise, stands a house on the left of the road. It is a tall red-brick house, narrow for its height; perhaps it was built about 1770. The top of the front is a low triangular pediment with a round window in the centre. Behind it are stables and offices, and such gardens as it has is behind them. Scraggy Scotch firs are near it: an expanse of gorse-covered land stretches away from it. It commands a view of the distant sea from the upper windows of the front. A sign on a post stands before the door, or did so stand, for though it was an inn of repute once, I believe it is so no longer.

To this inn came my acquaintance, Mr. Thomson, when he was a young man, on a fine spring day, coming from the

University of Cambridge, and desirous of solitude in tolerable quarters, and time for reading. These he found, for the landlord and his wife had been in service and could make a visitor comfortable, and there was no one else staying in the inn. He had a large room on the first floor commanding the road and the view, and if it faced east, why, that could not be helped; the house was well built and warm.

He spent very tranquil and uneventful days: work all the morning, an afternoon perambulation of the country round, a little conversation with country company or the people of the inn in the evening over the then fashionable drink of brandy and water, a little more reading and writing, and bed; and he would have been content that this should continue for the full month he had at disposal, so well was his work progressing, and so fine was the April of that year—which I have reason to believe was that which Orlando Whistlecraft chronicles in his weather record as the "Charming Year."

One of his walks took him along the northern road, which stands high and traverses a wide common, called a heath. On the bright afternoon when he first chose this direction his eye caught a white object some hundreds of yards to the left of the road, and he felt it necessary to make sure what this might be. It was not long before he was standing by it, and found himself looking at a square block of white stone fashioned somewhat like the base of a pillar, with a square hole in the upper surface. Just such another you may see at this day on Thetford Heath. After taking stock of it he contemplated for a few minutes the view, which offered a church tower or two, some red roofs of cottages, and windows winking in the sun, and the expanse of sea—also with an occasional wink and gleam upon it—and so pursued his way.

In the desultory evening talk in the bar, he asked why the white stone was there on the common.

"A old-fashioned thing, that is," said the landlord (Mr. Betts), "we was none of us alive when that was put there." "That's right," said another. "It stands pretty high," said Mr. Thomson, "I dare say a seamark was on it some time back." "Ah! yes," Mr. Betts agreed, "I 'ave 'eard they could see it from the boats; but whatever there was, it's fell to bits this long time." "Good job, too," said a third, "'twarn't a lucky mark, by what the old men used to say; not lucky for the fishin', I mean to say." "Why ever not?" said Thomson. "Well, I never see it myself," was the answer, "but they 'ad some funny ideas, what I mean, peculiar, them old chaps, and I shouldn't wonder but what they made away with it theirselves."

It was impossible to get anything clearer than this: the company, never very voluble, fell silent, and when next some one spoke it was of village affairs and crops. Mr. Betts was the speaker.

Not every day did Thomson consult his health by taking a country walk. One very fine afternoon found him busily writing at three o'clock. Then he stretched himself and rose, and walked out of his room into the passage. Facing him was another room, then the stairhead, then two more rooms, one looking out to the back, the other to the south. At the south end of the passage was a window, to which he went, considering with himself that it was rather a shame to waste such a fine afternoon. However, work was paramount just at the moment; he thought he would just take five minutes off and go back to it, and those five minutes he would employ—the Bettses could not possibly object—to looking at the other rooms in the passage, which he had never seen. Nobody at all, it seemed, was indoors; probably, as it was market day, they were all gone to the town, except perhaps a maid in the bar. Very still the house was, and the sun shone really hot; early flies buzzed in the window-panes. So he explored. The room facing his

own was undistinguished except for an old print of Bury
St. Edmunds; the two next him on his side of the passage
were gay and clean, with one window apiece, whereas his
had two. Remained the southwest room, opposite to the
last which he had entered. This was locked; but Thomson
was in a mood of quite indefensible curiosity, and feeling
confident that there could be no damaging secrets in a
place so easily got at, he proceeded to fetch the key of his
own room, and when that did not answer, to collect the
keys of the other three. One of them fitted and he opened
the door. The room had two windows looking south and
west, so it was as bright and the sun as hot upon it as
could be. Here there was no carpet, but bare boards; no
pictures, no washing-stand, only a bed in the farther corner: an iron bed, with mattress and bolster, covered with
a bluish check counterpane. As featureless a room as you
can well imagine, and yet there was something that made
Thomson close the door very quickly and quietly behind
him and lean against the windowsill in the passage, actually quivering all over. It was this, that under the counterpane some one lay, and not only lay, but stirred. That
it was some *one* and not some *thing* was certain, because
the shape of a head was unmistakable on the bolster; and
yet it was all covered, and no one lies with covered head,
but a dead person; and this was not dead, not truly dead,
for it heaved and shivered. If he had seen these things in
dusk or by the light of a flickering candle, Thomson could
have comforted himself and talked of fancy. On this bright
day that was impossible. What was to be done? First, lock
the door at all costs. Very gingerly he approached it and
bending down listened, holding his breath; perhaps there
might be a sound of heavy breathing, and a prosaic explanation. There was absolute silence. But, as with a rather
tremulous hand, he put the key into its hole and turned
it, it rattled, and on the instant a stumbling padding tread

was heard coming toward the door. Thomson fled like a
rabbit to his room and locked himself in: futile enough,
he knew it was; would doors and locks be any obstacle to
what he suspected? But it was all he could think of at the
moment, and in fact nothing happened; only there was a
time of acute suspense—followed by a misery of doubt as
to what to do. The impulse, of course, was to slip away
as soon as possible from a house which contained such an
inmate. But only the day before he had said he should be
staying for at least a week more, and how, if he changed
plans, could he avoid the suspicion of having pried into
places where he certainly had no business? Moreover,
either the Bettses knew all about the inmate, and yet
did not leave the house, or knew nothing, which equally
meant that there was nothing to be afraid of, or knew just
enough to make them shut up the room, but not enough to
weigh on their spirits; in any of these cases it seemed that
not much was to be feared, and certainly so far he had had
no sort of ugly experience. On the whole the line of least
resistance was to stay.

Well, he stayed out his week. Nothing took him past
that door, and, often as he would pause in a quiet hour
of day or night in the passage and listen, and listen, no
sound whatever issued from that direction. You might
have thought that he would have made some attempt at
ferreting out stories connected with the inn—hardly perhaps from Betts, but from the parson of the parish, or old
people in the village, but no, the reticence which commonly falls on people who have had strange experiences,
and believe in them, was upon him. Nevertheless, as the
end of his stay drew near, his yearning after some kind of
explanation grew more and more acute. On his solitary
walks he persisted in planning out some way, the least
obtrusive, of getting another daylight glimpse into that
room, and eventually arrived at this scheme. He would

leave by an afternoon train—about four o'clock. When his
fly was waiting, and his luggage on it, he would make one
last expedition upstairs to look round his own room and
see if anything was left unpacked, and then, with that key,
which he had contrived to oil (as if that made any difference!) the door should once more be opened for a moment,
and shut.

So it worked out. The bill was paid, the consequent
small talk gone through while the fly was loaded: "pleasant part of the country—been very comfortable, thanks
to you and Mrs. Betts—hope to come back some time,"
on one side: on the other, "very glad you've found satisfaction, sir, done our best—always glad to 'ave your good
word—very much favored we've been with the weather, to
be sure." Then, "I'll just take a look upstairs in case I've
left a book or something out—no, don't trouble, I'll be
back in a minute." And as noiselessly as possible he stole
to the door and opened it. The shattering of the illusion!
He almost laughed aloud. Propped, or you might say sitting, on the edge of the bed was—nothing in the round
world but a scarecrow! A scarecrow out of the garden, of
course, dumped into the deserted room. . . . Yes; but here
amusement ceased. Have scarecrows bare bony feet? Do
their heads loll on to their shoulders? Have they iron col-
lars and links of chain about their necks? Can they get up
and move, if never so stiffly, across a floor with wagging
head and arms close at their sides? And shiver?

The slam of the door, the dash to the stair-head, the
leap downstairs, were followed by a faint. Awaking Thomson saw Betts standing over him with the brandy bottle
and a very reproachful face. "You shouldn't a' done so,
sir, really you shouldn't. It ain't a kind way to act by persons as done the best they could for you." Thomson heard
words of this kind, but what he said in reply he did not
know. Mr. Betts, and perhaps even more Mrs. Betts, found

it hard to accept his apologies and his assurances that he
would say no word that could damage the good name of
the house. However, they were accepted. Since the train
could not now be caught, it was arranged that Thomson
should be driven to the town to sleep there. Before he
went the Bettses told him what little they knew. "They
says he was landlord 'ere a long time back, and was in with
the 'ighwaymen that 'ad their beat about the 'eath. That's
how he come by his end: 'ung in chains, they say, up where
you see that stone what the gallus stood in. Yes, the fish-
ermen made away with that, I believe, because they see it
out at sea and it kep' the fish off, according to their idea.
Yes, we 'ad the account from the people that 'ad the 'ouse
before we come. 'You keep that room shut up,' they says,
'but don't move the bed out, and you'll find there won't
be no trouble.' And no more there 'as been; not once he
haven't come out into the ouse, though what he may do
now their ain't no sayin'. Anyway, you're the first I know
on that's seen him since we've been 'ere; I never set eyes on
him myself, nor don't want. And ever since we've made the
servants' rooms in the stablin', we ain't 'ad no difficulty
that way. Only I do 'ope, sir, as you'll keep a close tongue,
considerin' 'ow an 'ouse do get talked about": with more
to this effect.

The promise of silence was kept for many years. The
occasion of my hearing the story at last was this: that when
Mr. Thomson came to stay with my father it fell to me to
show him to his room, and instead of letting me open
the door for him, he stepped forward and threw it open
himself, and then for some moments stood in the doorway
holding up his candle and looking narrowly into the inte-
rior. Then he seemed to recollect himself and said: "I beg
your pardon. Very absurd, but I can't help doing that, for
a particular reason." What that reason was I heard some
few days afterward and you have heard now.

The Stranger
Algernon Blackwood

The flat lay deadly quiet, voices were hushed, and all moved to and fro on tiptoe. In the room where she lay—the woman who refused to die—this quiet was, of course, most marked, for there her breathing, so faint it was scarcely perceptible, alone broke the pall of silence. The last clearly audible sound had been the lowered voice of the family physician: "I won't wait now. There is little I can do. I will come back within an hour," and his heels tapping softly across the tiled floor of the narrow hall toward the lift.

Yes, she might last an hour or two, possibly even till to-morrow, this woman who so hated death that she always refused even to acknowledge it; but she would not wake from unconsciousness. She was sinking fast, the doctor said; the intense vitality at length was unavailing; there was nothing he could do.

And so now it was that the lowered voice, the tap of boots on the tiled floor of the landing, the rumble of the lift, still echoed on in the mind where all else lay muted and repressed.

Apart from two members of the family, and these but nominally, dutifully, affectionate, Colonel Moreland alone was present in that room of silence. Elderly, grizzled, with features set in bronze, he sat motionless beside the bed. Looking like a Roman sentinel, he watched the grim,

155

silent figure, whose arena was a few square feet of human frailty, and his was the mind in which the recent sounds seemed still to echo. The others, a step-brother and an uncle, stood with their backs to him by the window, watching the dusk fall slowly over the dismal London street, not otherwise moved, probably, than by those practical considerations the approaching death of a tolerated relative involved. Priority of place, at any rate, they gave readily to the stern man who sat thus motionless beside the bed, almost a stranger to them, yet whose right, it seemed they admitted gladly.

With the lessening traffic and the dropping of the winter's night, the silence deepened. A slow wind mourned about the building. The stillness grew. If the faithful serving-woman in the kitchen wept, she wept inaudibly. That she did weep, however, is certain, for some half an hour later, when the Colonel looked into her face, the tears lay still upon her ashen cheeks. . . .

To her, indeed, as to himself, this stealthy approach of death seemed an incredible occurrence, painfully dramatic for all its quiet method of arrival. To the old Scottish woman, a mere lassie from the Highlands when first she entered the family service years before, it seemed impossible that a mistress with such fierce love of living should ever cease to breathe. It was unnatural, almost wicked. A loathing of death, so intense that it amounted to a fixed refusal to die, must surely—somehow—keep her alive forever! Death, in her mistress's presence, no one ever dared to mention. Had she not proved it again and again: she—*would* not die!

To both soldier and servant, at any rate, death now seemed an outrage, something almost against the normal order. Yet to Colonel Moreland, though he shared with the humble serving-woman that rare worship of true love which had held faithful over a quarter of a century, the silent battle was painful and dramatic for other, and very different reasons. From time to time, as the minutes crawled, his eyes would open, gaze for a moment on the face he so passionately loved, then quickly close again, lest the intensity of his inner realization be even by so much dimmed. His thoughts—pictures, rather than actual thoughts—were of long ago, of more recent years, to be exact, of two weeks before, when news of the dangerous seizure had brought him instantly to her side. No trivial, foolish convention had prevented then, as it had prevented years ago. No trumpery considerations of social rank, of thine and mine, differences that in youth appear so great, in later years so petty, had interfered with the over-mastering power that impelled, even commanded, him to see her, before, in the final sense, it was too late, and—to make his long-concealed confession face to face. . . .

Twenty-five years ago, ignorance and timidity had sealed his lips. The V. C., gained on the Northwest frontier, proved a quality in him which yet had not availed a young man, finely self-forgetful, fighting for a loveliness that seemed wholly beyond his reach; she, all unknowing, had given herself to another—and he had seen her go. Now, on his return from long sojourn in the East, he had heard in one and the same day both of her illness and of her present liberty. He had not hesitated. The late confession had been made that ought to have been made so many years before. She told him her own long secret, too. And in that very breath, which the doctor whispered might be well-nigh her last, she told him likewise—her whole being defiant with aggressive will:

"I shall get well again. I shall live for you. It is never too late for that . . . I *will* get well . . . !"

The pathetic ignominy of it struck even the unimaginative soldier—the defiant little human will now helpless and inoperative as the last cold Shadow stole toward the bed. Death reckoned not of human desire and intention, however fierce, and the desolate battle, it seemed to him, was a foregone conclusion. Any moment now, the remorseless Figure must stand at the door, approach the bed, and steal her from his world. Colonel Moreland, overwrought perhaps a little, pictured in his mind a relentless and unbending Outline. . . .

The step-brother turned from the window, lighted a softly shaded lamp, then moved back without a sound to the post he held somewhat awkwardly with his companion. But the bronze outline beside the bed was too intent upon his poignant inner pictures to take much notice of what they did. Only the doctor's lowered voice, the tap of his boots upon the tiled floor outside, the rumble of the descending lift, still echoed on across the background of his mind. . . . These, indeed, and the frail outline beneath the sheets, seemed his sole relations with the outer world. When a step, therefore, became audible in the passage, it was natural he hardly stirred at first, and that the opening and closing of the front door, the murmur of confused voices, too, should have merged in that continuous memory of a mental sound.

There was a cold air that sent a faint shiver over him, but it was the whispering by the window that really disturbed his profound reverie:

"The doctor probably . . . sooner than he meant . . ." he heard one say, and so was on his feet, startled rather, and out in the passage before either of them. But the woman from the kitchen was in front of him. He ran into her in his eagerness, noticed the tears upon her ashen cheeks, and saw at the same time the tall, thin outline of the stranger, who most certainly was not the doctor.

A very upright and unbending Outline it was—the stiffness, no doubt, adding to the appearance of the stature, beside which the woman seemed diminutive, almost dwarflike. The dreadful whiteness of her face he found unwelcome—more, it troubled him profoundly, though he recalled this only later. There was talk, confused and hurried, yet the voice of the stranger, he believed, was not once actually audible at all. It was the woman's voice and words he caught so distinctly, words whose incongruity must, at any other time, have brought a smile to his stern lips. This appearance, however, of rapid exchange between two persons was as clear to him as the certainty that there was a mistake as well, a mistake that seemed grossly stupid at this moment: the wrong name, the wrong door, the wrong building, of course.

Sharply, then, out of this muttering, the woman's words emerged, both fear and courage in the tone, as she repeated with insistent emphasis that her mistress was not at home: "She's *not* at home . . . to anybody. She's *dying*. . . . !"

Colonel Moreland, as he heard, found himself abruptly stopped. He stood stock still, arrested in his tracks. The incongruity of the language gave him a sense of intolerant impatience, of anger, even. The stupid disturbance, at such a moment, was more than he could bear, while yet he took no immediate steps to relieve the fierce vexation that consumed him. His deep annoyance found no outlet. His mind, as well as his muscles, were arrested. There was about the tall, unbending outline of the stranger something indefinable that produced a sudden shock, paralyzing him unaccountably on the instant, and with it a flash that struck cold as winter's ice against his heart. The power of it caught him full: he remained motionless where he stood. . . . Thus, his first impulse to send the caller peremptorily about his business, to push him out of the still open door, was not obeyed; and on turning an instant to see whether the others followed from the bedroom, he was aware of the woman close against him as though for protection, tears upon a face blanched like linen, terror in the staring eyes, and her body shaking like a leaf.

"I couldna' stop him," came her thick whisper. "He said he would—come back."

It was while she spoke he realized for the first time that she was no longer accompanied. She stood now at his side—alone.

The soldier found his voice, though not yet his entire self-possession. "Come back!" he managed to ejaculate. "Come back!" he repeated. "At a time like this . . . !"

Words failed him then. He glared at the trembling woman, who now pointed, with helpless, unintelligent gesture, to the drawing-room door behind her. Her body, he noticed, was still quivering all over.

"In there," she muttered. "He went in there!"

Something turned over in the soldier's heart. He did not argue; he made at first no comment. The one weapon he really understood, a blow, was useless, for he knew not where to aim. His sense of outrage, his anger, moreover, were of a sudden curiously stilled. The ice pressed closer, but if the hair upon his scalp rose, he denied it violently.

"You are mistaken," he said presently, in his curtest tone. "You made a mistake," he repeated firmly, the anger now oddly gone from his voice as well. "He—he went out by the front door. He will not come back. It was all a mistake, I tell you."

The woman, beneath his compelling eyes, mumbled submissively, yet keeping close against him:

"If ye say so, sir," he heard her whisper. Flustered beyond belief she was, but she was unconvinced, her gaze still fixed in terror on the drawing-room door.

The other found his sternest voice, the one the Army knew, the voice of action.

"Get back to your kitchen," he commanded. "Kneel down! Kneel down, I say, and pray to your God at once!"

She crept away, shuffling, looking back over her shoulder before she disappeared. Her lips were moving, though no words came forth.

Colonel Moreland strode over and closed the front door, peering first along the bare stone floor, across the narrow landing where the gas jet flared, then down the darkened passage. There was no one visible. No sound broke the silence. He paused an instant, then abruptly did a curious thing. He said something without knowing why he said it:

"Your mistress," his sudden whisper followed the trembling woman, though probably inaudible to her, "will not die. She will recover."

As he spoke the words, wondering whence came his marvellously sure conviction, he pushed into the drawing-room. He felt his courage ebbing. A second's hesitation and it must have failed him. He went in boldly.

Again, if the hair upon his scalp rose up, he denied it violently; if that touch of ice pressed nearer on his heart, he faced it; his muscles, if they trembled, were in a grip of iron.

Inside the threshold he felt for the light and switched it on. One glance at the chintz-covered furniture sufficed. There was no figure, there was no living presence. The room was empty.

Their marriage, late in life, proved beyond words a happy one, for passion's turbulence left no dread of a reaction, and the deeper ties were free to utter their fine call unhampered. If regret for unrealized glories tinged its glamour, it held at least no sordid pity for a gross remorse. To them it seemed unclouded, the gardened house in Kent, surrounded by gracious friends, its perfect setting.

The faithful serving-woman had gone her way, her curious problem with her—so far, at least, as Colonel Moreland had ever questioned. The soldier, indeed, kept his own counsel about a matter he had not cared to probe by cross-examination; his wife, on this point, was never in his confidence. The puzzle remained, for him, unsolved. The woman had seen; he, too, had seen. Yet, since both observers were in a condition of high nervous tension at the time—overwrought, he termed it—neither possibly, for that matter, had seen anything at all. This was the explanation laborious self-deception used; temperament selected it, and stiff self-restraint maintained it, with an effort.

In his own inmost mind, none the less, there lurked a doubt no deliberate effort wholly could stifle. A note of interrogation, like a hidden flame, glowed and would not fade. As soldier, as Englishman, he had that abhorrence of the unordinary which was his due; "supernatural" was a word not found in his vocabulary; hostility, scepticism rose automatically when anything of the kind was mentioned. He had seen, more than most perhaps, what mysterious India had to show, and had enjoyed it; for trickery might baffle the mind pleasurably without stretching it into uncomfortable postures. Through thick and thin he had always maintained this comfortable attitude; he was not going to change it now for anybody in the world. The doubt, the note of interrogation, none the less, persisted; there was a question, though a question never asked.

He was glad the serving-woman had gone to a world where questions were impossible, for the fear had been in him that one day he must ask her, worse still—that she might speak to him. He was now relieved of that anxiety. Yet there was another question, independent of an answerer. This was a faint, disturbing memory, though a memory he could never feel quite sure about, since he himself, the only person who might explain it, found no positive answer in him. Had he, indeed, caught that other voice, or had he not?

A fitful wind, he remembered, moaned in gusts about the building at the time; up the shaft it sighed, and through the opened door as well. A moaning wind could be responsible for sounds a strained mind might well twist into syllables, into the semblance of a voice with words, even into a definite sentence. It had made strange, restless noises, that fitful wind. He was a careful man: he would never positively swear to it. Yet to this sentence had been due his amazing conviction that recovery suddenly was certain, though only afterward did he realize why he used the words he actually had used to the woman. . . .

There remained this disquieting, persistent memory of another voice, almost a whisper, little more, perhaps, than a breath of wind; *"I will come back . . ."* and so gently uttered it seemed to have been sighed into his understanding, rather than spoken audibly: *"I will come back."*

Yet the doctor, he remembered, had used a similar phrase when he left half an hour earlier. Was not this second voice, perhaps, its reproduction in a mind troubled and overwrought, a mind still echoing the footsteps on the tiled floor, the rumble of the lift? He would not positively swear; as already said, he was a careful man. He realized only his sudden, positive assurance that recovery from that moment, had become a definite certainty.

The note of interrogation thus remained. It haunted and troubled him for years, till with the passage of time it grew less present, less discomforting, at any rate. But it did not die. He could never entirely forget it.

Their happiness, meanwhile, if calm, was of the radiant kind that nothing, least of all differences of opinion, could disturb. Firmly based upon fundamentals, it was securely anchored in a deep need each had of the other. They supplied, indeed, respectively, one another's deficiencies, finding life's harvest rich and wonderful; and tolerance seemed their native gift. Yet a single dread they shared in common: lest one should be taken and the other left. That the final harvesting might come for both together was their intense desire.

The house, as a rule, had voices ringing through it, young voices, for they were the kind young people love. Friends of earlier years came with their children, a married niece, a holiday group, so that corridors and garden paths were alive with footsteps, calling, laughter; everywhere among the lawns and shrubberies moving figures darted, little people climbed the stairs, the children's quarters echoed, and young life had its happy way.

On this particular Sunday in late September, for the first time, indeed, during the entire summer, they found themselves alone. The Colonel's niece, with her brood of boys and girls, had left the day before, preparatory to Black Monday when schools reopen. It seemed as if a school treat, rather than four children with their mother, now left the house and grounds so still, so strangely quiet. The servants, as a reward for recent special services, had been given afternoon leave. . . . There was a touch of melancholy about both house and grounds, of emptiness, almost of desertion, and in their own hearts, too, there lay a certain emptiness, a silence that held half-ghostly whispers of unspoken questions. Though neither gave it utterance, the same thought echoed in that inner chamber, where, but for the trick the years had played them, might now have sounded the pattering of little feet, the cries and laughter, the presences, indeed, of children of their own.

To this thought, tinged with inevitable regret, neither ever permitted utterance; but now, as they sat after tea upon the lawn, each knew full well that the other's inmost chamber was thus tenanted. There was a happy telepathy between them they did not question. Inexplicable it might be, but frequent custom had established it beyond argument, so that even to Colonel Moreland's strict habit of mind it had become a commonplace. Some incalculable sympathy of love had taught them the code, the soldier himself acknowledging the results without demur. . . .

He made his suggestion quietly, glancing at her through the cigar smoke the air hardly stirred: "Aloud, dear—won't you?" Then, seeing that she hesitated, he added: "You say them so beautifully always."

He touched her hand, yet turned his head away to listen, for poetry made him shy. He closed his eyes, as she began, his face in mask-like repose. It was the voice, perhaps, as much as the exquisite words that he enjoyed, floating to him over the still lawn and flower beds, where the sunset lay in slanting gold. Its music called up pictures of so many years ago . . . of bright, wondrous hours . . . of "hours that might have been, yet had not been . . ." and yet, it seems, of one Hour in particular:

> "The hour which might have been yet might
>   not be,
>   Which man's and woman's heart conceived
>   and bore
>   Yet whereof life was barren—on what shore
>   Bides it the breaking of Time's weary sea?"

She paused a moment. He was aware of her eyes upon his own, a question in them, so that he shyly turned to meet her gaze. Thrilled to a deeper understanding than he had ever known before, he divined that question instantly; but he spoke no word, because no word came to him to speak . . . while the stillness deepened about them, and the shadows lengthened on the lawn. There was a new, sudden stirring in the depths within him. His whole being listened; it was almost as though he waited, expecting something; and the breeze that just moved the rose leaves behind her hair seemed to mingle with the voice, as she continued:

"Bondchild of all consummate joys set free,
   It somewhere sighs and serves, and mute
      before
   The House of Love, hears through the
      echoing door
   His hours elect in choral consonancy . . ."

Again she paused a moment; and again she raised her eyes to his; listening, as it were, to the Hours Elect that had known realization, yet for themselves had never struck. He, too, listened; and, as he listened, understanding in him marvellously and sharply opened, so that his whole life rushed suddenly past, presenting with that lightning meaning due, they say, to drowning men, each separate item of failure or success, yet emphasized with its ultimate truth as wisdom or defeat. This lightning experience was abruptly his, lasting at most a second. The flash seemed timeless. . . . It passed . . . and he sat listening for her voice, and waiting with a sigh.

He remembered the lines to follow. That "Little Outcast Hour" lay in his inmost thought, perhaps, as he felt sure it lay in hers. There was a look in her eyes, he noticed, that gave him happiness and terror suddenly, the terror of some mighty happiness hitherto unknown, a happiness, he felt, that must be more than he could bear, unless she shared it with him.

The world he realized at this moment was, in any case, an inner world. Of this he was vividly aware. It held no shyness. In it, for him, only the mightier movements passed. . . .

A flooding wave broke over him. He took her hand.

"Beautiful," he stammered, "beautiful and true. How—how could he know—?"

His words halted, as the wave momentarily withdrew. An inner breathlessness caught him, a groping almost physical, lest his feet be swept from under him, lest he be borne away from his known foundations. He held tightly to the fingers in his own.

"Your hand, dear," he heard himself saying. "It's cold."

He waited a moment. It seemed to him he had been speaking for a long, long time; for days; for years; for centuries.

A new coolness, he noticed, had stolen into the air. It had been coming closer, ever closer; it had now invaded both of them.

Something was happening to her as well as to himself. The happiness, the terror, the returning wave. . . . His feet lost touch, his mind went groping. . . .

He made a prodigious effort, and it caused him an agony never before experienced.

"Shall we go in now," he managed to say, his breath difficult to control. "The damp—is rising."

The familiar words, the commonplace effort, made him realize abruptly that a few seconds only—a scarcely perceptible interval—had passed since her voice ceased on the spoken lines and she had looked into his eyes. But she was still looking into his eyes. Her lips, he saw, were moving. . . . Only a second had passed, he struggled to remember; only a fleeting second, after all. . . .

It was, perhaps a revelation that came upon them across that quiet English lawn, stealing past the roses, using the last sunset light to clothe itself, and taking the notes of a thrush that now burst suddenly into rapturous song in the cedar by the house. The low human tones surely came floating down the evening air rather than from her own lips.

> "But, lo! what wedded souls now hand in hand
> Together tread at last the immortal strand,
> *With eyes where burning memory lights love*
> *home?"*

The voice, the singing of the bird, hushed simultaneously, as a tide of happiness too great for human consciousness burst flooding over him, drowning all utterance in its wave. He saw her eyes—the way they now shifted from his own, searching the space behind him. She had stopped dead. His blood ebbed, then flushed again.

"Look!" He caught her low voice. "What is it? So upright, so unbending; and—by the hand—a little child?"

"Dear," he faltered, following the direction of her gaze, "but—I see no one—no one."

The lawn was empty.

The next lines—did she say them, or did he hear them singing within him as his feet lost their final touch with earth?

> "Lo! how the little outcast hour has turned
>   And leaped to them and in their faces
>   yearned:"

He saw her try to rise. Her hands were stretched out beyond him. Her face was radiant with a burning glory. The last line yet hung upon her lips.

He made once again a prodigious effort. "No, no!" he wanted to cry aloud. "Don't say it, dear—don't say it—"

It was too late. He struggled to his feet in vain. No muscle, either of tongue or limb obeyed. A flood of light drove down the evening air, awful yet lovely, and from the heart of it a voice—

> "I am your child: O parents, ye have come!"

It was the servant, returning in the dusk, who found them, not sitting in their chairs, but side by side upon the lawn, fallen, her right hand holding his, her other stretched out toward the house, as though . . . "as though," the old butler put in, "they had gone to meet some one. That's how they looked to me . . . and the faces both young and smiling." Between the roses they lay thus, close together.

Dispossession

C. H. B. Kitchin

I

July. Two hours after midnight. The small windows of the first-floor room of 15, Cherry Lane, Chelsea, were wide open, but the blue curtains, closely drawn behind them, were shaken by no breeze. The night was hot in the street, and even hotter in the dark bedroom. Flat on its back, on the middle of an old four-poster bed, lay the body of Harry Duke, still as a corpse, and almost as cold.

Suddenly a muscle twitched beneath the sheets. The body grew warmer. A leg stirred, then a hand. The spine and loins shuddered. Drops of sweat crept through the skin. The mouth opened and gasped. An eyelid fluttered. Then the whole body heaved, while two brown hands jerked upward over the chest and with one strong movement flung the bedclothes aside. The head shot forward. The unseeing eyes opened widely. The breath came quickly and violently.

Meanwhile the buried mind had taken shape, and struggled painfully upward like a seed lying deep down in the earth and putting out a frail shoot past strata of peculiar perils. Each moment new visions pressed upon it, while old fears, writhing in sudden coils from a limbo of the brain, would have encircled it and dragged it down, had not the steady impulse of a growing will urged it onward.

Half an hour later, the man got out of bed and, tottering to the door, switched on the light. At the sight of himself in a long mirror he stood for some minutes in bewilderment, and then, stripping off the silk pyjamas still drenched in sweat, looked with hesitant pride at his naked body, felt one hand with another, caressed with a lovers' fingers his lips, moustache and eyes, and turning himself this way and that, as if the glass had never before reflected such an image, stroked trunk and arms and legs. Yet even while he surveyed himself and rejoiced so strangely in his strength, a dizziness came over him, and scarce had he staggered onto the bed, before the whole room swam round him and his eyes shut as if never to open. In vain he grappled with his wandering mind, summoning all his wits to consider where he was, and the plans which were still to be made. His senses ebbed away, and left the body as it had been before, quiet and untormented and almost dead.

II

Harry Duke woke at eleven. By five minutes past, he had realized that the electric light was burning, that his pyjamas were lying on the floor and that he was hungry and unaccountably tired. He wondered, also why the alarm clock had not roused him at eight. He had not expected to be called, as the couple who attended to him had gone for their holiday and he had counted on being well able to look after himself for one night. But it was irritating to have missed the boat train, even though there were other services which he could take, and the hour of his arrival at Wimereux was of no great importance.

He went to the bathroom and lit the geyser. While the water was being heated, he felt so ravenous that he went downstairs in search of food. There were some biscuits in a canister in the sitting-room, and he ate them greedily, deciding to have a proper meal in a restaurant as soon as he had dressed. On his way back through the hall, he noticed two newspapers in the letter-box. He expected one; but why two? He hoped the Dennisons had remembered to stop the papers while he was away. He couldn't bother to go himself to the newsagent that morning. After all, a penny a day for ten days is only tenpence. Still, tenpence wasted. . . . Whatever had possessed the boy to leave two papers? With a jerk he pulled them through the slit in the door, and looked at them on the way upstairs. A glance showed him that they were different issues of the same paper. The head-lines were not the same. July 25, and July 26. He'd had yesterday's paper—but July 26—what could it mean? There must be a mistake. July 26 was to-morrow—Friday, July 26. To-day was Thursday. On Wednesday, the night before, the Dennisons had left. This was Thursday, the day he was to go to Wimereux. On Friday he'd arranged to play golf with Grimwade's party.

After a little time, it dawned on him that he had overslept not by a few minutes, but by more than twenty-four hours.

He lay in the bath and groaned. This time there was no escaping it. He was not well. He was—a moment's horror seized him. What could he do? How could he go on hiding it? What would be the end? He was unused to mental suffering, and longed suddenly for some one to give him sympathy, for contact with another person, for an almost bodily comfort. Only one person had seemed able to understand his trouble, even guess that he had one—that spectacled girl, Joan Averil, a damned inquisitive little fool. So far, she had been the only one to take him at a disadvantage, to realize the crisis when it came. He used the word "crisis" to describe one of a series of events which lay outside the process of his normal life. It was only lately that he had classed them together as a series. Having no gift for introspection, he had been very slow to notice any progress or similarity in the accidents which for the past eight months had been pursuing him. But now he was forced to "look facts in the face," to try to understand himself, to learn what it was that had to be cured, if cure there was.

He dried himself and, as he dressed, looked at "tomorrow's" paper. "Still no sign," he read, "of missing architect. Thousand pounds reward offered by solicitors." In his bedroom, he unlocked a drawer and brought out a bundle of manuscript, the very writing of which seemed full of fear and shame. The composition dated from his most serious attempt to take stock of himself—after the last crisis. At best, writing did not come easily to him.

The first page was headed October 26th, and the record was as follows:

"Dined with Embley and his wife and Mrs. Pole. About 10.30 went to party given by man called Grover (?) in St. John's Wood. Dancing and charades. E. said it would show me what Bohemian society was, though I must be careful not to use the word. I soon got too drunk to be shocked—not that I should have been if I'd kept sober. At 1.30 a good many people left and a man and a woman, whose names I never caught, proposed we should go round to a party in the Adelphi. Got separated from the E's. and Mrs. P., and faintly remember driving in a taxi with three women and another man. My head was rather clearer on arriving and I jibbed at going in, but it seemed rude to back out of it. The people at the new place were a very odd crew. I didn't know any of them and shouldn't recognize them again. There was some gambling, in which I felt too drunk to join, and some of the people seemed to be dressing and undressing and acting charades on their own. More drink. I was completely knocked out, and the last thing I remember is falling flat on a kind of divan, and some one saying, 'Come on, old chap, I'll see you home.'

"I awoke in my own bed the next day—feeling like death. My latch-key was on the dressing-table. I was too ill to get up, and as I felt even worse at night, I told Dennison to fetch a doctor. God knows I'd been drunk often enough before, but never like this. I thought I must have been poisoned—or doped. The doctor—a breezy fool—said there was nothing the matter with me except the obvious, and gave me some medicine. That night I had awful nightmares, which I can't remember. The day afterward I felt better, and got up. For about a week I had appalling dreams every night, though there seemed nothing the matter with me by day. I called in the doctor again, and he still didn't take me seriously. 'Constitution of an ox,' he said, and then murmured something about burning the candle at both ends. I paid him off, and decided to get better by myself. For a time I did."

December 2nd.
"I'd been living very soberly—nothing in the nature of a binge for weeks, no worries to speak of. Physically quite fit. Dennison called me as usual, he said, and couldn't awaken me. I slept till three, and woke up in a sweat, feeling that something had happened. All the energy seemed to have been sucked out of me, and there was a kind of whirling at the back of my head, as if I was a corkscrew being drawn backward through putty. I didn't want to eat, or read, or see any one, and yet was terrified of going to sleep. When I did fall asleep, nothing happened. Awoke the next day feeling weak but better. Day after, quite well."

December 15th.
"Same as December 2nd, but worse. Went to specialist to be overhauled. Cheered up on hearing there was absolutely nothing wrong with me."

December 23rd.
"Went to the Partingtons for Christmas. The usual crowd, except for a Miss Averil whom I hadn't met before—somebody's odd relation. Spectacles, no S.A., and very intelligent. She seemed to find me interesting."

Christmas Eve.
"After dinner we had some bridge and then all sat round the fire talking and drinking punch. A cheery scene, holly and all that. Somebody told a ghost story or two, rather poor ones, and then it was suggested that we should take turns in telling what we thought was the most thrilling event in our lives. Edgar P. began with his old yarn about the bomb at the Gare du Nord. Phoebe produced an affair with a burglar, Jimmy Hale another ghost, and so on. Then it came to my turn, and was racking my brains to see if I couldn't improve on my story of the puff adder, when the room swam round in circles, and I had the corkscrew feeling again, but somehow reversed. I managed to get out a few words, and then everything became a blank.

"N.B. The punch was fairly strong, and the room pretty hot, but I'll guarantee I've as good a head as most people, and I've never before found myself sensitive to heat or cold.

"I was naturally rather upset next day, and apologized to P. after breakfast. He seemed surprised and said he hadn't noticed anything unusual. 'How did I get to bed, then?' I asked. 'Why, by walking upstairs, I suppose,' he said. I pressed him a little further, but he seemed so convinced, in his dull way, that I hadn't done anything out of the ordinary, that I let the matter rest. He suggested I'd been having a nightmare as a result of the punch, and I half agreed with him.

"On Christmas afternoon I found myself alone with Miss Averill in the library. She made me feel uncomfortable, and I tried to escape, but couldn't.

"'What regiment were you with during the war?' she asked me suddenly. I told her, and she went on to ask if

I'd ever been attached to the Third Middlesex Rangers. I said I hadn't, and more than that, that I'd never even come across any one who had. I was a little annoyed by her curiosity, and was afraid she was going to bring out some appallingly sentimental memory, or tell me that I was the image of her dead fiancé. But she hadn't finished yet, and asked me several other questions. Where was I during the war? Partly in England and partly in France. Whereabouts in France? All over the place: Loos, Vimy, Arras, Fauquissart, Ypres, Cambrai, etc. Was I ever in Miraumont? No, never. It was one of the few bits of the line I'd given a miss to. 'But in your story,' she said, 'on which I congratulate you, you specially mentioned a dug-out beyond the front line between Miraumont and Grandcourt.' 'I was never nearer either than Albert,' I said, and went on to ask her what kind of a story I'd told. 'D'you mean to say you don't remember?' 'I don't. I'm afraid the punch must have gone to my head. I suppose it was absolute rot.' 'Not at all,' she replied. 'Well, then, what was it?' She seemed unwilling to tell me just then, and before I had time to get it out of her we were interrupted. She had to go to London that night, and all she managed to say to me before she left the house was: 'Give me your address and I'll write to you.' I gave her my card, and said good-by, hoping that I should neither see her nor hear from her again.

"The rest of the visit was quite ordinary, and I tried to put the business of Christmas Eve out of my mind."

Next in the bundle of manuscript came some sheets of blue note-paper covered with a careful and feminine hand.

January 4th.

> *Dear Mr. Duke,*
> *In case you have really forgotten the amazing story you told us on Christmas Eve, I send it you now. I have a good memory, and have tried to*

use your own phrases. You told it well. Indeed—
forgive me—I think you will find the style hard
to recognize.

I feel I understand something about you that
you don't. If I can help you at any time, I shall
be very glad to do so. I live normally with my
parents in Flat 50, Clarence House, Park Lane.

Yours sincerely,
Joan Averil.

Mr. Duke's Story

"In January 1917, I was a junior subaltern with the 3rd Middlesex Rangers. The battalion had charge of a vast and vague area of mud in the Somme district. The whereabouts of the enemy's lines was hardly known. All landmarks had been destroyed, and what with the mist that overhung the desolate region and the absence of all tracks, means of communication were hazardous and primitive.

"With a few men, I was in charge of an outpost, the position of which was at the time recorded on none of our maps, somewhere between two ruinous areas which had once been the villages of Miraumont and Grandcourt. Apart from visits to my chilled and sodden sentries, I had little to do—or rather, I did little; for I dare say I could have found many duties had I sought them. The deep dug-out left to us by the retreating enemy, in which I spent my idle hours, was divided into two parts, separated by a hanging blanket. My men lived in the larger and I in the smaller, which was so small that, though they were eight or nine, and I was only one, I was almost as cramped for room as they.

"One morning, before daybreak, my sergeant was shot in a sudden burst of machine-gun fire while on patrol. The men with him brought the body to the dugout and I told them to let it rest in my cell till night; for it was impossible to carry it back to our headquarters during daylight.

"The body lay on the floor, covered by a waterproof sheet, and I on a wire trestle beside it. I had no horror of corpses that had met with a clean death. Indeed, it seemed companionable to have it there, and before long I lifted the waterproof sheet and looked at what lay beneath with sad curiosity. The only sign of the wound was a little stain on the tunic near the heart. Except for the absence of all breathing, you would have taken the body for that of a man who was asleep.

"It was a fine sergeant we had lost—a little stupid, but brave and magnificently strong. I remembered having seen him stripped at the baths, and noticing his healthy skin and well-built powerful limbs. And now, as I looked at his calm face, it was not without a sense of jealous inferiority that I thought of my own poor body, stunted and thin, never free from some ache or uneasiness. You laugh as I say this *but perhaps I am not the man I seem.* How wretchedly unjust, I thought, that I should go through life burdened with this corpse of mine, this miserable mass of nerves and skin perpetually hampering the exercise of my will and brain, and destined one day to harry me to death. Why could I not fall asleep and find myself rid of it, wake up as a new creature with a body equal in vigor to my mind? Must it be that these legs and arms beside me—and as the thought came to me, I stroked them gently—that firm flesh, those splendid muscles, still fully fit for living, even though dead, should moulder into decay and no use be found for them? So great was my disgust with Nature's law, so intense my despair at falling so far short of a perfection which, strangely enough, seemed almost attainable, that a mood of reckless agony came over me, and, hardly knowing what I did, I stretched myself out over the sergeant's body, my mouth on his mouth, my legs along his legs, as Elisha stretched himself upon the Shunammite's son whom he raised from the dead. . . .

"When I opened my eyes, it was my own face, pale and horrible, that I saw above me, my own body that lay on the top of me, but when I thrust it away, it was the sergeant's hand that moved. Triumphant in my new form, I stood up, and, gazing with hatred at the prostrate body that had been mine, I kicked it heavily in the ribs and covered it with the waterproof sheet that had covered the sergeant's body. Then, being still somewhat unsteady on my new-found legs, I sat down on the floor, lay back and laughed with joy.

"An hour later, my servant found me, bruised and numb, under the waterproof sheet."

III

At this point Duke pushed the bundle of papers aside, and lit a cigarette with nervous fingers. The story, not being written by himself, still moved him. When he had first received it, he had almost been amused. Later, when chastened by the next "crisis," he had written a short note to the sender, begging her not to bewilder him any more. Her reply, from the South of France, assured him that the story was substantially as he had told it. Then why, he had wondered, if by any strange chance this was the truth, had none of the others spoken to him about it? Of course, they were a dull and stupid crowd. Perhaps they had all, except for the one attentive listener, been half asleep, half drunk, and hadn't understood what he was saying—or if they had, disliked it and did not wish to mention it again.

One thing reassured him. The story was objectively untrue. Apart from regimental records, there were many living people who could vouch for his never having been near Miraumont and Grandcourt. At the beginning of

1917, he had been a company commander in a battalion stationed near Merville. This was a crumb of comfort, but his telling of the story, and its reference to himself, if any, was still mysterious. Was it a dream? Had he talked in his sleep? Perhaps. But he had had too many strange dreams to feel easy about even them.

Forgetting the need of breakfast, he walked round his bedroom in agitation. The newspaper—"to-morrow's" newspaper—was lying on a chair, and caught his eye. He picked it up and read it as he walked.

"Still no sign of missing architect. Thousand pounds offered by solicitors. . . .

"The whereabout of Mr. de Milas are still unknown. He was last seen at his residence, 22, Amboyne Road, Adelphi Terrace, by his housekeeper, Mrs. Garley, about half past two on Wednesday afternoon. He was then going upstairs to rest in his bedroom. Mrs. Garley first became uneasy at nine o'clock, when a manservant, sent to the bedroom, reported that it was empty.

"Mr. de Milas is a gentleman of considerable means and somewhat eccentric habits. He is described as an architect, but it is not known when or where he exercised that profession. He served with the infantry during the war, and his age is now about forty-five. For some time his health has given cause for anxiety."

Anxiety, anxiety, anxiety, thought Duke, throwing the paper down in disgust. Was there no escape from trouble, other people's and one's own? Was he never to get back to ordinary life, cheerful society, cards, games and horses? How had this blight come upon him, this train of odd symptoms that seemed to pursue him from within, drawing him inward, making him think too much about himself? Yet it had to be faced. He was worse, not better. With a sigh, he sat down and turned again to the manuscript:—

February 16th.

"I was to ride Lady Foyle's Halsettia in the Lauderbrake Steeplechase. A year ago I came in third on Diamond Claw, and this year hoped to win. The evening of the day before the race I had a feeling that something was wrong. A bad night, but no dream that I can remember. Felt very low at breakfast. Took my temperature. Normal. Very angry with myself. Wondered if it was simply funk, though I'd never been taken that way before. Decided to force myself to carry on, even if I broke my neck. Anything's better than being out of things. 11 a.m. violent headache. Had to go to bed, in great pain. Wired unwell. Headache easier by 4 p.m. Fit as a fiddle by 6. Johnson, who rode instead of me, was thrown and killed at the second jump. Outcry in papers about course being too dangerous."

March 25th.

"Awoke very late. Dazed. Felt like a sleep-walker. Early to bed."

March 26th.

"Too feeble to get up. Dozed most of the day. Refused to have doctor sent for."

March 27th.

"The same. At night an extraordinary dream. These are the only bits I can remember.

"I seemed to be in a kind of orderly-room—bare boards and tables, and army forms, etc. Through holes in the wall, I could see wild flowers bending in the wind. The sun was setting, and I got caught in a long red ray, which made me unable to turn round. Suddenly a voice—behind me or in the ceiling—said, 'Is it impossible for us to get on better?' 'Who are you?' I asked. 'Can't you see?' I made a great effort and turned round, but could see no one.

"I went out into the fields, and all at once the voice said again, 'You must take me for granted without seeing me, then. You laugh, *but I am not the man I seem*. After all, what have I done to you? I have caused you really so little pain. Of course, I apologize for the Christmas joke. But I saved your life, though you may not know it. Oh, don't think I'm a clairvoyant. You are a good rider and might perhaps not have been killed. But you were too valuable for me to take the risk.'

"The voice went on speaking for a long time, till I found myself alone with some one in the room in the Adelphi where the party of October 26th was given. 'If ever you want a refuge,' the voice said, 'you can have what I can provide. Even you might be ill, or in trouble. Look!' At this point I felt as if I was going to learn an amazing secret, but the room was suddenly draped in thick red curtains, which opened and closed, showing me little pieces of something and blotting it out again. I can't remember what it was that I was so eager to see, but each time I looked, I had the sensation that I was escaping from my body. Then the curtains swooped down on me and smothered me till I died. After my death, which wasn't painful, I looked into the orderly-room, and saw myself lying on the table. I longed terribly to be alive again, and took my body in my arms, intending to carry it home, but wherever I went, I found red curtains in the way. Then the voice spoke again, but I have forgotten what it said.

"Woke up very late the next day, weak, but better."

April 2nd.
"To Vinton, nerve-specialist. Talked a lot about dual personalities and psycho-analysis. Don't trust him."

April 6th.
"Hear that Phillips—poor chap—had been to Vinton for

two months before he committed suicide. Panicked, and decided not to go to V. again."

May 18th.
"No crisis, but since I've decided to keep notes on my 'case,' had better put this down. Met Miss Averil, at the Jordans' party—only for a few minutes. She asked me if I had been telling any more stories. I felt very awkward, and she saw it. Suddenly I blurted out, 'Do you think I have a double personality?' She said, 'No, not exactly, in the ordinary sense of the words. Won't you tell me more about your trouble?' Then we were interrupted, and feeling a fool, I managed to slip away."

June 4th and 5th.
"Very like March 4th, 5th and 6th, but no dream. Worried on 'recovering,' whether I'm becoming different from what I was. In my body, I feel as well as I ever did, but I can't be so certain of my mind. Remembered Jekyll and Hyde, which frightened me. If I have a 'double personality,' can anything be done about it? But Miss A. seemed to think it wasn't that. What does she know about these things?"

IV

For luncheon, he had gone to a quiet restaurant near his house. He had given up all intention of going to France, but had made no other plans. He could think of nothing but himself, his mind and his body, and something that seemed to be occurring in both of them. As he walked back home, he noticed the newspaper placards. "Missing architect still untraced."

When he reached his house, he had a strong impulse to go to bed, but was afraid to do so. He felt himself to be in a state receptive of extraordinary influences. There was a continual drag on his brain, paralyzing his capacity for action and urging him to look inward. More and more, he seemed to be dreaming, and wondered how it is that we ever know the difference between dreams and waking life. Some of his thoughts seemed to be his own, and others the product of an alien mind. These would come suddenly, in the midst of his own mental sentences, interrupting them as a heckler might interrupt an orator. *"Give in, give in. Cease to struggle,"* an inner voice kept saying, and again with an insidious sweetness, *"Come with me. Follow me. Find where I am."*

At four o'clock, when for a few moments the tension relaxed, he looked out Miss Averil's number in the telephone book.

"Miss Averil?"

"Yes."

"My name is Duke."

"I remember. What is it?"

"I'm in great trouble. I need some one to help me, badly. I'm slipping away—slipping out of myself. Can you help me?"

"I'm in bed, recovering from measles—not ill, but infectious. Tell me everything from the beginning."

"Wait a minute then. I've got some stuff written down, which I could read you."

He put down the receiver, and went upstairs.

"Come with me. Follow me. Find where I am."

He looked for his manuscript in the wrong drawer.

"Give in. Give in. Let yourself go. Sleep, while I wake."

At length he found the manuscript, and went downstairs: "Miss Averil?"

There was no answer. He looked hurriedly in the directory and rang up again.

"Can Mr. Duke speak to Miss Averil, please?"

"Speak to whom?" asked the voice of an old woman.

"Miss Averil."

"I'm afraid you've got the wrong number. This is Mr. de Milas's house."

"Is there any news of Mr. de Milas?"

"Who is that speaking, please?"

Horrified, he rang off.

A newspaper boy was shouting in the street. Duke went to the door, bought a paper, and took it with him to the telephone. "Three o'clock results." . . . *Follow me. Find me. . . .*" "Missing Architect. . . . Mrs. Garley admitted that she had been surprised by her master's absence from the house on one or two previous occasions, and on being pressed for the dates of these, identified one of them with February 16th, which she remembered because it was the day of the Lauderbrake Steeplechase. Her nephew had persuaded her to put five shillings on Halsettia, the ill-fated horse which was killed with its rider, Captain Johnson. But her master had walked into the dining-room at about nine o'clock that evening, and she had thought no more of the matter. . . ."

"Follow me. Follow me. Follow me home."

"Mr. de Milas also, it seems, disappeared toward the end of March. It is true he had told Mrs. Garley that he might find it necessary to be absent from the house for a time, but as he seemed far from well, and gave no instructions about his luggage, she was uneasy till she him sitting in the drawing-room at tea-time three days later. . . ."

"Sleep, while I wake."

"He was also away on the 4th and 5th of June, but as he had packed a small hand-bag, she felt no anxiety. The strangest part of the mystery is that on none of these occasions did Mrs. Garley see her master leave his house or return to it. . . ."

"You laugh, but you are not the man you seem."

Very quietly, Duke picked up the telephone receiver, and asked for a number.

"Can I speak to Miss Averil, please?"

"This is 22, Amboyne Road, Mr. de Milas's house. Who is that speaking please?"

"I am the missing architect, Mr. de Milas."

"Oh, sir, is that you? This is Mrs. Garley speaking, sir. Dr. Polder made me notify the police the day before yesterday, that you were missing from home. We've all been very anxious about you, sir."

"I shall soon be home."

"I'm sure I'm very glad to hear that, sir. We've—"

He put down the receiver, went up to his bedroom, and lay on the bed. A force seemed to be entering him, in spiral fashion like a corkscrew, while at the same time his normal will drained away, leaving the body without resistance. And yet at that very moment he had a sense, that he had never had before, of the preciousness of his body, its vigor and the perfection of all its organs. "This is your treasure," a voice seemed to murmur, "this is what you can give me. Forget your foolish little mind with its racing debts, its games of golf, its dances. Be generous to me, and give all you can freely. I have great need of you."

Then, after a period of silence during which Duke opened his eyes and saw the familiar things in the room shrinking and dwindling away, a rhythmical whisper seemed to flow gently along his spine. At first the words, if they were words, were too indistinct for him to catch, and sounded like a mere pulsation in common time. But soon the beat quickened, and became more staccato and articulate. "Go and find me. Go and find me. Leave this body. Go to mine. Go to mine. Leave this body free for me." The words were repeated monotonously, and at the same time Duke seemed to assent of his own volition and to be persuading himself to yield. "After all," he thought, "why shouldn't I do as he asks, poor devil? Why shouldn't I give him a chance? He may make better use of me than I can. Come! I'm ready."

But as if even this generous submission were not enough, the rhythm of the summons grew suddenly more imperious, irregular and desperate. "Let me in. The time is so short. Let me in. Your place is in the black box, in the cupboard. Go and hide there, in what I'm leaving you. Five minutes! Only five minutes! Give me yourself for five minutes! The black box in the little room. You've been there before. Go again now, just this once, and save me. Save me, and give me peace. Help! Help! I'm choking . . ."

The last word went through Duke's body as if a claw were tearing him apart. For an instant, he seemed poised on the edge of an unfathomable void, while the smell and touch of clammy flesh came over him and squeezed him together in a small and narrow space. "The grave," he thought, "the grave!" and with a convulsive movement, he threw out his arms and legs.

All at once the rhythm ceased, and he was filled with a sane and miraculous calm. A distant lorry rumbled toward the river. The clock on the mantelpiece ticked gently. Duke opened his eyes and looked at it. Five minutes past six. Then urgently the telephone bell rang downstairs.

"Hello. Is that you at last, Mr. Duke? Joan Averil speaking. I've tried eight times to get you."

They had a long conversation, in which, full of wisdom, she told him what to do.

V

"Missing Architect Found
"Mrs. Garley's Extraordinary Story

"The mystery of the disappearance of Mr. de Milas was solved yesterday evening in an amazing and tragic fashion. Mrs. Garley states that she was disturbed several times during the afternoon by telephone calls from persons who had, as they thought, recognized Mr. de Milas from his photograph in the press, and were eager to give information as to when and where they had seen him. In each case, Mrs. Garley requested the speaker to communicate at once with Mr. de Milas' solicitors or the police. Two of the calls, however, were of an unusual nature. On both occasions a man's voice began by asking to speak to a lady, whose name Mrs. Garley did not catch. On Mrs. Garley's suggestion of a wrong number, the speaker did not ring off at once, but, in his first call asked for news of Mr. de Milas, and in his second call announced that he was Mr. de Milas himself. It is now thought that the inquiry was a piece of facetiousness on the part of some irresponsible person who had accidentally been given Mr. de Milas number instead of the number he required, and that on a repetition of the same accident, the unknown was so far exasperated as to be guilty of a joke in exceedingly bad taste, pardonable only on the assumption that he was ignorant of the circumstances into which he was intruding.

"No further incident occurred till shortly after seven, when Dr. Polder, who had attended Mr. de Milas during his illness, called at the house and asked Mrs. Garley if she knew of a black box belonging to her master. It seems that the doctor had been rung up about a quarter to seven by a man who purported to be speaking for Mr. de Milas. The speaker had requested him with great urgency to visit Mr. de Milas' residence and search it for a black box, which he was to open immediately. He was assured that the opening of the box would throw a light on Mr. de Milas' disappearance, and that circumstances might arise in which medical skill would be essential. Mrs. Garley replied that there was such a box in a big cupboard opening out of Mr. de Milas' bedroom. To her knowledge the box—an old-fashioned leather trunk—had not been used or opened for some years. She accompanied Dr. Polder to the cupboard in question and saw the box in its usual position. The doctor attempted to lift it into the light, but

could not do so owing to its great weight. He then asked
Mrs. Garley to bring him a candle or lamp, and when she
had left the room, he raised the lid of the box, which was
unlocked. *Inside, huddled up on some blankets, was the dead
body of Mr. de Milas.* The body was fully clad, and covered
in part by a water-proof sheet such as was used exten-
sively by soldiers during the war. . . . It is the opinion of
Dr. Polder that death occurred about six o'clock the same
afternoon, though the body might have been in a trance or
state of catalepsy for several hours beforehand."

STOP PRESS
"Call to Dr. Polder traced to Piccadilly subway."

So ran the account of the finding of the missing architect as given to the public. Two people alone could have
added substantially to it—Harry Duke, who was playing
golf at Wimereux, and that devotee of psychical research,
Joan Averil, who was recovering from measles in Park Lane.
But neither of them cared to do so.

The Lord-in-Waiting

Shane Leslie

I spent my last and happiest fortnight as an undergraduate at Cambridge indulging myself in the leisure which rowing and reading had previously not permitted. A friend, whom I will call Peter Enright, was with me most of the time. We had both secured our release from final examinations and we spent day after day in voyages of discovery on the Cam. They began in a desire to find the native swallow-tailed butterfly. They ended in our paddling down as far as the sea. The more important result was that from henceforth we became very resolute friends. We decided to sign on for life-long friendship. Life was simple then, and the children of Victorians could not conceive any change affecting the structure of society. The Victorian age seemed bound to reproduce itself over and over again with variations. Oxford and Cambridge seemed to symbolize eternal truths. Germany appeared inefficient in professordom, futile in diplomacy and fantastic in armor. Definitely the German was unsporting, and the Great War, which swept Peter Enright out of past, present and future, was as incredible to the imagination as the story of the Deluge to the people of the Sahara.

Peter's life was destined to be remarkably short, had he known it. All his hardly earned knowledge of mathematics (for he was a seventeenth Wrangler) as well as his

fine physical development were destined to be quenched
in a moment of time. Fortunately of that moment he had
no prevision and his few years subsequent to Cambridge
were very cheerful. He was destined however to add more
than one singular experience to the normal collection of
reactions with which Cambridge had endowed him. Peter
told me, while we were paddling among the Fens, that
he had decided to take a Curacy in the country under
very old-fashioned conditions. That he was willing to take
Orders in the Church of England showed what a very normal and unmetaphysical person he was. He was no doubt
a muscular Christian, though not in any offensive sense.
We had both belonged to one of the minor and neglected
Colleges, which for that reason imposed a certain freema-
sonry among their Fellows and followers. We were sworn
to help each other in the after-passages of life, and though
I immediately rehearsed the names of people I knew in
possession of livings suitable to my friend's talents, I had
a feeling that it would be long before he needed my help
or influence. At the same time I always believed that Peter
was one of those protected beings who had unseen powers
working for them. At a lecture on Spiritualism given in the
College he had once been selected to his huge amusement
by the lecturer as possessing the makings of a first-class
medium. As he looked more like a medium-weight boxer
the amusement became general, and he was called "Mrs.
Piper" after a well-known sorceress for some time to come.

Though Peter never strayed into the paths of psychical
science so called, a singular thing had happened to him
in his first year, which caused him no little scruple conscience. He had entered for a minor prize or scholarship,
which he was anxious to obtain rather for the ready pock-
et-money than for its distinction. He had crammed himself
steadily for several weeks and worked abnormal hours at
night until his brain was no doubt in a worried condition,

but in those days there was no other acceptable manner of preparing for examinations, and Peter underwent the process with a wet towel round his head, stewing over gallons of hot tea. The night previous to the examination he fell asleep over his books and dreamed that he was already in the examination room. He found himself confronted there by a paper which he was unable to answer very well. When he woke in the early hours he carried it in his head, and referring to his books he learnt the answers by heart. In the morning he found himself a surprised but easy examinee sitting in front of the same identical questions. It was not the figures which surprised him so much as the color of the examination paper on which he was expected to write. In his dream during the night he remembered that the paper was tinted a greenish color. To his genuine amazement this was the case in daylight. The paper was tinted green. There was nothing for him to do but to write a very successful paper and inquire quietly afterward why the paper was of such unusual color. The explanation was simple. The examiner was suffering from a disease of the eyes which made it necessary for him to use tinted paper. Peter was awarded the prize and was filled with distress. Finally he explained to his tutor that he did not believe he had come by the reward fairly, that he must have wandered and found the paper somewhere in his sleep. How else could he have known beforehand that green was the color of the paper to be given him in the examination room? His tutor, having kept the papers locked in his drawer the night previous to the examination, dismissed the idea as the fancy of an overwrought brain, and insisted on giving Peter his *exeat* for a few days holiday. Any further discussion was thus pleasantly squashed and Peter was not allowed to dream of refusing the prize. As his tutor had expected, a few days holiday restored his normality and for two years he worked and rowed steadily until academical freedom and honor had been attained. Nothing of the kind ever remotely occurred to him again during his Cambridge time, and his desire to receive Orders from some ghostly Father and Lord of the Established Church seemed to arise from a healthy optimism in life rather than from any wish to wrestle with the terrors of the spiritual world.

To the outer world in those days we fancied ourselves impregnable. Why three years of unflagging rowing should have bred so hearty a contempt for the world, that doth not row nor give instruction in rowing, I could never guess. Even in a Cambridge degree each imagined he had secured a combined shield and spear to present to the outside hosts of folly, disorder and unsportingness. Incidentally we had each escaped damage to our hearts on the river or elsewhere. We felt so successful in advance that it seemed a little difficult to know what the world would do with us.

Before we left the college portals for good, Peter decided he must make some deal with the world, into which he was entering with less than the price of a clerical outfit, so he took a tutorship in the County of Huntingdon, hoping to clear a few pounds by the end of the Long Vacation. Let us say that he engaged himself to coach the son of Lord Mountstable at Mountstable Towers. It covers all identities. It was falsely called Towers, if Towers it was called, for it bore no resemblance to any castle. It was Georgian and highly modernized at the time when the Victorians were putting their houses in order for the Millennium so abundantly foreshown at the Great Exhibition of 1851.

We parted promising to meet regularly in life; at the Boat Race, at the annual tea-crawl given to the senile of the College on Founders' Day, at the Oxford and Cambridge cricket match at Lords, and to help and succor each other whenever overwhelmed by debts, taxes or Christmas collections. We went our ways and in a few hours our College life had passed out of the realm of working reality into the pleasant background of a dream. Our whole year scattered, never to meet again. Peter undertook his tutorship and I spent the Long in the Touraine, where the weeks of perfect health and weather passed by as quickly as the sunlit fields seen from a passing railway-carriage. Though Peter never left my general remembrance, it was a surprise to receive a telegram from him at the little French post-office a week before I intended to return. It was simple:

> *Remember old promises can you join me imme-diately wire Mountstable Rectory Mountstable.*
> *Peter.*

There was no refusing so direct a call, and that evening I was following my own reply as fast as the train could take me to Paris. The next day I was met by Peter at a Huntingdonshire station and driven in a horse-gig to Mountstable Towers. "I thought you had better have a preliminary look at it," he said, when we drew within sight of a singularly modern and ugly building. It seemed deprived of all romance or history, exhibiting only the squat and gilded squalor by which the Victorian middle-class announced their arrival among the County families. "It's not much to look at," added Peter. "It looks like the College kitchens worked up into a Ritz hotel. It's modern and new, and everything is as comfortable as you could wish, but I am not going to sleep there again till I have finished my tutorship. I'm staying in the Rectory over there and I hope you'll stay with me as my friend." Otherwise he had absolutely no communication to make. I was curious and acquiescent.

Beyond the elm avenue was a much more ancient structure, an old broken-down Rectory apparently only held together by festoons of wisteria and passionflowers. Behind the tithe barn in the background was a neat mediaeval

church. Peter introduced me to the Rector, who gave us
supper and left us to ourselves. The Rector nervous, tact-
ful, silent and an ardent Baconian as I quickly learnt,
was also the happy possessor of a cook who could make
good coffee. Peter and I sat up till midnight, our quickened wits wrestling with each other, for Peter would not
broach what had induced him to send me such a pressing
telegram. I learnt a good deal else of his circumstances.
It seemed a comfortable billet. The present Lord Mountstable was a recluse. He was delicate and almost deformed.
His poor twisted limbs had never allowed him to share the
life of public school or university. But he was anxious that
his son, who was a healthy youngster in his teens, should
enjoy those advantages to the full. He had made Peter
comfortable in every way. There was a squash tennis court
at his disposal. Every suggestion he made was met regard-
less of cost. The boy was intelligent and showed no particular contempt for the Binomial Theorem. As to his change
of quarters, Peter would only say that he preferred not to
sleep in the Towers. He had given his host and employer
no reason, but, as he was an admirable tutor, he had been
given rooms in the Rectory, whence he telegraphed to me
and whither I had come. Peter said that he liked his pupil immensely. He had found traces of real mathematical
power. "Such a curious brain. He has had no grounding,
but he often knows the answers of difficult problems before he understands the nature of the problems at all. He
is a really queer boy. I am told by the Rector that he takes
after his grandfather, the first in the present line. He was
an amazing man. Made his great fortune in business and
then educated himself into a very learned personage. His
hobby was science and he had a wonderful collection of
mediaeval scientific books. Instead of a racehorse stable
he used to keep a laboratory with trained assistants. There
was an awful explosion once or twice and the assistants

were killed. When the second happened, the Government gave him a hint to close his laboratory. He still carried on experiments in the house, but nobody saw him except his servants, and often days passed during which they prepared and left his food in a locked room without catching a glimpse of their employer. I learnt all this from the Rector." And, as it was midnight, Peter suggested we should go to bed.

Night in the quiet old house was peaceful, and the awakening was lovely and benign. In the morning the Rector took us round the Church. There was little of the picturesque to note as the result of three thorough restorations, but in the vestry there was a small chained library, of which he showed us the catalogue. Most of the books were still on their chains, but bibliophiles during the years had wrested a number away from their places. Some of the most tantalizing in the catalogue, especially as they were in manuscript, had disappeared. For instance I looked in vain for a tome that had been inscribed *De succubis et incubis animadversaria*. . . . The rest of the title had been erased. The Rector informed us that they had disappeared with some others in his predecessor's time, under the first Lord Mountstable. Until then they had been known to mediaeval scholars. Unfortunately they had never been printed, though the editing had often been mooted. Something had always happened to prevent it. One scholar had died while actually transcribing them. Another, in Germany curiously enough, had never brought out his edition although he lived past his century of years. Eventually the books had disappeared and no inquiries had ever replaced them. In that way a definite scrap of mediaeval superstition had perished forever.

Peter returned to his charge, and after the morning's work and lunch at the Towers returned to the Rectory. That afternoon we went a long walk together and he

began to expound. "I'm dreadfully ashamed to haul you
back from France and all because of a bad dream." I assured
him that I knew that he must have felt abundant reasons
or he would never have sent me the telegram. "Well, there
was a reason. It was more than a dream and I will show
you something that I didn't dream, for it remained over.
They gave me the room at the top of the house where the
old grandfather had lived the last years of his life. I can't
say it's haunted for I shouldn't mind that much. A ghost is
a ghost and nothing more. The room felt unpleasant and I
shouldn't have minded however much it continued to feel
unpleasant. I never heard a step or a sound. Nobody ever
has from those rooms, but then nobody ever slept in them
since the last man died. That's all I know about the place
and I slept five nights there and each was worse than the
other. I intend to sleep a sixth night when my tutorship
is over if you will stay in the room with me. That's why
I telegraphed to you. I wanted you here for a few days to
prepare you. I should feel a coward if I quitted that house
without going upstairs again."

I agreed to stand by him, but out of more than personal
curiosity I inquired what manner of visitation had befall-
en him. "It is difficult to say what it is, but I dreamed
horribly every night. The dream was the same with more
or less intensity each time. I could not remember what it
was except that it was terrible. The moment I awoke, it
seemed to go, only leaving me with a feeling that there
was something in the bed beside me, something not alive,
but cold and prickly. When I woke, it was to dead silence.
I could hear and see nothing nor could I feel anything in
the physical sense of feeling. It is more truthful to say that
I couldn't feel at all. At last there came the night when I
couldn't stand it any longer. I woke, but so quickly this
time, that I carried a clearer reminiscence of my dream
with me. In the anguish of a moment I found myself tied

by cords to some being, some person or some spirit who was wriggling and writhing in my embrace as though we were both drowning together at the bottom of a well. It was so appalling that I had to let my mind race through and through my state of awakenedness until I could assure myself that it was all a dream. Even so I found myself lying on the floor with the bedclothes twisted in knots, and round and round the clothes these old electric wires. I could not imagine where they came from, for all the wires lighting the room were intact. I must have walked in my sleep and dragged them out of some old corner. I still have them. Here they are."

Peter handed me a heavy entanglement of old wires wrapped on worn silk, rusty, bent and twisted. They were thicker than modern wires, they were knotted and held in a design, but Peter had not tried to unravel them. "Come, let us play cat's-cradle," I said, and gradually we pulled them into some shape. Five sets of wiring could be pulled away from the main body. It was not for an hour that we smoothed them out. There was then no need to remark that as a whole it made a cage for a human body. It struck us both rather horribly at the same time. Then I suggested that it was the sort of thing that might be used to hang criminals who had been condemned to be gibbetted. But that was not likely. What on earth would it be doing here? We preferred not to think and returned to spend a second night of peace and rest in the Rectory. It seemed decidedly cowardly to let that room keep its mystery to itself. That had been Peter's chief feeling in telegraphing to me, and the adventurous challenge of youth rose in our blood.

The next day was the last of the tutorship, and we both made up our minds to pass the last night in that room. We told the Rector of our purpose. He wished us well but he would not encourage or dissuade us. Toward evening he appeared a little nervous and asked us if we held to our determination. We replied that we did, as we felt there was something to be explained and that if we did not find an explanation, nobody ever would.

"There are many things which have never been explained in that house," said the Rector. But he remained uncommunicative until tea-time. . . . He talked to us a good deal before we set out for Mountstable Towers after dinner. His tale was more or less this—

"You must do what you feel best. I cannot advise you. Lord Mountstable may be grateful to you if you penetrate the mystery, if there is a mystery. He is certainly pleased with the progress which his boy has made and was very distressed that you could not remain under his roof at night. Unfortunately that was the only wing on which he could offer accommodation. It has never had the repute of being haunted. Frankly there is no ghost, but, if there is any trouble, it can only date from the first lord. All I know about him comes to me from my predecessor.

"Lord Mountstable was of ancient but poverty-stricken origin. He made money quickly and easily and retired from business. He rebuilt the old house that was standing here and he experimented in advance of his days. He certainly frightened the neighborhood thoroughly. When they saw his electric flashes at night they thought he was in league with the devil. It used to be said with some terror that oil and tallow were never needed for lighting at the Towers. Whence I presume he had hit upon incandescent light in a glass bulb before the great American discoveries. He was supposed to have raised fiends from below, when voices were heard resounding from hollow boards attached to wires at a distance from the house. I presume again that he had stumbled on the telephone before his time. He was never able to make any commercial use of his weird pre-knowledge, and after a few years he passed on to another series of experiments which may have been

premonitions of that future which still remains undis-
closed. They necessitated a laboratory and assistants.

"About this time he very unexpectedly inherited a peer-
age, which made him the first of a new line in his family. This, together with his self-made fortune and his very
Radical opinions, called attention to him for the first time
in his life and there was a proposal that the Liberal Government should make him a Lord-in-Waiting. But this he
declined very firmly and consequently was never heard of
again, except for some unfortunate accidents, which befell
his laboratory.

"He was looked upon as a remarkable amateur, and
from time to time he communicated theories to the University of Oxford, which brought him an honorary degree
though the scientists seldom carried his papers into the
experimental stage. They took him seriously enough to
supply him with laboratory assistants whom he paid well.
All would have proceeded well, had not one been found
dead for no assignable cause. Lord Mountstable alleged the
explosion of a new gas. There were no witnesses or traces
of chemical disaster and nobody had heard an explosion.
The young man was allowed by the Coroner to be buried
on Lord Mountstable's explanations and nothing could be
said. Four years later the same thing happened. Only the
second time there remained nothing of the assistant at all.
A coroner sat again and there was an inquiry, which was
regarded rather grimly in the neighborhood.

"It was then that counsel published the fact that Lord
Mountstable had once been offered a Lordship-in-Waiting
at Court. No particular conclusions could be reached. Lord
Mountstable evidenced a silent and internal explosion and
showed some molten glass and twisted wires, which ex-
perts agreed had been subjected at some time to tremen-
dous forces. There was a good deal of ill-natured comment,
for the total disappearance of the assistant could scarcely

be accounted for according to known rules of chemistry. An Oxford professor admitted that the papers, which his Lordship had been submitting of late, were considerably in advance of such laws as were accepted or dreamed of in the world of science, but he remained non-committal. The best evidence in Lord Mountstable's favor was the fact that he had been very seriously burnt himself and appeared in court with bandages over his shoulders. He could remember little except that he had left his assistant at one end of the laboratory while he was making tests at the other, when an unexpected accident wrenched the whole building. The electrical fire, which followed, had reduced glass and metal to a solvent condition. His assistant had been caught in the wires and had perished in the glow. He himself had only been saved by being precipitated from the window. He could not explain his own wounds, but it looked as though the wires had entered his own flesh. When he was asked questions on the nature of his experiments he distanced his questioners by a knowledge which the Professor of Chemistry in Oxford described as uncanny. In the end he was asked to close his laboratory and to pay a pension to the assistant's family, which he consented to do. He was asked whether he thought his experiments would lead to any result beneficial to the human race. He answered that he had already proposed means for the electrical transmission of the human voice. He also thought that electrical currents would be used to cure the most malignant diseases in time. Both these suggestions caused a great deal of amusement. Lord Mountstable was considered eccentric to the verge of insanity, but he was cloaked from general ridicule by the veneration which then happily hedged a peer."

The Rector had paused in his narrative and fumbled with the leaves of his Bacon. "There is a quotation from the 'Novum Organum,' which might well have been applied that the race of chemists out of a few experiments of the furnace have built up a fantastic philosophy." Peter asked whether it was not possible to regard Lord Mountstable as a pioneer. There had been Darwinians before Darwin. It was possible that there had been a prae-Edisonian in England. The Rector replied again from Bacon in the philosopher's words, that the subtlety of Nature is greater many times than the subtlety of the understanding. Undoubtedly the understanding of early Victorian times was not equal to the subtlety which Lord Mountstable suspected in Nature. As to initiating any celebration of his name the Rector spoke doubtfully: "I have every belief that his mind was as remarkable a mind for his own day as Bacon was for his. I would be the first to encourage national recognition and I am sure a very good case could be made from his papers. But I should feel uneasy of booming what appears to me now in the light of a sinister character.

"As I think I told you, there have been occurrences at the Towers which have never been properly explained. Some fame could be attached to his earlier speculations, but I think his latter series of experiments had better remain out of notice. The inquests held at the time left matters veiled, and veiled they will probably always remain. The public suspicion at the time that all was not well was based on a truer instinct than Juries or Coroners could follow. Even at this distant time I think it is best for the sake of the family and especially of the boy, on whom the good wishes of the neighborhood continue to rest, that mystery should be left even where it is most mysterious. For that reason I do not particularly encourage your expedition this evening. I can quite understand your wishing to settle the restlessness begotten of your unpleasant experiences, which we may call hallucinations until we know better. At the same time you may catch the clew to certain grave matters, of which I shall speak to you before you leave tomorrow. You would be only confused if I mentioned them to-night and your imagination might be set upon a wrong track. It is possible that you may find no cause for feeling that the place is in the least haunted. In this case it would be better to let sleeping dogs lie, or shall we say, to leave Lords-in-Waiting to continue waiting."

All this the old gentleman said in the wisest and kindest way. It was obvious that his long knowledge of the neighborhood had made him aware of things, of which he was unwilling to speak unless they proved to correspond with some new happening. Before we started for the Towers we could not help inviting him to divulge a little more. "I really cannot give you more facts," he answered. "I have only put together suspicions of what may have been the nature of those latter experiments of the first lord. The present lord has never spoken to me once on the subject of his father, whom he holds in incredible hatred. So much so that it is dangerous to allude to him, for the son appears to foam at the mouth at such mention. Although he was brought up entirely outside any religious belief, he has not been unfriendly to me, and it was on my advice that you were selected as the tutor of his son, who I regret to say has been brought up in the same negative opinions. When he goes to Cambridge I hope he will meet redeeming influences. Meantime, I can only assume a position of watchful benevolence."

We still begged him to advise what we might understand by the influences which had troubled Peter during the nights he had spent at the Towers. He hesitated and answered us rather nervously. "You must not regard me as either superstitious or professional in what I say. The present Lord Mountstable was never baptized. It was given out at the time that he was too delicate, but this my predecessor never admitted. His old nurse, who lived for years, almost half a century, at the Towers, passed through

my hands at the end. Hers was a very troubled deathbed.
I could not take all she told me seriously, but certainly
she took blame upon herself that she had never brought
the child to be baptized in spite of his father's positive
orders. One thing she insisted upon was that when under
her charge he had been a strong well-built boy. Whatever
happened to him after he passed out of her care, she
attributed to the vengeance of God. Of course I could not
encourage such a detestable view of the Divinity. Lord
Mountstable's deformity could only have been caused by a
natural accident or by some condition dating from birth.
He has always given me the appearance of a shrunken man
and one who has suffered from a sense of inferiority. The
old nurse used to speak of him as though he were not the
same being as the bonny bairn she had tended, and as
though some changeling had taken his place. I felt that
there was always something which she dared not tell me.
But she was a pensionary of the family and perhaps it was
not until the close of her life that a desire to cleanse her
soul of horrible memories affected her. Certainly I shall
always remember her agony and terror at the approach of
death. It was only with the greatest will-power that I composed her and caused her to die in comparative peace."

   As we all walked together on our way, we passed the
churchyard and he pointed out her grave. "Yes, there have
been inexplicable things over a considerable time and they
do not necessarily dovetail. I shall give you my general
deduction to-morrow, but of facts I have no more. There
is one thing I shall show you to-morrow and that is one
of the chained books which was a long time missing from
the vestry library. It was returned after many years anony-
mously from Oxford, but I understand it had remained
in the possession of the family of one of the assistants,
who must have abstracted it before he met with the fatal
explosion. I have never restored it to the library. I keep it

in the parish Safe but you may examine it before you leave to-morrow."

That night, with Lord Mountstable's permission, we both took up quarters in the unoccupied wing of the Towers. We did not undress as we had already packed our suitcases nor did we occupy beds. We each took blankets and prepared opposite corners. To begin with, we made a thorough search through the whole wing, rooms and corridors. It was all strictly Victorian and in order. There was not a worm-bite nor a crack in the heavy carved panelling surmounted with crockets made of deal. It was a solid example of carpenter's Gothic. The furniture and fittings were added in similar taste. Curtains, staircase rods and brass bedsteads all signified an era of materialism tinged by Pharisaism. On the stairs was a cupboard which showed signs of recent opening. The lock had been forced at some time. It was a housekeeper's receptacle, the height of a man, and it was crammed with dusty old apparatus, apparently all the relics of the destroyed laboratory. There were large copper batteries greened by the breath of time, and coils of heavy silk-coated wires. "This is the most prehistoric thing here," I observed. "This is where I must have picked up my little sample in my sleep," laughed Peter. "Now we know where it came from."

We pulled the cupboard inside out. It was a melancholy collection, as grim as a dead man's suit of clothes when it has been given over to the moth. This was the mechanical outfit occupied once by a strenuous and possibly sinister mind, now gone utterly from amongst mankind. It is always difficult to place such minds as Lord Mountstable's in the hereafter. They seem equally unfitted for Heaven or Hell. We replaced the stuff and returned to our room. It might have been pictured as the model of a comfortable and unhaunted room. We lay down in our respective corners and became somnolent.

But we were not heavily sunk in sleep. If a board cracked for dryness or a breath of air rustled the blinds, we both found ourselves awake and staring at each other across the room. Sometimes we dozed and sometimes we dreamed. And all the while the night hours were creeping along. If our bodies slept, our minds were subconsciously awake. Certainly they were not resting themselves, for our vigil charged them with that mental heaviness which comes from a strain. And as the hours passed, the autumn dawn floated into the atmosphere. The window sashes became clearly discernible against the light like great squares of arid phosphoresence. Still there was no stir within or without. Not a moth moved out of a curtain and for all the herbal treasures surrounding us in the park no bird sang. The sunrise itself, as though it were intimidated by the general lack of welcome, seemed to hang and hesitate. It was only a dull ray which filtered finally through the panes, and we had both fallen into the last lap of the night's slumber, when a distinct cry woke us from the corridor.

We both sat up instantly and Peter rushed to open the door. The cry came to us again. We could only see the gray clamminess streak down the empty passage. We moved toward the other wing when we heard a voice. "Good God, it is the boy!" shouted Peter and we ran into the next wing where we found his door was ajar. We entered, but the bed was empty and the linen lay in a heap. I felt it. It was warm and wet, as though the last drop of his sweat had been wrung out of him. We returned down the corridor in time to catch a groan from the direction of the cupboard we had fingered that evening. I thrust it open and Peter caught the boy as he fell out in a swoon. "Hold him!" called Peter and we both closed our arms round him. He was swaying to and fro as though in the clutch of another. His face was pallid, his eyes were tightly closed and his tongue was hanging. We could feel and hold him, but our combined strength was insufficient to keep him still. He eluded our strength like one of the demoniacs of the Bible.

As he swayed in our arms without exerting any muscular effort on us, I became subject to a growing sensation of horror. There was nothing between my elbows except this bundled youth, but my limbs seemed to be tied to his. I felt as a very sensitive fly might feel when engaged in its first struggle against the flypaper before losing all hope. I could feel nothing external, but in my own skin I felt cold and prickly, but colder than I had ever felt before, and more prickly than any attack of pins and needles in bed had ever left me. Something that I could not define or disengage from was drawing the very marrow out of my bones. A faintness overcame me, which was not that which arises from physical pain, but rather from the senses when they are sinking under a subtle narcotic. One latent sense remained only too vividly awake, that sense which human beings possess between dormant superstition and the stupor of the reason. I felt that I was giving up the ghost and began to sway limply with the unfortunate boy whom we held like a corpse between us . . . but a galvanized corpse. . . . Seconds seemed swollen into hours. A minute would have been as long as a day. . . . I felt my head becoming larger and larger until it seemed on the point of dissolving itself into a cloud of chill mist . . . Peter, gradually exerting all his sturdiness of body and mind, was able to soothe the unconscious boy in his arms. He seemed to be passing from rigidity into languor. Peter picked him up and replaced him in his bed. I followed and we spent some time rearranging the blankets around him. He was profoundly asleep but his heart beat normally and we thought it safer to leave him where he lay. The atmosphere cleared rapidly. The sun had extracted itself out of the cloud and a warmer light was penetrating the corridors. We fell into two or three hours of ordinary sleep. When we awoke, it was past breakfast-time and all seemed very like a dream.

We tidied ourselves and made our way down for breakfast, where Peter's pupil greeted us as though nothing had happened. He appeared paler than usual but showed no hectic sign. Apparently he had slept directly through his experiences and, whatever they had been to him, they had flown forgotten as a dream. We, remembering more of the night, were far more upset and found it difficult to eat more than one of the many courses which make the rural British breakfast. Peter went along afterward to say good-by to his host, who hoped he had had one good night at least under his roof. Peter felt bound to say that he had not been personally disturbed. He would not promise to return the next Vacation, as he expected to secure his Curacy by then. He thought the boy would do very well under a regular coach and eventually be able to face the Mathematical Tripos.

We strolled back to the Rectory where our venerable friend awaited us, and behind closed doors we repeated our experiences of the night. He listened with fascinated attention. "I am not surprised," he remarked. "It does not explain everything but it shows in what direction explanation may lie."

We begged him to suggest his ideas. "I think," he resumed, "the late Lord Mountstable carried out some very advanced experiments. I think that late in life he read some mediaeval ideas of the kind which used to appeal to the alchemists and which he endeavored to subject to modern appliances. I think his assistants formed part of the experiment and that they perished under his wires. The body of the first assistant was reported to have been marked as though strangled with red-hot wire. The body of the second was probably disposed of for reasons best known to the experimenter. I imagine that last experiment was a failure. He never tried it again, at least during his own life-time. The nickname of Lord-in-Waiting seemed to suit him thereafter rather grimly, for I feel he was always waiting to complete his experiment as far as a disembodied spirit is able to frequent the plane which he has left."

He then opened a drawer and showed us the missing chained book which had been returned by the assistant's family. "They were of course unable to read the characters and always mistook it for a chemical note-book. In time they heard of the collection here and made a gift." He pulled out the heavy vellum MSS. It was written in black letters with cabalistic designs. It had been scored by modern pencil marks.

"I have read it," said the Rector, "and it makes ill-reading for Christian folks. It is in cipher at times, but I think I can read through the lines. Discoveries were always handed down in the form of secret anagram during the Middle Ages. This book describes demoniacal possession and the transference of personality, and includes speculations on the possibility of transference of natural forces from a young body into an older one. The requisite of the mediaeval sorcerer was always some magical medium. It was that which failed him all the centuries he spent questing for the Philosopher's Stone. Nor did he succeed in attaining the conservation of youthful energy by foul means or fair. This book must have come under the notice of Lord Mountstable soon after two attempts had been made to edit and translate it. Both editors died before they made any publication from the volume, unless you care to imagine that the one, who became a centenarian, had profited by his secret reading. Lord Mountstable had completed his magnetic discoveries without any idea how richly they would affect modern life. Then he took a wrong turning. To apply electricity while still an unknown force to a mediaeval theory appealed to him disastrously. Personally I have no doubt of the use of his assistants and I only pray that their ends were not prolonged. . . .

"The experimenter's survival in time and space after death may be attributed to laws which even the Society for Psychical Research has not yet penetrated. The force of his mind has remained in solution in the atmosphere, which it would not be untrue to describe at times as electrical, and it has been posthumously turned against his own kin. The present Lord no doubt received his disfigurement while that force was still virulent. Its recent manifestations seem to have shown a decreasing potency. I trust sincerely that it has exhausted itself in this final attempt at obsession. Bacon wrote that the study of Nature is engaged in by the mechanic, the mathematician, the physician, the alchemist and the magician. But the latter two are only the illegitimate fore-runners of the others. In the fresh-eyed beginning of religious and scientific movements the pioneers sometimes received glimpses that were concealed from their successors. When the laws of Nature have been discovered in their entirety, it will be found that though all things are not permitted, all things are possible. . . ."

The Last Man In
W. B. Maxwell

The usual evening visitors were assembled in the taproom of the Stag Inn, and Mr. Judd the landlord, serving unassisted, had full employment. The "Stag" was a humble tavern in a poor street of a country town, but no doubt it seemed to its frequenters on this cold winter's night a snug and agreeable little club—a place of brightness and ease after the long day's toil.

Behind the tap-room was the commonly furnished and rather bare living-room, and here Mrs. Judd, the landlady, sat with a certain air of state. For her too, the day's work was done. She amused herself, but did not labor, with some repairs to a large pile of Mr. Judd's socks and undergarments; and, as she stitched and darned, she paused often to glance reflectively at the coal fire, the shabby armchair by the hearth, the brass clock, and the oleograph pictures, or to listen to the voices in the other room. The small-paned window between the two rooms had a red curtain drawn across it, so that one could not see the company; but the open door permitted one to enjoy much of their jovial chaff, laughter, and argument.

"Good evenin', Mrs. Judd."

Mr. Billett, an old customer, had appeared in the doorway, smoking his pipe and carrying his pot of beer.

"Good evenin', Mr. Billett. You're very noisy in there to-night. What's all the fun about?"

"It isn't exactly fun," said Mr. Billett pompously. "We've been arguing out this London murder."

"Oh, Lor'."

"'Orrible business, ain't it? But there's something very fascinating to me in a murder"; and Mr. Billett put his pot of beer on the ledge just inside the door, and came forward into the room.

"Yes," said Mrs. Judd. "I like a good secret murder as much as anything in the paper. But not this sort—to be butchered in the open street. It makes my flesh creep to think of." She folded a garment with a decisive manner, and laid it in her work-basket "If that's London ways, I say you can 'ave London. Give me Bratford."

"Oh, don't be down on London. I lived there once. There's life in London."

"Yes, and death too—seemingly."

"The attraction to me of a murder," said Mr. Billett sententiously, "is the problem it offers the int'lect. To pierce the mystery, and put your 'and on the culprit. I argue in this case they'll catch him—the one as done it—the London P'lice will. The detection of crim'nals has been brought to a fine art in London."

While he spoke, a hand and arm appeared round the door jamb, and Mr. Billett's pot of beer was cautiously and stealthily withdrawn into the tap-room. Mr. Billett did not observe this action, and he smiled superciliously when the loud and jovial voice of an unseen friend addressed him.

"You talk too much, old boy," said the voice, and there were sounds of general merriment in the taproom.

"I don't mind them," said Mr. Billett. "I won the argument in there. I was about to tell you, ma'am, that a cousin of mine belonged to the London P'lice Force once—but he dropped out of it. In many respects my cousin resembled me, for he—"

The appearance of the landlord interrupted Mr. Billett's stream of reminiscences. Mr. Judd, a red-haired, dry old fellow, had a short clay pipe in his mouth, and he carried a tray with a whisky bottle, glass, and water jug. On his way to his wife's table, he stopped and asked Mr. Billett a question in a confidential whisper.

"Who's that man in the corner—him that came in last?"

"I dunno 'im. A new customer."

"None of the chaps seems to know him. And I don't care for the look of him. . . . Here y'are, Missus," and Mr. Judd placed the tray beside the workbasket, and mixed a glass of whisky and water for his wife.

"Doctor's orders," said Mrs. Judd, with an explanatory wave of her needle toward Mr. Billett. "Doctor Page tells me I want it."

"I don't require a doctor to tell me that," said Mr. Billett facetiously. "I *know* I want it."

Mrs. Judd assumed considerable dignity.

"I'm not as young as I was—I'm over sixty-two years of age—and I do all my own housework still."

"That's a fact, Mr. Billett."

"We don't keep no servant," continued Mrs. Judd, "and I'm tired by the end of the day."

Mr. Judd handed her the glass. "There's your nightcap."

"Nightcap!" cried Mr. Billett. "He hasn't *laced* it like a nightcap should be. *That* ain't my style."

Mrs. Judd took the glass with the utmost dignity; but as she raised it, her manner relaxed. The wrinkles about her eyes deepened, and her lips twitched under the stress of a humorous idea. "The King: God bless 'im," and she took a sip. "Gentlemen, you may smoke." She looked round, and pretended to be greatly surprised. "But you *are* smoking. Without permission—in a lady's drawn'n room? Oh, what manners!" And she laughed merrily.

"Mother," said Mr. Judd, grinning at her. "Your good news has gone to yer 'ead," and he hurried back to his noisy guests.

"Ah, yes," said Mr. Billett, coming to the table. "My congratulations, ma'am—and fully sincere. And may all the tale be true."

"What's the tale indeed?"

"Why, your son coming home."

"That's true—so far."

"And you to buy this place for your own—yes, and keep what servants you please."

"Oh, that's all neighbors' gossip." Mrs. Judd picked up a tattered sock briskly and cheerfully. "They know we expect our son, so they make him out to come home with a fortune."

"Ah, but there's more at the back of it than mere chatter-boxing," and Mr. Billett's tone had a friendly knowingness in it. "He said himself he was returning with money in his pockets."

"Yes."

"That was the expression in his letter, wasn't it? Well, such words may mean a lot. It's how a rich man might put it—modest. A rich man don't want to boast—least of all to his own parents."

"We'll know what he meant in another month." Mrs. Judd was threading her needle with slightly tremulous fingers. "Sober and kind, Mr. Billett, is as good to a mother's heart as rich and free."

"You'll get both. Mark my words. It's the wild 'uns that turn out best in the end."

"I 'ope so," said Mrs. Judd, rather sadly.

"From what Mr. Judd has let fall now and again, I take it he *was* a wild 'un, but never a *wrong* 'un."

Mrs. Judd ignored the implied question.

"Eleven years, Mr. Billett! That's what he's been away from us. It's a long time—a long time."

"I'll drink you luck—and don't forget sincere old friends when the luck comes."

Then Mr. Billett, going back to the ledge by the doorway, discovered that his pot of beer had been removed.

"Who's taken my beer?" he asked excitedly and angrily, as he plunged into the tap-room. "Which of you done this?"

"You talk too long-winded," said a voice. "Makes us dry to listen to you."

"I ask, who done it?"

"You know so much," said another voice, "about the detection of criminals, you can find it for yourself."

A chorus of laughter greeted this sally; one heard many voices mingling, and in the midst of the noise Mr. Billett still angrily protesting. Presently, during a lull of the animated chatter, Mrs. Judd looked up from her work and poised the darning needle in a listening attitude.

"'Ark! That's the paper boy. He's behind his time," and she glanced at the clock. "More'n 'arf an 'our."

The shrill voice of the newspaper boy could be heard approaching in the narrow street.

"Horrible murder. . . . Latest particulars. . . . The London mur-der. . . ."

Mrs. Judd called to the opened doorway.

"One of you gentlemen be so kind as get my paper for me—will you kindly? Don't let the boy pass the house. Young imp'll do that if there's—"

"Here he is."

The boy's shrill voice sounded at the outer door.

"Mrs. Judd's paper."

"That's right, sonnie."

Mr. Billett brought the newspaper to the doorway, and stood there unfolding the double sheet.

"Would you, ma'am, grant me a glance at it? . . . Yes—here we are. 'London's atroshus murder,'" and he began to read.

"Well," said a voice, "have they caught him?"

"Not yet. . . . Would you, ma'am, allow me to read it out, for the benefit of all parties?"

"Certainly."

"'It seems,' read Mr. Billett, with careful elocution, "'that while Scotland Yard has been completely baffled—'"

"What price the P'lice now?" asked a derisive voice.

"Don't be in an 'urry," said Mr. Billett. "Give 'em time. They're watching and waitin'. It's like a mouse in a hole, and a cat watchin'. She doesn't make any mewing. But when he shows himself, then *pounce!*"

"Go on with the print," said one of the voices.

"'An important clew has been provided by a private individual—'"

"Brayvo, puss," and a mocking voice attempted to imitate a cat. "Meeaw. Meeaw."

"'The victim'—Mr. Billett read on, loudly and pompously—"'is now practically identified as a sailor from a Montevideo cargo ship which has just left for the port of Hamburg. The evidence at the adjourned inquest to-day was of a shockin' description,'"—Mr. Billett paused, looked round, and repeated with evident relish—"'shockin' description. . . . It would seem that the face was totally unrecognizable as a human visage—'"

"O Lor'," said Mrs. Judd shudderingly.

"'So that the whole ship's company, were they here, might be unable to swear to a late comrade. The unhappy creature was prob'ly struck down from the back and then with unparalleled ferocity the head was lit'rally beaten to a pulp.'"

"Oh!" said Mrs. Judd, "it's too dreadful," and she hid her face in her hands, as if to shut out the ugly vision that had been created by the newspaper report.

"'But the problem becomes the more difficult of solution'"—Mr. Billett looked round with an air of proud satisfaction. "That's what I said. It's the problem—very word I used."

"Go on with the print," said a voice, in subdued tones.

"'The myst'ry deepens. Here is a person of almost colossal statue and presoom—presoom'ble stren'th, done to death in a public, and by no mean unfrequented street, within fifty yards of a main art'ry of traffic, i, and e, the Commercial Road.'—(Bin there meself a score o' times.)

"'Was the deed perpetrated by one man or by a gang? Was the motive plunder or revenge? It is like a crime woven by the morbid fancy of a sensashnal nov'list. One would say a horde o' madmen had broke loose, or demons possessed of power to render themselves invisible, or—'"

"Is that the print?" asked a voice, subdued now to a whisper.

"Yes," said Mr. Billett. "But he ain't got no more news. He runs on—embroidering like."

"Then that's enough of it."

"Yes," echoed Mrs. Judd with conviction, "that's more'n enough. It's too horrible."

Mr. Billett refolded the paper, laid it on the table, and returned to the convivial company of the front room.

Somehow or other the gaiety and light-heartedness of the assembled drinkers were evaporating. Mrs. Judd, stitching and listening musingly, heard no more laughter; the conversation had taken a serious turn; the voices, as they mingled, seemed to be sinking lower and lower toward a hushed solemnity of tone.

"Did you ever see the Tower Bridge from underneath?"

"No, I seen it from the train."

"There was a woman fell off it without hurting herself."

"Oh, that's a good 'un."

"What took you there? The football match?"

"No, the Guv'nor sent me to the warehouses."

Thus the talk proceeded but it was no longer spontaneous and easy. A silence fell once or twice, and there was a perceptible effort in the voice of the speaker who started a fresh topic. It was very curious, but it seemed as if an oppression of mind had descended upon all in the front room; and then soon it seemed as if the oppressive discomfort was spreading to the back room too.

Mrs. Judd got up, crossed to the fireplace, and put some coals on the fire.

"You're very quiet all at once," she said, turning toward the doorway.

No one answered; a silence had fallen. Mrs. Judd put on some more coals, dropped the shovel noisily, and went back to the table. Giving herself a shake she sat down again and resumed her task.

"Well," said a voice, "I'll be saying good night."

"Good night, Mr. Price. . . . Excuse me a moment, gen'elmen."

Mr. Judd had appeared in the doorway, and he came to his wife's side.

"You're very quiet," she said, "in there to-night."

"Yes—you notice too?"

"What's caused it? Mr. Billett's reading?"

"No," said Mr. Judd confidentially, "it's the man in the corner—him as came in last. We don't know him—and it's a damper."

"Is he unpleasant? I haven't heard any strange voice all evening."

"He hasn't spoken. Just a damper. I wish he'd go."

Somebody called to the landlord, and he withdrew to fulfil the order.

"If I may trouble you again, Mr. Judd."

"Coming, Mr. Yates."

Left to herself, Mrs. Judd made a few thoughtful stitches; then she put down her work abruptly, got up, and moving to the doorway, glanced into the tap-room without showing herself to customers, old or new. Moving again, she softly drew a chair to the red-curtained window, stood upon the seat of the chair, and cautiously peered through the glass above the curtain. Then she returned to her table once more, and picked up her work. But in a moment or two the work was again abandoned with a jerk, and she called to her husband sharply.

"Judd."

"That's the missus calling you."

"What is it?" asked Mr. Judd, in the doorway.

"Come here. . . . Speak low. I took a peep, but I couldn't see him."

"No, I tell you, he sits in the corner."

"D'you say he don't talk—at all?"

"Not a word."

"What's he had?"

"Three glasses."

"Has he paid?"

"No. He don't offer to pay or to go. He just sits there like a toad. And I see the others feel it same as me. Can't talk jolly. I on'y wish he'd go."

Mrs. Judd whispered sharply and decisively.

"Tell him to go."

"Shall I?"

"Yes, you tell him to pay his score, and clear out of this."

"Suppose he turns nasty?"

"Then make the excuse that you want to shut up. It *is* nigh on time. Let the lot go—and shut the door."

"Well, they're going a'ready—one after another."

"Don't stand here gaping. Do it, quick! Tell that man to go."

The landlord went to dismiss the unwelcome guest; and Mrs. Judd stood by her table, watching the doorway and listening intently. Her lips twitched nervously, and her hand, as it rested on the table, trembled.

"'Ow goes the hour, eh?"

The little company was apparently breaking up; a cold breath of air came creeping in when somebody opened the street door; one heard a note of leave-taking in the low-pitched voices.

"They say"—that was Mr. Veal's voice, slow and grave—"they say there's bin more influenza of the sort there has bin this winter than what there *ever* has been."

"Great deal o' sickness"—That was Mr. Carter's voice, low and solemn—"and, mind you, distress too—real distress—throughout the land."

"Good night, old boy."

"I'm on the move myself," said Mr. Billett.

"Good night to you."

Mrs. Judd, straining her ears, caught no sound of the stranger's voice.

"Well?" she whispered anxiously, when her husband reappeared. "Has he gone?"

Mr. Judd put his finger to his lips as he approached.

"Has he gone?"

"No."

"Did you tell him?"

"No. But I've been speaking to him. Listen. He asks this! May he sleep here? Any shake-down will do. And he'll pay handsome."

"No, no. Don't you let him stop." Mrs. Judd had shown sudden fear. She seized her husband's arm, dragging it to her; her face was white, and she trembled violently. "Get rid of him. Get rid of him quick before all the others go. I'm scared."

"You needn't be afeared."

"It's the thought that come into my mind. . . . Suppose it was him they read of—the *murderer.*"

"Oh!" Mr. Judd was looking at his wife in blank surprise. He added, very feebly: "That ain't likely—at all."

"You go back—quick. No time to lose."

"Gentlemen," said Mr. Judd, hurrying into the tap-room, "you'll excuse me, but it's time I shut up—if you please. . . . What—are you off a'ready?"

The voices sounded in the street now, outside the tap-room door. "Good night. . . . Good night. . . And good luck to you." The voices were dying away; soon all was silence.

Mr. Judd returned, rubbing his hands, and speaking with unfeigned cheerfulness.

"Don't be afeared. He's gone."

"Thank goodness! It scared me."

"Must have gone while I was talkin' to you."

"Thank goodness!" Mrs. Judd gave herself a shake. "That's what I say. Thank goodness!"

"But he's sneaked off without paying."

"Never mind," cried Mrs. Judd vehemently. "I don't want that man's money. . . . Now you shut up carefully," and she packed her work into the basket. "Draw them door-bolts full—and see the chain's fast."

From the tap-room there came the noise of bolts and bars as the fastenings were adjusted.

"And put the rod firm across the shutter."

"That's firm enough," said Mr. Judd.

"Did you latch the window first?"

"Of course I did."

Then Mr. Judd turned out the gas in the tap-room, and came back to the sitting-room. He laid his pipe on the mantelpiece, warmed his legs at the fire, and laughed.

"You *are* a one to get hold of rum ideas—"

Mrs. Judd had picked up a bedroom candlestick and was about to light the candle when suddenly she raised her hand as if signalling to her husband to keep quiet.

"'Ark," she whispered. "What was that? I swear I 'eard something in there."

Judd moved hastily to his wife's side, and they both stood staring at the darkness behind the tap-room window.

"God! What's that?"

It was a tinkling crash of broken glass somewhere in the darkness; a tumbler had fallen on the tap-room floor.

"Wha—wha—what is it?" stammered Mr. Judd quaveringly.

There came a vague noise of movement; then more plainly, unmistakably heard—some one moving in the darkness of the tap-room.

"Look. Look."

A man was standing in the doorway. A slouch hat concealed the upper part of his face, but his red beard, growing high to the cheek bones, gave him a fierce and terrible aspect. He seemed clumsy, loutish, stupid; and he spoke deliberately and slowly, with a rather thick utterance, but not as if he was drunk.

"All right," said the man. "I 'adn't gone. I was 'id be'ind the bar."

"Then outside you go now," said Mr. Judd feebly.

"I 'adn't sneaked off without paying," the man continued slowly, and with a slight chuckle. "I pay my debts. . . . You must let me stop here."

"Lis'n to me," said Mr. Judd, frightened but blustering. "You go straight to that door and draw the bolts and step out precious quick. You ought to be ashamed o' yourself."

"You can't turn me out. See? Because I want rest. I'm a boner fidy trav'ler"—the man took off his hat, and came forward into the room—"and I'm your own son."

Mr. Judd and his wife had drawn away to the wall as the man advanced. They were staring at him fearfully.

"Tom? No! I don't reco'nize *you* as my son."

"'Adn't grown me beard, 'ad I? It's all right. You can prove me. I wrote and told you I was coming. Well, I'm back sooner than I expected."

Mrs. Judd moved a few steps nearer to the man, stared at his eyes, and spoke with a breathless falter.

"Where did you write from?"

"Rio der lar Plarter."

"Yes!" Mrs. Judd took another step toward him. "Yes— but that's no proof."

"Prove me by the fam'ly hist'ry. . . . You buried two before I was born. My sister Loo, what followed me, died o' the scarlet fever. I left for foreign parts because I'd disgraced meself over the club money that was left in the till. . . . But what's use? Mother, don't yer *know* I'm yer son?"

There was a pause, and then Mrs. Judd turned to her husband.

"Yes. It's Tom."

"Then what are you playing at?" Mr. Judd looked at the man half timidly, half angrily, and, bringing out a handkerchief, wiped the perspiration from his forehead. "Where's the fun of scaring people? Why couldn't you announce yerself like a reas'nable being?"

"Didn't want to be messing about with a pack of strangers. . . . I'm a bit queer. See? . . . But I was all right when I wrote. I was all right till I left Montevideo."

Mrs. Judd started and drew back.

"Montyvidyer!"

Mr. Judd echoed the word meaninglessly.

"Montyvidyer."

"When you been to Montyvidyer?" asked Mrs. Judd in a shaky voice. "That's not the place you said. Lar Plarter?"

"Same thing. That's the river. Montevideo's the city."
The man put his hand to his brow, and spoke with a dreamy
air. "It's a grand city—Mon-te-vid-yo. . . ." He dropped
his head, and turned to Mrs. Judd with surly anger. "What
yer looking at me like that? What's the matter with you?"

Mrs. Judd had drawn right away to the wall again; there
was horror as well as fear in her starting eyes; her lips were
twitching.

"Well? . . . Is this yer welcome 'ome? Mother! Aren't yer
goin' ter kiss me?"

There was a brief silence. Then Mrs. Judd shook herself, as if making a final successful effort to shake off the
dark fears that oppressed her.

"Yes, of course I'm goin' ter kiss yer." She came from
the wall, embraced her son, and with her arms round his
neck, began to cry. "My boy. My own boy."

"That's all right," and the son offered his hand to Mr.
Judd. "Father!"

"How are yer?" and Mr. Judd shook hands. "Will you
have another drink?"

"No. I mustn't drink. I tell you I'm queer—queer about
the 'ead. Felt so dazed I could scarce find me way 'ome
'ere."

"Is that so?" Mr. Judd looked at his wife, who made
a sign and whispered a few words to him. "I say, I think
I best fetch the doctor to *you*. Dr. Page! Just acrost the
road," and he moved toward the door. "He won't be gone
to bed. He's a late bird—Dr. Page."

The son moved clumsily and intercepted him.

"No. You mustn't do that. I've seen a doctor—and I
told him how it was. Bin pretty near choked—and then
the inj'ry to th' 'ead." He looked at his parents stupidly
and dreamily; then roused himself, as if trying to continue, but forgetting what he intended to say. "Yes, that's
it. The doctor tells me, 'You're very queer, my fren.' See?

'Take care,' he says, 'or you'll go off in a fit—and no doctors won't pull you out of that.'"

He went to the hearth, drew the armchair before the fire and put another chair by it to form his couch.

"I've money in my pockets—but I'm in trouble. See? I'm goin' on first thing mornin'." He said this slowly and dreamily. "Let me sleep and let me go. What yer lookin' at me, mother? Want to hear my story, eh?" With an exertion he roused himself again to continue speaking. "Montevideo's a grand city—so's the river. Wonderful place." He stood staring in front of him; then once again roused himself. "You'd like to hear my story. Well, it's a wonderful place. Paradise for a sailorman—with money in his pockets. There's the drinking saloons by the water, and these tamb'reen gals—Spanish half-breeds—dancing while you lap down yer liquor. Diff'rent from this set-out," and he waved his arm in the direction of the tap-room. "'Andsome and bright as parakeets—them tamb'reen gals," and he snapped his fingers. "Chikeeta! Chikeeta!"

He shuffled his feet, moved his hands as if beating a tambourine, and sang an unmelodious snatch of song. Then he stared in front of him fixedly, and there was a long silence before he went on, dreamily.

"I wish I was in Montevideo now. That's where I wish I was now—down by the water, but out o' the sunshine."

Mrs. Judd had gone back to her table. She stood motionless, listening fearfully. Mr. Judd was at her side, by the table, listening stolidly and stupidly.

"Roughest lot ever I shipped with—and one as bullied me. Brought his grudge aboard with 'im." The man dropped his voice in a low grumble. "Bullying devil from hell. Thinks he'll choke me—out me in my bunk. See?" He put his hands to his throat, and gasped and grunted as if he really felt suffocation. "But they pulls 'im off of me. . . . Next time, he goes for me with an iron bolt"—and he put his hands to his head—"something cruel." Then he added dreamily, "You didn't ought to hit a man with iron.

"So that's my story, mother," and he sat down in the armchair, and stretched his legs upon the other chair. "I'm dead beat. You must let me sleep. And you must watch and wake me. Rouse me daylight. I must go on," and he was about to settle himself in the chair when he looked round quickly. "See though. Wake me if I dream. Don't let me dream. I've been dreaming ever since— Promise you'll wake me if I dream."

"Yes," said Mrs. Judd, in a dry, husky whisper, "I promise."

The man lay back in the armchair, and almost immediately fell asleep. For a little while Mrs. Judd stood by her table watching him. Mr. Judd looked at her stupidly.

"Should I turn out the gas?"

"Yes," said Mrs. Judd. "No. Turn it down—not out. Do it soft—so's not to disturb him."

Mr. Judd obeyed her; then he pulled a chair to the table and sat down, making a slight rattling noise as his hand blundered against the tray and jug.

"Shush!"

She took a shawl, slowly crossed to the sleeping man, and softly put it over his chest. In all her movements she showed dread and fear of the man. Watching him apprehensively, she knelt on the hearth and replenished the fire, picking the lumps of coal from the scuttle with her fingers, making no noise. She remained kneeling till the fire began to burn brighter, to light up the figure of the sleeper, to throw monstrous shadows on the ceiling and the wall. Then she rose from her knees, went back to her chair, and, leaning her elbows on the table, hid her face in her hands.

The minutes dragged slowly and heavily. Not a sound now broke the silence, except the crisp ticking of the clock and the stertorous breathing of the man.

"'Ark!"

The man was faintly muttering in his sleep.

"Chikeeta. . . . Chikeeta."

He muttered indistinctly, but one could catch a sentence here and there among the confused series of words.

"Chikeeta. . . . All tamb'reen gals the same. She's my gal. . . . Yes—my gal."

"He's on the dream," said Mrs. Judd. "Go and wake 'im."

"Wake 'im so soon?"

"Yes—now."

Mr. Judd got up, went across to the fire, and stood by the man's side. The man muttered again.

"Do as I tell you. Wake 'im."

Mr. Judd laid his hand on the man's shoulder. "Look 'ere. Yer mother says time to wake up."

Then the man spoke loudly and distinctly.

"Let me and my gal alone. See? My gal—an' me—my gal."

"'Ere. Stop it." Mr. Judd shook the man's shoulder. "Wake up."

"Let me alone," said the man loudly and snarlingly. "Let me alone, I say," and he threw off the shawl that covered his shoulders.

Judd drew back alarmed, and his wife, springing from her chair, came and seized the man's left hand.

"Wake," she cried. "It's I—yer own mother. . . . God, there's something wrong with his sleeping like this. Wake—can't you?" and she pulled at his hand violently.

The man slowly released his hand and pressed it against his breast, leaned forward in the chair, and went on talking. His eyes were still shut.

"No more your gal than my gal."

He spoke these words with an appalling fierceness; and Mrs. Judd shrank away from him, terrified.

"Any man's gal, while there's money in yer pockets. . . . Son of a dog, am I?" He was speaking with increasing passion. "Monkey-face, am I? If I am, *she* don't mind. She's chosen her monkey. See!" And his voice subsided again to indistinct mutterings.

Mrs. Judd in her terror had got behind the table; she was leaning on the table for support, as though all strength had gone from her knees.

"For the love o' mercy, wake 'im."

"I—I can't. I—I daren't."

Mrs. Judd frantically swept the tray, the jug, and glass off the table, and they fell with a clatter and a smash.

"Wake. Why don't you wake?"

"Look 'ere. I—I'll fetch the doctor."

"No, no, don't leave me alone with 'im," and the terrified woman clutched at her husband's arm. "I can't bear it . . . Yes, yes, I can. . . . Fetch Dr. . . . Bring Dr. Page to wake 'im."

Her husband rushed through the tap-room, noisily drew the bolts of the outer door, and ran into the street, leaving the door open behind him.

The cold air crept into the warm room and seemed to freeze one's blood; the flames flickered behind the bars of the grate, lighting up the sleeper's face and his closed eyes, making fantastic shadows dance behind him on the wall; in the silence the ticking of the clock sounded like heavy, bursting heart-beats. Then the silence was broken; the man had begun to speak again.

"I'm not afraid of you—ashore or afloat. You don't put fear into me—on land or sea. . . . Bullying devil from hell."

"Wake."

Mrs. Judd came from behind the table and took two steps toward the dreaming man, as if she intended to try once more to rouse him. But her fear was too great. She stopped, with her hand on the table, as if paralyzed by terror.

"Take your hands from me throat." He had lifted his hands to his neck, was struggling in the chair. He pulled at his scarf, gasped and spluttered, as though choking. "Let me go. Let go o' me." He sank back on the chair, panting. "Thank ye, mates. Thank you kindly. He near done me that time."

"Wake."

He was slowly coming forward in the chair.

"See here—ye swab. This don't end it. I'll pay you when we get ashore. I pay my debts. . . . Ye'll call me son of a dog! All right—but I'll pay you back. I'll swing for it—but I'll pay you."

"Wake!" The word came in a shrill scream of terror. "Wake."

"There he goes—there he goes. . . He was whispering now; and, as he whispered, he raised himself, leaning right forward and pointing with an outstretched hand.

"There—there he goes," and his eyes opened, and he stared in front of him. The eyes were glassy, glittering, most horrible to watch in the silence while one waited with shuddering awe for the voice.

"Take that. Take that."

The voice had sounded loud and strong, bestially ferocious, and the dreamer was stooping from the chair and looking down at the floor.

"Where's your answer now? Speak up now. . . . There's more," and he made violent, frightful gestures with the right hand. "There's more for you," he gasped. "And more, and more. . . . That's how I pay my debts."

He was breathless, panting; and, as he looked down at the floor, the words came in a low snarling rage.

"Answer back now. Now who's Monkey-face? Why, your own mother wouldn't know you now."

He drew back into the chair suddenly, shivering and gasping.

"No, no—not the dead man. Dead men can't—can't—can't. . . ."

He raised both hands to his head with a swift motion, and dropped back in the chair. Then his arms fell, hanging loosely; his head sank upon his left shoulder; and he lay quite still.

"'Ere. This way—this way. 'Ere's 'elp at last."

Mr. Judd came hurrying through the tap-room, followed by the doctor.

Mrs. Judd stood by her table, unable to move, scarcely able to speak, in a frenzy of horror. Mr. Judd had turned up the gas, and brought a lighted candle for the doctor. The doctor was stooping over the man, lifting his head, scrutinizing his eyes, feeling his breast.

"Wake 'im. Oh, wake 'im."

The doctor, looking round, spoke gravely.

"No one can wake him now. He will never wake."

"Dead?"

"Yes."

Mrs. Judd stepped forward, dropped upon her knees, and raised her arms.

"Thank God. Thank God for that," and, sobbing and shaking, she covered her face with her hands.

The End of the Flight
W. Somerset Maugham

I shook hands with the skipper and he wished me good luck. Then I went down to the lower deck crowded with natives, Malays, Chinese, and Dyaks, and made my way to the ladder; looking over the ship's side I saw that my luggage was already in the boat. It was a large, clumsy-looking craft, with a great square sail of bamboo matting, and it was crammed full of gesticulating natives. I scrambled in and a place was made for me. We were about three miles from the shore and a stiff breeze was blowing. As we drew near I saw that the cocoanut trees in green abundance grew to the water's edge, and among them I saw the brown roofs of the village. A Chinese who spoke English pointed out to me a white bungalow as the residence of the District Officer; though he did not know it, it was with him I was going to stay. I had a letter of introduction to him in my pocket.

I felt somewhat forlorn when I landed and my bags were set down beside me on the glistening beach. This was a remote spot to find myself in, this little town on the north coast of Borneo, and I felt a trifle shy at the thought of presenting myself to a total stranger with the announcement that I was going to sleep under his roof, eat his food and drink his whisky, till another boat came in to take me to the port to which I was bound.

But I might have spared myself these misgivings, for the moment I reached the bungalow and sent in my letter, he came out, a sturdy, ruddy, jovial man, of thirty-five perhaps, and greeted me with heartiness. While he held my hand he shouted to a boy to bring drinks and to another to look after my luggage. He cut short my apologies.

"Good God, man, you have no idea how glad I am to see you. Don't think I'm doing anything for you in putting you up. The boot's on the other leg. And stay as long as you damned well like. Stay a year."

I laughed. He put away his day's work, assuring me that he had nothing to do that could not wait till the morrow, and threw himself into a long chair. We talked and drank and talked. When the heat of the day wore off we went for a long tramp in the jungle and came back wet to the skin. A bath and a change were very grateful, and then we dined. I was tired out and though my host was plainly willing to go on talking straight through the night I was obliged to beg him to allow me to go to bed.

"All right, I'll just come along to your room, and see everything's all right."

It was a large room with verandas on two sides of it, sparsely furnished, but with a huge bed protected by mosquito netting.

"The bed is rather hard," said my host "Do you mind?"

"Not a bit. I shall sleep without rocking to-night."

My host looked at the bed reflectively.

"It was a Dutchman who slept in it last. Do you want to hear a funny story?"

I wanted chiefly to go to bed, but he *was* my host, and being at times somewhat of a humorist myself I know that it is hard to have an amusing story to tell and find no listener.

"He came on the boat that brought you, on its last journey along the coast; he came into my office and asked where the dak bungalow was. I told him there wasn't one, but if he hadn't anywhere to go I didn't mind putting him up. He jumped at the invitation. I told him to have his kit sent along.

"'This is all I've got,' he said.

"He held out a little shiny black grip. It seemed a bit scanty, but it was no business of mine, so I told him to go along to the bungalow and I'd come as soon as I was through with my work. While I was speaking the door of my office was opened and my clerk came in. The Dutchman had his back to the door and it may be that my clerk opened it a bit suddenly. Anyhow the Dutchman gave a shout, he jumped about two feet into the air and whipped out a revolver.

"'What the hell are you doing?' I said.

"When he saw it was the clerk he collapsed. He leaned against the desk, panting, and upon my word he was shaking as though he'd got fever.

"'I beg your pardon,' he said. 'It's my nerves. My nerves are terrible.'

"'It looks like it,' I said.

"I was rather short with him. To tell you the truth I wished I hadn't asked him to stop with me. He didn't look as though he'd been drinking a lot and I wondered if he was some fellow the police were after. If he were, I said to myself, he could hardly be such a fool as to walk right into the lion's den.

"'You'd better go and lie down,' I said.

"He took himself off, and when I got back to my bungalow I found him sitting quite quietly, but bolt upright, on the veranda. He'd had a bath and shaved, and put on clean things and he looked fairly presentable.

"'Why are you sitting in the middle of the place like that?' I asked him. 'You'll be much more comfortable in one of the long chairs.'

"'I prefer to sit up,' he said.

"Queer, I thought. But if a man in this heat would rather sit up than lie down it's his own look out. He wasn't much to look at, tallish and heavily built, with a square head and close-cropped bristly hair. I should think he was about forty. The thing that chiefly struck me about him was his expression. There was a look in his eyes, blue eyes they were and rather small, that beat me altogether, and his face sagged as it were; it gave you the feeling he was going to cry. He had a way of looking quickly over his left shoulder as though he thought he heard something. By God, he was nervous. But we had a couple of drinks and he began to talk. He spoke English very well; except for a slight accent you'd never have known that he was a foreigner, and I'm bound to admit he was a good talker. He'd been everywhere and he'd read any amount. It was a treat to listen to him.

"We had three or four whiskies in the afternoon and a lot of gin pahits later on, so that when dinner came along we were by way of being rather hilarious, and I'd come to the conclusion that he was a damned good fellow. Of course we had a lot of whisky at dinner and I happened to have a bottle of Benedictine so we had some liqueurs afterward. I can't help thinking we both got very tight.

"And at last he told me why he'd come. It was a rum story."

My host stopped and looked at me with his mouth slightly open as though, remembering it now, he was struck again with its rumness.

"He came from Sumatra, the Dutchman, and he'd done something to an Achinese and the Achinese had sworn to kill him. At first he made light of it, but the fellow tried two or three times and it began to be rather a nuisance, so he thought he'd better go away for a bit. He went over to Batavia and made up his mind to have a good time.

But when he'd been there a week he saw the fellow slink-
ing along a wall. By God, he'd followed him. It looked as
though he meant business. The Dutchman began to think
it was getting beyond a joke and he thought the best thing
he could do would be to skip off to Soerabaya. You know
how crowded the streets are there; he was strolling about
one day when he happened to turn round and saw the Achinese walking quite quietly just behind him. It gave him a
turn. It would give any one a turn.

"The Dutchman went straight back to his hotel, packed
his things, and took the next boat to Singapore. Of course
he put up at the Van Wyck, all the Dutch stay there, and
one day when he was having a drink in the courtyard
in front of the hotel, the Achinese walked in as bold as
brass, looked at him for a minute, and walked out again.
The Dutchman told me he was just paralyzed. The fellow
could have stuck his kriss into him there and then and he
wouldn't have been able to move a hand to defend himself. The Dutchman knew he was just biding his time; that
damned native was going to kill him, he saw it in his eyes,
and he went all to pieces."

"But why didn't he go to the police?" I asked.

"I don't know. I expect it wasn't a thing he wanted the
police to be mixed up in."

"But what had he done to the man?"

"I don't know that either. He wouldn't tell me. But the
look he gave when I asked him, I expect it was something
pretty rotten. I have an idea he knew he deserved whatever
the Achinese could do."

My host lit a cigarette.

"Go on," I said.

"The skipper of the boat that runs between Singapore
and Kuching lives at the Van Wyck between trips and the
boat was starting at dawn. The Dutchman thought it a
grand chance to give the fellow the slip; he left his luggage

at the hotel and walked down to the ship with the skipper, as if he were just going to see him off, and stayed on her when she sailed. His nerves were all anyhow by then. He didn't care about anything but getting rid of the Achinese. He felt pretty safe at Kuching. He got a room at the rest-house and bought himself a couple of suits and some shirts in the Chinese shops. But he told me he couldn't sleep. He dreamed of that man, and half a dozen times he awakened just as he thought a kriss was being drawn across his throat. By God, I felt quite sorry for him. He just shook as he talked to me and his voice was hoarse with terror. That was the meaning of the look I had noticed. You remember, I told you he had a funny look on his face and I couldn't tell what it meant. Well, it was fear.

"And one day when he was in the club at Kuching he looked out of the window and saw the Achinese sitting there. Their eyes met. The Dutchman just crumpled up and fainted. When he came to, his first idea was to get out. Well, you know, there's not a hell of a lot of traffic at Kuching and this boat that brought you was the only one that gave him a chance to get away quickly. He got on her. He was positive the man was not on board."

"But what made him come here?"

"Well, the old tramp stops at a dozen places on the coast and the Achinese couldn't possibly guess he'd chosen this one because he only made up his mind to get off when he saw there was only one boat to take the passengers ashore, and there weren't more than a dozen people in it.

"'I'm safe here for a bit at all events,' he said, 'and if I can only be quiet for a while I shall get my nerve back.'

"'Stay as long as you like,' I said. 'You're all right here, at all events till the boat comes along next month, and if you like we'll watch the people who come off.'

"He was all over me. I could see what a relief it was to him.

"It was pretty late and I suggested to him that we should turn in. I took him to his room to see that it was all right. He locked the door of the bath-house and bolted the shutters, though I told him there was no risk, and when I left him I heard him lock the door I had just gone out of.

"Next morning when the boy brought me my tea I asked him if he'd called the Dutchman. He said he was just going to—I heard him knock and knock again. Funny, I thought. The boy hammered on the door, but there was no answer. I felt a little nervous, so I got up. I knocked too. We made enough noise to rouse the dead, but the Dutchman slept on. Then I broke down the door. The mosquito curtains were neatly tucked in round the bed. I pulled them open. He was lying there on his back with his eyes wide open. He was as dead as mutton. A kriss lay across his throat, and say I'm a liar if you like, but I swear to God it's true, there wasn't a wound about him anywhere. The room was empty.

"Funny, wasn't it?"

"Well, that all depends on your idea of humor," I replied.

My host looked at me quickly.

"You don't mind sleeping in that bed, do you?"

"N-no. But I'd just as soon you'd told me the story to-morrow morning."

Her Judgment Day
Mrs. Belloc Lowndes

I

With a sudden cry of fear Enid Rayburn sat up in the Jacobean four-post bed where she had spent a broken night. She was still plunged in the heavy sleep induced by a big dose of her favorite sleeping draught; but any one standing, say, by the large half-moon window of the delightful old-world country bedroom, would have thought Mrs. Rayburn awake, for her violet-blue eyes were wide open, and dilated, as if with terror.

How lovely she looked! How childlike was the pure delicate contour of her face, and the droop of her little red mouth. Her dimpled shoulders rose from a nightgown which even to the indulgent eyes of her spinster hostess, the quaintly-named Matilda Fidgett, looked more like a ball dress than what Miss Fidgett understood was now called a "nighty." Enid's nightie was of pale pink crêpe de Chine, and the sleeveless bodice was edged with a deep band of real lace. Even in her own and her late husband's worse financial straits, Mrs. Rayburn had always achieved the possession of beautiful clothes, and Miss Fidgett was perhaps the only one of her women friends who believed the legend that she herself made many of the charming things she wore, with the aid of her one devoted maid.

Who, looking at her now, framed in the shadowed delicious stillness of Miss Fidgett s principal guest-chamber, could have believed that the lovely girl—for she still looked a girl—had just gone through the most terrible ordeal which can fall to the lot of a civilized woman?

Yet, so it was, for Enid Rayburn had been the principal witness for the Crown in a murder trial, which had excited the whole country. The man in the dock had been a brilliant medical student named Godfrey Lynworth, and for unrequited love of Mrs. Rayburn, he had committed that most dastardly of crimes, secret murder by poison. *This morning at nine o'clock he was to expiate his crime.*

There were tens of thousands of human beings who, had they been privileged to see Mrs. Rayburn as she was now, this morning, would have felt their hearts contract with intense pity for the woman they regarded as the innocent victim of an extraordinary set of ironic circumstances. There were also tens of thousands who, having had a doubt as to the part she had played in the singular tragedy, would have told themselves that their half-suspicions had been cruelly unjust, could they have looked into that flower-like face, and heard the words now escaping from her half-opened mouth. For those words were uttered in an appealing, broken tone:

"Don't hurt him! Please don't hurt him,"—and then:

"Oh, Godfrey, I *am* so sorry for you!"

She was not here, in this pretty country bedroom. She was standing in the door of a small, bare room which she knew to be the condemned cell of the prison where a judgment of death was to be executed that morning. There stood by the pallet bed the tall fine figure of the youth who had loved her with so passionate and absorbing a love, and by whose wish, according to the statement made by the famous counsel who had defended him, not a word concerning her, or their friendship, had been uttered in extenuation of anything, he, Godfrey Lynworth, had done, or left undone.

Lynworth, collarless, was clad in an old tweed suit—a suit which Enid remembered well, and which she had once told him she liked to see him wear. He held himself upright, with his head thrown back in what had been a characteristic attitude.

Two men were pinioning his arms and legs, and it was to them that Enid Rayburn had just addressed her piteous plea.

All at once, the chaplain, together with the governor of the prison, walked in. It was all happening exactly as she had once seen it happen—in a horrible scene in a play.

Godfrey now left the cell, and he began walking with steady steps, his head still thrown back, down a narrow passage.

And then Enid gave a stifled shriek, for suddenly she saw the gallows, through the open door at the end of the passage.

She covered her face with her hands, yet something seemed to force her to peep through her fingers; and, for a fleeting moment, Godfrey Lynworth turned and looked at her. His look was so charged with mute, terrible reproach, that with an anguished cry of protest, she awoke—awoke to the blessed reality that she was sixty miles from the prison where that awful drama was to be enacted this morning.

Her shaking hand felt for her watch on the tiny Chippendale table by the bed, and having found it she held it close before her eyes.

It was only seven o'clock, and Mrs. Rayburn sighed heavily, for that meant that there were two more awful hours of misery and suspense to be lived through. Nay, two hours and a half, for the faithful friend who had promised to stand near the prison gate till the death notice was put up, and who was then to telephone to her from a house near by, had thought it unlikely she could get a trunk call through before half past nine. Enid told herself that it was cruel, cruel, that she should have waked like this at seven, when the same dose of chloral taken by her the night after her cross-examination had given her a measure of merciful oblivion for fourteen hours!

The tears began rolling down her cheeks; yet it was not for him, Godfrey Lynworth, and his awful fate that she was weeping. It was for pity of herself, for all she had gone through, and for what remained for her to go through, till she heard the blessed news that Lynworth had died, as he had lived, silent. She knew, deep down in her heart, that not only his counsel, Sir Marcus Tristram, had believed him innocent, but also that Godfrey's heart-broken father and mother had hoped, to the last moment of his trial, that he would clear himself by shifting the burden of guilt on her.

Why those heartless old people had actually found out where she was hiding, and had made her a frantic appeal to save their boy, their Benjamin, by incriminating herself!

That had been the one time when she had felt really frightened. Every one else had been so kind; even during that long cross-examination by Sir Marcus Tristram, she had been supported by the feeling that every one, judge, jury, and all the spectators in that horrible crowded court, had been on her side, and intensely sorry for her. Indeed at more than one of the probing, cruel queries put to her by Sir Marcus, there had run a murmur of disapproval among the spectators, and once the judge had said: "Sir Marcus, I must disallow that question."

But when these two old people, Mr. and Mrs. Lynworth, had forced themselves upon her, she had gone through some terrible moments. Yet she had taken what she had thought to be a very kind and sympathetic line with those unfortunate parents, for she had told them that she, too, did not believe their son could be guilty, and that she was still racking her brain to think who could be. They had not dared, either of them, to say right out that they believed her to be guilty. But at the very end of that horrible interview, Mrs. Lynworth, looking straight into her eyes, had exclaimed in a strangled voice: "You know who did it, Mrs. Rayburn. But I suppose we cannot expect you to tell the truth, for you never loved Godfrey. He adored you, but you only—" and then the old woman had used a most horrible word, a word that Enid had never heard uttered aloud by any human being. Godfrey's mother, that fine-bred lady, had actually so lost herself as to say, "you only lusted after him." No wonder Mr. Lynworth had taken his wife's arm and said: "You forget yourself, my dear. Saying that kind of thing will not help Godfrey."

When she had told her own counsel, the great Sir John Watling, something of that terrible interview, he had expressed strong indignation. Nothing, he had exclaimed, could excuse the impropriety, the cruelty, of such an action on the Lynworths' part. "But you must forgive them, Mrs. Rayburn—after all, that wretched young fellow is their son." "I have forgiven them," she had answered, in an angelic voice. "Their behavior is the more astonishing," he had gone on vigorously, "because of the noble way you have behaved to that misguided boy—your brave asseveration, in spite of all that was proved against him, that you could not believe him to be guilty." It was then that she had taken the opportunity to say in a deeply troubled voice: "He wants to see me, Sir John. Do you think I ought to see him? He was very, very fond of me—once. But oh! I so dread the idea."

And the great counsel had shaken his head decidedly.

"You have already borne enough misery and torture over this terrible affair. You are in no way bound to see young Lynworth, and I'm amazed at his asking you to do so," he had answered.

So she had written the condemned man a letter, first showing it to Sir John, who had unwillingly passed it, while declaring it to be the noblest epistle ever written by a woman!

She had made so many rough copies of that short letter that she knew it by heart; and she repeated it to herself now, this morning, rocking her slight body this way and that in the large bed.

> *Dear Godfrey,*
> *I am ill, so I cannot come to you. Otherwise I would do so. You know that I believe you inno-cent; and I want now to tell you how grateful I am for all your kindness to me—for the love, however wrong it may have been, that you lav-ished on me.*
>
> *Enid.*

She had hoped this letter would give poor Godfrey pleasure, and, above all, that he would read between the lines and see how sorry she was—how terribly sorry—that everything had fallen out as it had fallen out. Indeed she had twice underlined the word *"grateful."*

And then suddenly she felt that she could not go on remembering any more. It was too horrible—too horrible. So she took a bottle off the little table where her watch was lying, and measured out a small dose into a medicine glass. They would wake her surely, when that longed-for message came through?

Soon she was once more plunged into an uneasy slumber, but alas! again there came that hideous, hideous nightmare. Once more she seemed transported to the condemned cell. And this time, in addition to the warders, the governor of the prison and the chaplain, there was the man, Sir Marcus Tristram, who had cross-examined her with such pitiless severity when she had been in the witness-box, and she listened even now, with a feeling of indignation and dread to his cold concise voice uttering the cruel dangerous words: "I adjure you, Lynworth, to tell the truth for the sake of your father and your poor mother, who have always believed in your innocence." There was a pause. Enid Rayburn clasped her hands together in supplication, and it was as if she at once knew that she there, standing at the door of that dreadful cell, and that she was here, in this quiet Sussex village, miles and miles away from that condemned cell.

She heard Lynworth's deep voice answer: "It is as you have always thought it was, Sir Marcus. I die innocent. Enid Rayburn poisoned her husband."

Outside that quiet bedroom, Miss Fidgett, already on the way down to breakfast, heard a fearful cry—"No! No! *No!*—that isn't true!"

She opened the door and saw that Enid was fast asleep.

"Poor child, poor child," she murmured. "No wonder she has the nightmare. Thank God that unhappy man is to be hanged this morning." And, being the manner of woman she was, she stopped and offered up a wordless prayer for the murderer, that he might make his peace with God.

There came a sharp knock on the bedroom door, and Enid Rayburn awoke with a stifled cry.

She jumped straight out of bed and stood, her hands clasped together, waiting.

There came another knock, and then, "Come in!" she cried shrilly, and Miss Fidgett's old parlormaid came in.

Enid had never liked the woman, and the woman had never liked her. It was a curious fact that most of the servants brought in contact with her did not care for Mrs. Rayburn, although some of the kindest letters written to her had been from domestic servants, warmly sympathizing with the heroine of their favorite Sunday paper.

"Mrs. Doghill is on the telephone, ma'am. Miss Fidgett's holding the line till you come."

Enid snatched up her periwinkle-blue satin dressing-gown and wrapped it about her. Then she thrust her tiny white feet into slippers that matched the dressing-gown, and ran downstairs, telling herself, not for the first time, how foolish it was of Matty to have her telephone in so public a place as in the hall.

Miss Fidgett, a comfortable, old-fashioned looking lady, was standing there, the telephone receiver to her ear. When she saw her friend, the words formed themselves on her lips: "It's all over." But she did not utter them aloud. Instead she silently handed her the receiver, and turning into her sitting-room, discreetly shut the door.

"Is that you, Jenny? Yes—yes! I can hear quite well." She waited in an agony of mingled hope and fear till, with startling distinctness, came the measured words that were being uttered seventy miles away.

"It's all over, Enid. And I *could* have telephoned twenty minutes ago. But I fortunately managed—as I told you I hoped to do—to speak to a reporter who was present. You will be glad to hear that it was all incredibly quick—not two minutes, the man said, from when they first went into the cell to—you know where."

Enid remained silent. She was trying to summon up courage to ask a certain difficult question.

"I want to ask you something—" her voice sank to a whisper. "Did he confess?"

"No, he said nothing. The reporter particularly mentioned that. They seem to have hoped he would say something. But he remained absolutely silent."

She heard a cross voice interject: "You've had six minutes. I can't allow you to have any more now."

Enid turned toward the sitting-room door, where she knew her hostess was waiting full of sympathy and curiosity.

She opened the door. "Matty," she muttered. "Matty? It's—it's—" and before she could say "all over," she had fallen fainting at the older woman's feet.

Miss Fidgett would not have believed an angel—had an angel come and told her that dear little Enid Rayburn had fainted not from anguish, but from sheer relief, and agonizing heart anxiety.

She spent the rest of the morning in bed. For the first time, for oh! ever so long—she made an excellent breakfast, looking so cheerful the while, that it had even shocked her faithful Matty, and that though Matty had herself said that she must put the past entirely behind her.

At twelve o'clock the old parlormaid came in, with a silver salver on which lay a telegram. Enid tore open the envelope: *Hope to be with you to-morrow evening.—Henry Bonnington.*

The telegram had been sent from Paris the day before, and delayed in transmission.

"There is no answer," said Mrs. Rayburn, in her soft, pleasant voice, and then she lay back happy—happy at last.

II

All through those terrible days of suspense and horror there had run for Enid Rayburn a wonderful secret thread of bright, delicious romance. It had been begun by a letter, written by herself, about ten days after the exhumation of her husband, and the awful revelation that he had died of a huge dose of arsenic, and it had been addressed to a man called Henry Bonnington, who was in Madeira by the bedside of a dearly-loved dying sister. Enid and her husband had met this wealthy, generous bachelor about a year ago, oddly enough through Miss Fidgett, who was a friend of his mother. He had made friends with them both, invited them to accompany him on a delightful trip in his big yacht to Greece.

There had been several other people on Bonnington's yacht, among them a girl named Alice Flint, whom Enid had disliked from the first, for she had guessed that Miss Flint cared for Bonnington, and she thought that Bonnington was making up his mind to marry the girl. Enid always felt annoyed when any rich bachelor of her acquaintance married.

Luckily, Miss Flint left the yacht to join her mother at a point on the Italian coast, and then a delightful thing had happened! Bonnington had fallen in love with her, Enid Rayburn, in a crazy, headlong, almost boyish way.

Even so, he behaved in a way she couldn't make out. It was as if he wished to keep himself from loving her. But on the last day of their trip they had had it out, and he had spoken to her in a way that had amazed and also, it must be confessed, irritated her.

"Look here," he had said without preamble, "the day I became one-and-twenty I promised my old dad that I'd never make love to a married woman. Up to now I've kept my word, and I mean to keep it still, Enid. I love you—I can't help loving you—though I've fought against it, God knows. And it's too bad"—there had come a humorous twist over his face, a smile Enid Rayburn had not understood—"for I should have been happy enough with poor little Alice Flint, if I'd never met you. But now I can't marry her, feeling as I do about you."

She had begun to cry. Her tears always had such a wonderful effect on men, and they had an effect even on this queer man.

"Don't cry," he said. "I can't bear to see you cry! If you cry I'll have to go away—"

Quickly she dried her eyes, and it was well that she had, for, "It's your birthday next week—I heard you say so yesterday," exclaimed Bonnington, "so here's a little present for you," and he handed her an envelope containing a bearer check for a thousand pounds made out to, and indorsed by, himself.

As with real gratitude—for money was a thing the value of which Enid Rayburn thoroughly understood—she faltered out her thanks, he suddenly bent forward and caught her roughly in his arms. They exchanged a long, long kiss—and then, "There," he cried, "I've broken my word to my old dad, but it's the last time I'll do it. You're dangerous, young woman? This means I must keep away from you."

And they had never met since that day. Even so, at intervals, she and Bonnington had exchanged letters. His had been funny letters, not love-letters as she understood the term, but in the last letter he had written to her before the terrible tragedy of her husband's sudden death he had put in a postscript: "I'm sorry to say my heart is still true to Poll."

In answer to her letter telling him of the terrible thing which had happened, and when he understood the awful predicament in which she found herself, the tone of his letters became suddenly lover-like. He had proved his devotion, too, in a way that had made Enid feel she did really love him, by cabling her a considerable sum of money.

As she read his telegram over for the third time she told herself how noble, how generous, how *devoted* he was, and what a wonderful life lay before her as the cherished, sheltered wife of a great business magnate.

III

As he walked up the gangway of the channel boat at Folkestone, Henry Bonnington's heart was full of two women—

his dead sister, and the young widow of whom he knew so little, save that she was exquisitely lovely, and that he was passionately in love with her.

Every fibre of his being longed consciously, hungrily, thirstily, for Enid Rayburn. During his long, dreary journey home he had often wondered if all she had gone through had changed her from the deliciously pretty, kind-hearted, rather irresponsible little creature he remembered her as being, into a more serious woman. Not that he really wanted her different, but her letters had grown shorter as his had grown longer, and vaguely they had disappointed him.

While the porter was looking out for a first-class smoker, for Bonnington hated Pullman cars, he told himself that he might as well buy an evening paper.

He looked down at the placards lying in front of the bookstalls, and then he experienced a most unpleasant shock, for "Lynworth Dies Game"—"Godfrey Lynworth Executed"—"Lynworth Pays the Penalty," was what met his eyes.

Sharply he turned on his heel, and hurried down the platform. He had no wish to buy an evening paper now.

Godfrey Lynworth? How often had Bonnington tried to visualize the young man who had committed so dastardly a form of murder in order to free the woman he loved hopelessly, and without return, from the degradation of being tied to such a waster as had been Hugo Rayburn. Though the papers had been full of the wretched fellow's handsome face, Bonnington had no clear vision of him, and Enid had never once mentioned him in any of her letters.

Suddenly the fact, Enid's absolute silence concerning Lynworth, struck him as being very strange. Those placards also caused him to realize what he had not realized till now, that poor lovely Enid could not but be all her life long, even after she changed her name, a marked woman.

She would be always pointed at as the heroine of a great *cause célèbre*.

Yet, stop! Under the circumstances would it not only be right, but reasonable, that she should marry him almost at once? As his wife he could take her away to some quiet place on the Continent, where they two could be hidden in a dream of love, while people forgot the terrible story of the murder of which she had been the innocent cause.

"I've got you a place at last, sir! It is in a carriage reserved for a party of three. But one of the two gentlemen saw the name on your bag, and he said he knew you, sir, and would be very pleased if you'd share his carriage."

Bonnington felt a touch of quick annoyance. He didn't want to see any one he knew just now. But when he got up into the railway carriage he saw that his hospitable friend was a certain Mr. Francis Fox, with whom he had but a slight business acquaintance.

In addition to Mr. Fox there were two other people—a thin, active-looking, middle-aged man with whose face he felt vaguely familiar—could he be a well-known actor?—and a middle-aged lady with a clever, plain, good-humored face.

Bonnington said quietly: "I'm just back from Madeira; my sister died there ten days ago."

Fox murmured a word of sympathy, and then he said: "I expect you'd rather not be introduced to my two friends, Sir Marcus Tristram and Lady Annabel FitzCharles?"

Bonnington nodded gratefully, and settled himself in a corner seat, away from the other three. He knew now why the other man's face had seemed vaguely familiar. He was a famous K.C., and he had defended Godfrey Lynworth in the great murder trial which had lately taken place.

The train slid out of the harbor station, and all at once Lady Annabel FitzCharles observed: "I see that that poor young fellow, Godfrey Lynworth, was hung this morning.

Some one told me the other day, that he was very clever and would have had a brilliant career before him."

Bonnington's friend, Fox, looked significantly across at Sir Marcus Tristram. "I suppose it's not etiquette, even now, to ask you if you really thought the young chap innocent?"

The answer was rapped out at once in quick sharp tones. "I'm convinced that he was innocent!"

Lady Annabel leant forward. "But if he was innocent, Sir Marcus, what an awful thing that he should have been hung! I thought that there wasn't a doubt of his guilt?"

"My dear Lady Annabel," Sir Marcus leant forward. He was not speaking loudly, but every word he said was heard by the man in the farther corner, "I'm willing to bet you a hundred to one that within, say, a year—though I think it will be much sooner—we shall see, tucked away in some corner of our daily paper, a paragraph informing us that the beautiful Mrs. Rayburn, whose husband died under tragic circumstances, is about to be married, very quietly, to Mr. Popsy-Wopsy, a gentleman of great wealth and of considerable position."

Bonnington moved slightly in his seat. He would have liked to strike across the face the sneering devil who had just uttered those horrible words. But he knew that if not for his own, then for Enid's sake, he must refrain from even saying one word in her defense. So he opened the French paper which had been brought along by the porter with his other things, and hid his face behind it.

"What we look for in murder," went on the great barrister more quietly, "is *motive*. Poor Godfrey Lynworth had no reason to wish that futile fool, Hugo Rayburn, dead. Mrs. Rayburn was already his mistress—"

The stranger in the corner made a sudden movement, and Sir Marcus looked round for a moment, while Lady Annabel murmured: "I had no idea of that."

"Perhaps I'm a brute to say so, for the one thought of that unfortunate fellow, Lynworth, was to prevent the fact becoming known. And he had his wish, for the fact—and it is a fact, Lady Annabel—is only known to a comparatively small circle of people."

"What sort of a woman is she—really?" asked Lady Annabel.

"She is one of those women whom people now style amoral. I found out a good deal about the fair Enid while I was getting up the case for that unfortunate young man. Up to the very end I hoped he would, at any rate, allow sufficient suspicion to be cast on her to give him the benefit of the doubt. But Lynworth was like iron—he would never talk of her, nor discuss her, and he charged me most solemnly not once, but several times, to avoid any allusion to her that could be avoided, during my speech for the defense."

"Then you think Mrs. Rayburn was in love with some one else?" interjected Mr. Fox.

"I think nothing of the kind! My view is, that among the many men who had made love to her in the last year or two, she had marked down some rich man as more than a possible, a probable, almost a certain, husband—were she only free. We discovered that she had made great efforts to persuade Rayburn to consent to an arranged divorce a few months before the wretched fellow was poisoned. But he refused, for unluckily for himself, he adored the woman."

Mr. Fox again intervened. "But how did she procure the poison, Tristram? Surely the arsenic was traced to Lynworth's possession—or d'you think he gave it to her?"

Sir Marcus shook his head. "When they became lovers he hired two rooms from a friend of his—a man who had a slum practice. These two rooms were part of a surgery, though they had a separate entrance. I think you can guess *now* when and where Mrs. Rayburn procured the arsenic."

"And have you any suspicion as to who is the happy man who will be her second?" asked Lady Annabel, with a smile.

"No, there you have me! But some one has been supplying her with money during the last few months. I have very little doubt that it is the man she intends to marry."

"D'you think he was her accomplice?" put in Mr. Fox.

"Good Heavens, no! The man who is giving her money, the man whose wife she'll almost certainly become, probably thinks her an angel—as seem to do most of the fools who live in this island. And, mind you, it's quite possible that henceforth pretty little Enid will run straight. She's been through a bad time. She must have dreaded up to this very morning that Lynworth might give her away. I was present at a most painful meeting between the poor boy and his father. His father implored him to tell the truth, and that was the only time he broke down. But though he sobbed—sobbed like a child—he shook his head, and swore that he believed her innocent."

He waited a moment, and then he said, slowly: "You'll think me a sentimental fool, but I'm glad I've told you two-all this. Of course, what I've said is highly libellous. But the greater the truth, the greater the libel! Even if I were to repeat what I trusted to be true to every one I meet, which I shall not do, Mrs. Rayburn would never take any action. *I know too much.*"

The train drew up in the station where Bonnington was to change for the Sussex village where the woman he had now loved so faithfully, for what seemed a lifetime to him, was staying with their mutual friend, good-natured, rather foolish, Matty Fidgett. But he made no effort to get out of the train. For one thing, he felt very ill, it was as if he was numbed, as if he had lost his power of judgment.

When they reached Victoria Station he paid the excess on his ticket, and then he went to the telegraph office. For the last time in his life he wrote Enid's name:

> *Mrs. Rayburn, Baycombe*
> *Manor, Farnaker, Sussex.*
> *Prevented coming to-night. Will be with you*
> *some time to-morrow.*

He was a brave man, and it never occurred to him that he need never see her again.

Feeling in a maze of anguish and horror—though not of doubt, for he had been convinced—he wandered out of the station. He did not know what to do, or where to go, for he was no Londoner. And then he remembered, with a sudden lightening of the heart, that his kind old friends, Mrs. Flint and her daughter, were in town. After a moment's thought he threw their address to a cabman.

IV

It was late the following afternoon before Bonnington reached Baycombe Manor. Though in a sense the day he had spent in London had been a peaceful, even a happy day, he looked haggard, stern and sad, as he stood in the pretty upstairs boudoir of the old house. When Miss Fidgett came in to him, she told herself that so devoted a brother would surely make a good husband. She knew, or thought she knew, that Henry Bonnington loved her sorely tried, delightful friend, Enid Rayburn, and that after a decent interval he would make her his wife.

"Considering all she has gone through, our dear Enid is wonderfully well," she exclaimed. "She was in a dreadful state of nerves after that wretched young man's conviction. But I have persuaded her that she must put the past behind her, and forget, as far as she can, the whole terrible affair; for, after all, Hugo Rayburn was a poor sort of a fellow—no husband for a woman like Enid."

"May I see her at once? I've a train to catch back to town under an hour from now."

She looked at him in mild astonishment. She had never known him discourteous before. "I'll go and fetch her."

And then she tried to prepare her friend: "He looks far from well, my dear. Remember to speak to him of his poor sister."

Mrs. Rayburn had a sweet temper. But now she shrugged her shoulders a little pettishly. What a foolish old maid Matty was!

All the same, when she walked into the charming old-world room where the man she now considered her lover was waiting for her, she told herself that Matty was right, and that it was of his dead sister, not of her, that his heart was full. But the dead are soon forgotten. Why, she hardly ever thought of poor Hugo now!

Bonnington stared at her. She looked very young, very lovely, very appealing, in her plain black dress. She held out her hand, and as he took it in his she exclaimed involuntarily, "How cold your hand is!"

There was a terrible, a sombre, look on his stern face, and all at once she realized that he was avoiding looking into her eyes.

"I felt so sad, even in the midst of my own troubles, when I got your telegram about your sister."

He put up his hand. "Please don't speak of her!" he exclaimed almost violently. And involuntarily she said, "I beg your pardon."

Then in a curiously detached tone, he asked: "D'you remember Alice Flint?"

Enid looked at him; it was a quick, troubled glance. "D'you mean the girl who was on the yacht last year?"

"She was my sister's dearest friend," he said, "I went and saw her yesterday, and we are now engaged."

And then he could not but admire her, for she threw back her head, and then, in a hard clear tone, "I wish you joy, Mr. Bonnington!" she exclaimed. "Also I thank you, from the bottom of my heart, for all you've done for me."

"I want to do something more." His voice was almost inaudible now, and there was a long pause. Then he pulled himself together, and, in a firm voice, he said: "I've arranged for ten thousand pounds to be placed to your account, in any bank you may select. I know you must need a change—"

And then at last she did break down, and began to sob bitterly, telling herself, in her bewildered disappointment, that men were strange, fickle, brutes.

"It's been terrible, terrible! And I long to get away, though people have been so good, and kind and understanding. I have some dear friends in India, so I think I shall go out there for the winter," and she dabbed her eyes with her tiny handkerchief. But as they shook hands quietly, she saw *that he knew.*

THE SUPERNATURAL
STORIES OF MONSIGNOR
ROBERT H. BENSON

THE LIGHT INVISIBLE
A MIRROR OF SHALOTT

DANCING SHADOWS

TALES OF THE SUPERNATURAL
BY BERNARD CAPES

BLACK SPIRITS
AND WHITE
RALPH ADAMS CRAM

TALES OF THE
SUPERNATURAL
JAMES PLATT

SHADOWS GOTHIC
AND GROTESQUE

STRANGE
HAUNTS

STORIES BY
F. MARION CRAWFORD &
H. B. MARRIOTT WATSON

Coachwhip Publications

CoachwhipBooks.com

TALES OF FRIGHT
AND FANTASY BY
E. F. BENSON

SECRET
WELLS

THE
SPECULATIVE FICTION
OF
A. C. BENSON

INTRODUCTION BY TIM PRASIL

ARTHUR MACHEN

THE DYSON
CHRONICLES

THE INMOST LIGHT · THE SHINING PYRAMID
THE RED HAND · THE THREE IMPOSTORS

LONELY HAUNTS

Coachwhip Publications

CoachwhipBooks.com

LIGHT SPIRITS

*Horrific Specters, Comedic Shades,
and Criminous Phantasms in
Vintage Periodical
Ghost Stories*

**LURKING
SHADOWS**

Shadow Tales in
Classic Short Fiction

**ANCIENT
HAUNTS**

The Stoneground
Ghost Tales
by E. G. Swain

Tedious Brief Tales
of Granta and Gramarye
by Arthur Gray

CATS OF SHADOW,
CLAWS OF DARKNESS

Stories of Were-Cats, Ghost Cats,
and Other Supernatural Felines

Coachwhip Publications
CoachwhipBooks.com

Coachwhip Publications

CoachwhipBooks.com

Bestiarium Cryptozoologicum

Mystery Animals and Unknown Species in Classic Science Fiction and Fantasy

zoologica fantastica

TALES OF THE WEIRD AND SUPERNATURAL

H. G. WELLS

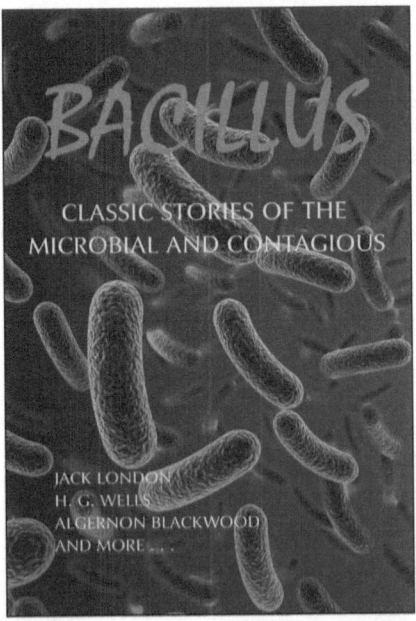

BACILLUS

CLASSIC STORIES OF THE MICROBIAL AND CONTAGIOUS

JACK LONDON
H. G. WELLS
ALGERNON BLACKWOOD
AND MORE . . .

Coachwhip Publications

CoachwhipBooks.com

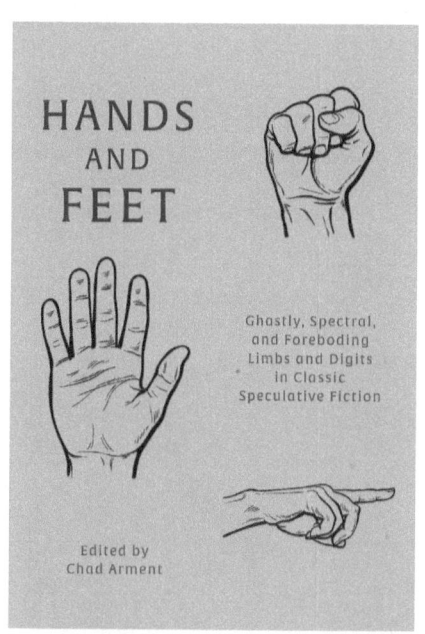

HANDS
AND
FEET

Ghastly, Spectral,
and Foreboding
Limbs and Digits
in Classic
Speculative Fiction

Edited by
Chad Arment

HORTUS
DIABOLICUS

Further Twisting Tales of
Menacing Flora and
Malignant Fungi

Edited by Chad Arment

OTHER LIFE

An Anthology of
Non-Terrestrial Biology

DAYS OF DOOM

APOCALYPTIC VISIONS &
UNEARTHLY NIGHTMARES

OWEN OLIVER

Coachwhip Publications

CoachwhipBooks.com